The Captured Heart

(The Claiming Games 1)

By

Beverly Rae

Copyright © 2014 by Beverly Rae (all rights reserved)
Print Edition
Edited by Kasi Alexander & Riane Holt
Cover by P & N Graphics

Published by Rae Publishing
E-book ISBN 978-1-941974-01-8
Print ISBN 978-1-941974-02-5

PLEASE NOTE: This work contains graphic sexual situations and language and is intended for readers 18 years and older. This work includes depictions of sex, violence, alcohol, suicide, and self-harm. Please be advised. Some of the material contained in this book may be a trigger for those who self-harm. However, no liability is assumed for any acts of self-harm or acts resulting in injury, deliberate or otherwise, by those who read this book.

This is not the typical romance story.

All characters and events in this book are fictitious. Any resemblance to actual persons living or dead, events or establishments, is solely coincidental.

Acknowledgments

The Captured Heart is not only the beginning of the Claiming Games series, but the beginning of my life as a self-published author. Writing my first self-published book took more time and effort than I'd ever dreamed it would. However, in the end, all the sacrifice, all the late hours and long weekends were worth it. It's difficult to bring a book to life, to give it to the world and hope someone likes it. Yet, as an author, it's also my joy.

A special thank you goes out to those who supported me and helped me do what I love. Thank you to all my readers. Thanks also goes to Vella Day and Jenika Snow who patiently answered many questions about the self-publishing process. Thank you to my brilliant editors, Kasi Alexander and Riane Holt, who made my book better than I'd hoped it could be. A huge thank you goes out to my husband, the man who is the inspiration for all my heroes.

Thank you,
Beverly Rae

Chapter One

Erin

"Erin, pay attention."

I heard Maddy, but as it usually was whenever I was with Mike, I paid more attention to him than to my friend. But Maddy Wheller, one of my best friends since we'd cheated off each other's test in Lit 101, wasn't the type to be ignored.

"Damn it, Erin. Will you get your shit together?"

"Maddy, leave her alone. It won't do any good anyway." Nina Winters, my other best friend, was the complete opposite of Maddy. She was quiet, shy, and rarely raised her voice.

My friends hated hanging around while Mike was with me. But as friends, they suffered through it. That and the fact that I'd forked over hard-earned money to buy their favorite brew at Caffeine Charlie's coffee shop. My job at the local art supply store paid minimum wage and money was always tight. But if buying coffee could help bring Mike and my two girlfriends closer, then it was worth it. I considered it an investment in our future friendship.

We stood outside the coffee shop, joining the throng of students who'd grabbed a caffeine boost between classes. Caffeine Charlie's had a monopoly in Chambers and the place was packed to standing room only with other drinkers like us spreading out onto the patio.

I hugged Mike a little harder, but he pushed my arm off his waist and turned so his back was toward me. I smiled and shoved down the sick feeling. That was okay. I knew he loved me. After all, we'd been together for a while and had even talked about the future. Kind of. Not with the details ironed out, but enough to know that a long-time future with him existed. I never would've believed I was the kind of girl who dreamed about the cottage with the picket fence and the kids playing in the backyard with our black-and-white dog. All while Mike and I sat on the back porch and shared a bottle of wine.

Yeah. That girl.

But who could blame me? Mike Rollingwood was the perfect guy. He was tall and blond, with movie star looks and a body made for sexy sin. His expression-filled deep blue eyes reminded me of the ocean. He was a football player at Rollingwood University—as in his great-great-great something or other who founded the place—and one of those students everyone knew and wanted to be friends with. We'd met at a frat party where I'd basically drooled over him the entire time. I hadn't had the nerve to approach him until he'd bumped into me and knocked the red Solo cup out of my hand. He was way out of my league and we both knew it. Which was why it had shocked the hell out of me when he'd gotten my number from a girl in my Econ class and had called me the next day to ask me out. We went on a fairy tale of a first date and had been inseparable ever since.

He was considerate, both in and out of bed, clever and funny. But the best part was that he wanted to be around me as much as I wanted to be around him. By some lucky twist of fate, my life had become like a romance movie. Once the word was out, all those girls who had snubbed me, telling me I wasn't pretty or popular enough to be in their sorority, were suddenly eating their hearts out. And I loved every minute of it.

"Damn it, Erin. Can't you see what he's doing? And right in front of you, too."

I frowned at Maddy, not understanding what her problem was. Mike stood a foot away from me talking to a friend of his. Big deal. Granted, the friend was a very pretty blonde with boobs that announced her presence five minutes before she entered a room, but I didn't have to worry. Although she was the girl every guy on campus wanted, Mike was with me and I wasn't the jealous type. I didn't need to be. After all, how many times had Mike told me that he was friends with a lot of girls and that it didn't mean anything whenever he hung around with them? He was in love with me.

Okay, maybe he hadn't actually said the word *love*, but he was. I could feel it.

"Maddy, it's fine. I told you what Mike said."

"Oh, my God. Will you snap out of it? He's hitting on her right in front of you."

He wasn't. He couldn't be. If that were true, I didn't know what I'd do. My faith in Mike was everything. If I didn't have that, then what did I have? I started to say as much when the roar of motorcycles drew everyone's attention to the street.

Chambers, Georgia was a fair-sized town where almost all the economy centered on the college and its conference-leading football team. Because of the team, Chambers got a lot of visitors, including parents of students, football enthusiasts, and those just out to enjoy the after-parties. But I'd never seen a motorcycle club riding down the main street.

Only one woman rode with the men, who were all dressed in black. They lined up into rows with enough riders beside each other to span the width of the street. A few had on black shirts or sleeveless vests with a roaring lion's head logo embossed on the back and the words *Kings of Beasts MC* below it. Even I could tell that their motorcycles were monster machines only a few regular riders could ever own. The chrome sparkled in the bright afternoon sun and the sound of their engines drowned out everything else. The riders commanded attention and they got it.

"Wow. Now that's what I call hot men." Maddy leaned closer, raising her voice as she tossed a scowl toward Mike. "And I mean men. Not college boys."

I agreed with Maddy—except about the boy thing, of course. Sure, most guys I'd met at college were more interested in getting laid than thinking about their future, but Mike was different. He was more mature, worldly, everything I'd ever wanted.

Still, the bikers were hot.

"Aren't they supposed to be wearing helmets?"

Leave it to Nina to point it out. Either the bikers didn't know about the law—which I doubted big-time—or they didn't give a crap.

The riders seemed around our age except for the big, burly man in the front who rode with the woman seated behind him, her arms wrapped around his waist. Her long white hair flowed around her shoulders like the mane of a lion. I got the impression that he was the leader of the group and she was his... His what? His Old Lady? The other riders fanned out behind them. I watched, fascinated until the last, lone rider coasted by us.

Oh, shit.

The rider stared straight at me. I could see the strange blue-silver of his eyes even from where I stood. Mike's eyes were blue, too, but they didn't hold the same intensity this man's eyes did. Longish black hair framed his face, curling around his ears to point out the chiseled jaw. His body was lean, mean, strong and insanely sexy in his tight black T-shirt. His legs looked hard and solid in his black jeans and slid my attention down to black biker boots. He oozed masculinity and a confidence that was as natural as his tan.

He's way hotter than Mike. I wonder what it would be like to be with him?

I blinked, shaken by the adulterous thought. With one look, one awful and unexpected idea, I'd betrayed Mike. I forced myself to turn away from the man on the motorcycle, needing to reassure Mike that no one, not even the hottest man I'd ever seen, could come between us.

To see Mike bent over the blonde, his mouth to her ear, tore at my gut. The Darkness worked its fingers into me, whispering that I wasn't enough, that Mike would soon figure it out and leave me just as so many had done in the past.

The Darkness was what I called my black thoughts. It had been with me a long time, ever since that awful day years earlier when my life had been thrown upside down and had never completely righted itself. Like a living entity clawing to get free from inside me, it ate at me. The Darkness was what drove me to do the thing others didn't do. It told me I wasn't pretty or smart or brave. It warned me to keep my secrets hidden. If Mike found out, he'd finally see the ugly side of me. Then he'd hate me, whispered The Darkness, and he'd be right to do so.

Since meeting Mike, I'd kept The Darkness controlled, pushing it down until I could almost forget it was there. I'd kept The Darkness at bay, all while resisting the urge to cut.

Still, I worried that it would break free, lashing out its torment until I had no choice but to listen. Cutting relieved the pressure The Darkness gave me, but one day I feared it would grow too strong and cutting wouldn't be enough. Then it would keep on pushing, battering me down until, at last, I gave in.

Closing my eyes, I shoved The Darkness back into its cave. When I opened them again, it was easier to ignore Mike whispering to the pretty blonde and smiling the special smile he'd promised was only for me.

"Hey, you, how about getting a refill?" He'd promised to buy a second cup for everyone. I tugged on his arm, but he still resisted, ignoring me as though I'd said nothing at all. But I was determined to get his attention back on me where it belonged. "Mike? We need refills."

Nina and Maddy sandwiched me between them. "Come on. We'll get our own. He's too busy trying to pick her up."

"That's not what he's doing, Maddy." Yet the churning in my stomach didn't ease up. My irritation should've been aimed at Mike. Instead, I focused it on Maddy.

"Maddy's right." Nina hooked her arm in mine, bringing me along with her inside the coffee shop. "Besides, I want one of those chocolate chip cookies with my next cup."

After a few minutes, I craned my neck around, searching out the door to see Mike. But he wasn't there. Where had he gone?

"He left with the blonde."

The cruel whisper crawled to the forefront of my mind. I hadn't wanted to let The Darkness speak, but I'd been too late to stop it. I stiffened, ready to fight more traitorous thoughts.

He'd probably just seen one of his football buddies and had gone to say hello. At least, that's what I wanted to believe.

"Erin? Do you want another one?"

I couldn't hide my worry as I turned to Maddy. "Did you see where Mike went?"

She rolled her eyes. "I'm buying this time, along with a cookie. What kind do you want?"

One more look outside and still I couldn't find him. I calmed myself by saying I would soon enough. He wouldn't leave me. He loved me.

"Peanut butter for me. And the same drink as before."

Maddy hugged me as though I'd said something wonderful. "Cool. I think I'll get three cookies. One chocolate, one sugar, and one peanut butter. Then we can all share."

"But I wanted chocolate chip," whined Nina.

"Either one sounds good to me." While my two friends argued about the virtues of a chocolate chip cookie versus a plain chocolate one, I let my irritation at Maddy go. We didn't treat ourselves to Caffeine Charlie's often. All three of us were paying our way through school, relying on our abilities to pay off our huge loans later. We rarely splurged on specialty coffee drinks and cookies, but every once in a while we needed a treat.

Thinking about how much debt I was in made me nervous. By the time I graduated law school, my student loans would amount to a small fortune. I could already imagine them as sinister black crows like in horror movies, following me wherever I went. Provided I could find a job, I'd start my career owing more than I'd make my first two years as an attorney. But that worry was for later. I already had more than enough to worry about. I checked again, hoping to see that Mike had returned, but he hadn't.

Mike, where are you?

Colter

I leaned against my Harley, the one I'd inherited from my Uncle Jake after he'd gotten his gut torn out in a bar fight, and listened to Burke and Roberta, the alphas of our pride, discuss the candidates. I'd come along on the ride down from our home in Cripple Creek, North Carolina, to get Burke and Roberta off my back, but I still wasn't going to take part in all of it.

That is, until I got a good look at the girl standing outside the coffee shop. She had shoulder-length brown hair that glistened with red highlights. She looked like she was a little younger than me, but not by much. It was hard to tell with girls between the ages of sixteen and twenty-five. Young girls looked older. Not that I'd ever deal with any jail bait. I stuck to the legal ones every time. And so did Burke and Roberta when it came time to find girls for The Claiming Games.

The games weren't anything new. I'd been old enough to take my turn for the past few years, but hadn't wanted to. I didn't like the way things sometimes went down. People, mainly the girls, got hurt, even dead. But it was a Kings of Beasts Motorcycle Club tradition and I wasn't about to go against the pride. I valued my hide and my heritage too much to do that.

"See anything you like, man?"

I crossed my arms and started to tell Burke no, but then, since I was getting hauled into the games this year anyway, why not have my say in it? "Yeah. There were a few outside the coffee shop."

Roberta flipped her hair over her shoulders. "Let me guess.

The leggy blonde, right? She looked like she was ready to fuck the guy wearing the football shirt. If she'll do him, then why not your sorry ass?"

It figures she'd think that. She knew men picked with their cocks instead of their brains. And that's what I was doing. Thing was, I hadn't cared for the blonde. She'd put off an "I'm better than you" vibe that had hit me the wrong way. I figured she was high maintenance from her high heels up to her perfect hair. High maintenance wouldn't last a day in our group.

We'd parked next to the curb to survey the local talent and I'd watched the girls as they'd gone inside the coffee shop. "Naw. She's one of the three at the counter now." The other two weren't bad, either. Just not my type.

"How about all three?" Burke slid his hand down Roberta's back. "They're more likely to come if a friend or two's tagging along."

I could sense his horniness kicking in and leaned away. As long as he and Roberta didn't start fucking right there on the main street, I could handle it.

"Yeah. Sure. Are we done?" I couldn't wait to get back on the road. The only places I felt at ease were on a long stretch of highway and in the mountains. I didn't like towns, with all the traffic and the people.

The other riders had already gone on ahead of us, riding back to the mountains and the rest of the pride. Some of the mated men had come along for the ride while their women stayed at home, but most of us were single guys hoping to scope out the girls. I wanted to get the hell out of town and catch up with them.

"Keep your shirt on. We still need to get their info. I'll ask around and see if anyone knows them."

Roberta was our go-to person for digging up their names and addresses. I couldn't have cared less how she did it. I lifted a lip, the silent snarl a direct message to Burke. "You do that. I'm outta here."

Burke didn't tell me to hold up. He knew better than to press me to stay. I swung my leg over my bike and was back on the road in a couple of minutes.

It didn't take long before I was out of town and cruising down the highway. But a strange sensation, a knot in my gut made me rip over the median in a U-turn and start heading back. Before long, however, I pulled off onto the shoulder. What the fuck was I doing? I'd sworn I wasn't interested in the games this year any more than I'd been all the previous years, but I couldn't ignore the fact that I was curious. Could the brown-haired girl be the one I'd take?

Erin

Two weeks later ~

I snuggled next to Mike. If there was a heaven on earth, lying in Mike's bed after having amazing sex was it. He was my present and my future. While I was with him, my past was wiped away. I tugged on a strand of my hair and impulsively decided it was time.

"Do you love me, Mike?"

He pulled me closer, showing me how much he loved me. "Come on, baby. You know how I feel."

I did. Saying the *L* word—or not—didn't mean a thing. We'd already talked about marriage, kids, and a house. What more did I need? I'd never felt closer to him. I trusted him with all my heart.

"Um, can I tell you something?"

"Sure. What is it?"

I leaned back a little so I could see his handsome face. The love in his eyes gave me the courage I needed. "It's not an easy thing for me to talk about."

"You can tell me anything. Don't you know that by now?"

I did. He'd never lied to me. No matter what Nina and Maddy said. Unlike them, I'd believed him when he said he'd gone off with the blonde to study for a final exam. Even if he hadn't told me he was leaving. Mike always had a good explanation. Still, I hesitated and pushed away the whispers telling me not to confide in him.

"You know the scars on my ankles?" The words came out in a rush. I'd kept them hidden as much as possible, for as long as possible, but I'd messed up and he'd seen them.

"Yeah?"

I heard the trust in his tone, urging me to continue. "I, uh, didn't get them the way I said I did." I'd told him I'd gotten wound up in sharp wire as a kid and the wire had cut into my skin, leaving me with the scars.

He twisted away from me and frowned, running lines across his forehead. "You didn't?"

Was that a flash of realization I'd just seen? Suddenly, I couldn't look at him and wished I'd never said anything at all. "No."

"Then how?" He pulled his body from mine, lifting up to study me even harder.

The Darkness spoke to me, telling me what a fool I was to open up to him. But I couldn't stop now. I should've planned what I'd say. Instead, I fumbled, trying to find the right words. But there were no words to make it sound better.

Instead, I blurted out the truth, trusting our love. "I used to cut myself."

A pain struck me dead center like a heart attack as he moved a little farther away.

"You cut yourself?" He pulled the sheet off me, his gaze going to my ankles.

I felt exposed, vulnerable, my heart entirely in his hands. "Yeah. I do it to help relieve stress." Realizing what I'd said, I hurriedly added, "But not since I've been with you."

"Fuck."

I had no choice but to look at him. What I saw made the pain go even deeper. "Mike, let me explain."

"So you're one of those sickos who cut? What's it called? Self-mutilation?"

"Self-harm. But I don't do it anymore." At least, not since I'd met him.

"Naw. You're lying. You said you *do* it. Not *did* it." The horror mixed with disgust on his face. "You still do it, don't you? Don't fuckin' lie to me."

But I wanted to lie. I needed to lie. Yet I couldn't. "Not since we got together."

"But since you came to college?"

"A little. But only when I had to."

"Oh, fuck." He snagged my wrist and studied it. "Do you cut your wrists, too? Have you tried to off yourself?"

I sucked in air, but couldn't get enough into my lungs to keep them from burning. "Mike, please—"

"Tell me, Erin. Have you tried to kill yourself?"

I wasn't going to tell him, but he'd already seen the truth in my face. "Once. But it was a long time ago."

He scrambled out of bed as though I'd changed into a poisonous snake.

"Get your scarred ass out!"

I went cold. He didn't mean it. He couldn't. He loved me. "Mike, please, don't."

"You're a mental case. You're fucked up. Did you hear me? Get the fuck out! Get out or I'll call the cops and have your ass hauled out." He tugged on his jeans then snatched a shirt off his dresser while shoving his feet into his sandals.

"You don't mean it. Please, let me explain." Not that I knew what to say. How could I explain away what he'd never understand? I hurried out of bed and tried to grab him, to hold him, to keep him with me.

He grabbed his phone. "Get away from me." He shoved me, throwing me back onto the bed.

"But we love each other." Tears blurred my eyesight as I pushed off the bed and dashed after him. "We're going to get married."

He strode away from me, then whirled to confront me. I slammed to a stop, stunned by the hatred on his face.

"Are you fucking kidding me? We're kids in college. That shit's just what guys tell their girlfriends to make them happy. Fuck, Erin. Are you that stupid?"

"No. We're going to have children." He'd stopped calling me *baby*.

"Like hell we are. I wouldn't have a family with a mental case like you." He turned and headed for the door.

He already had it opened by the time I got to him. His neighbors, two of his football friends who lived in the apartment across the hall, gawked at my naked body as I tugged on Mike's arm. Their surprise soon turned into jeering laughter.

But I didn't care. I'd run naked across campus during class change if it would change Mike's mind.

"I told you, Erin. Get your shit out by the end of the day. And stay the hell away from me." He shoved me back again, sending me crashing to my butt.

Sobs racked me as he slammed the door behind him.

Erin

The Darkness wouldn't let me go. I fought against it, but trying to strike a blow at the invisible monster was impossible. Pain was its constant companion, tearing me apart from the inside, urging me to slash my body as it slashed my soul. Urging me to go beyond the superficial cuts that would release the pressure inside me. Sobbing and wailing came next, but I was already worn out from crying and ached to release the agony inside me. The urge was so strong, demanding I give in. Only then would my pain go away. Only then would I keep from risking my life the way I'd done years earlier. I didn't want to give in at all, but if I didn't cut, the pain would only get worse until, one day, The Darkness would lift its ugly head, grin its evil grin, and shove me over the edge.

Mike dumped me. Mike dumped me. Mike dumped me.

My world had become divided between the time *Before Mike* and the time *After Mike.*

Like the pounding of a bass drum, the endless litany continued in my head until I was on the verge of screaming. It wouldn't stop. If I could've reached into my brain and ripped the chant out, I would have.

Why had I told him? Had I purposely sabotaged our relationship knowing I didn't deserve him? I had to have known how he'd react. So many people in my past had turned away from me in disgust and fear. Why else would I have stashed a shiny new razor blade in the corner of the nightstand? I still had my own apartment, but in the tradition of boyfriend-girlfriend relationships, I'd brought some of my things over and left them at his place, including the razor.

If Mike hadn't called Nina demanding that she get me out of his place, and if she hadn't shown up in time, would The Darkness have pushed me to cut? And if it had, would the lines of red across my skin have saved me from giving in, from allowing The Darkness to force me into a grand release that would finally end my pain for good?

But I didn't want to die. I really didn't even want to cut. I only wanted the pain gone and my life back.

If a life *After Mike* could be called living.

Mike had called her after he'd stormed out. Didn't that mean he still cared? At least a little? Or had he'd called just to get me out of his life after he'd broken my heart?

I lay crumpled on Nina's bed, numb and cold. I couldn't remember how long I'd been there. What did it matter? With Mike gone, life was worthless, a shit-hole of one lonely day followed by another.

"Please, Erin, let me call someone. Maybe your mom? Or Mr. Latham, your psych prof? You like Mr. Latham, right?"

I felt Nina's hand on my leg, felt her give me a little shake, but I didn't move. She wouldn't touch the scars that ran across my ankles. She knew I didn't like anyone touching them. She and Maddy were two of the few people who had seen the faded scars, and knew how they'd gotten there. I'd talked to them about my secret, even about my suicide attempt when I was sixteen. They'd been shocked, but I'd been shocked even more when they'd stuck by me. I'd asked them to keep my secrets and they had.

Yet I'd heard them whispering, conspiring to keep razors and other sharp items out of sight. As if that would keep me from finding another tool to slice my flesh and add new scars to my collection. For weeks after I'd confided in them, I'd seen their worried gazes flick to my ankles. They hadn't stopped checking me out until recently, and now I'd blown it.

Why did I tell Mike? How could I have been so stupid?

Please just make it all go away.

I couldn't remember how Nina had gotten me from Mike's apartment to hers. Or how many days it had been since she'd tucked me into her bed.

The Darkness was back, stronger than ever, tormenting me, threatening my very desire to draw breath. I wanted to rid myself of the agony, but no matter what I did, it stayed. The urge to cut was enormous, but the look in Nina's eyes as she'd seen what I was about to do haunted me.

Why, Mike? Why couldn't you love me enough?

After one and a half years of dating, sex, college fun, and half way moving in with him, he'd declared our relationship over.

As though it had never existed.

As though I was nothing more than a girl he'd picked up at a frat party to fuck and forget.

As though I had no feelings.

If Nina hadn't shown up, I'd probably still be in his apartment, a crumpled mass of human flesh, sobbing on the floor of the bedroom with his football jersey clutched to my chest. The scattered remains of the symbols of our love encircled me. I couldn't remember doing it, but the love notes he'd written were torn to shreds, along with photos and other tokens of his love. Even the promise bracelet he'd given me was broken.

Broken. Just like my heart.

If not for Nina, I might have stayed there, my back resting against the side of the bed, the bottle of tequila on the floor next to me, and the razor in my hand as I turned it over, watching the morning sun glint on the steel. Would I give in and cut? Would I go even farther, pushed on by the horrible whispers? Or would I win the battle?

"Erin, please. I don't know what else to do. Maybe if I call the school clinic they could help."

Nina's voice sounded strange, but why shouldn't it? Her best friend had wanted to hurt herself. She had a difficult time understanding why anyone would want to do such ugliness to their body.

"Erin Emily Pierce, I've had enough of this."

Maddy's here.

"You need to pull yourself together. We can't stay with you twenty-four-seven any longer. We both have classes and finals to get through. Now open your eyes and get your ass moving. I'm not going to let you waste away over Mike or any other stupid boy."

I opened my eyes as far as possible, but the puffiness kept me from seeing clearly. Or was it my non-functioning brain that was responsible?

"Erin, come on. Do it for me." Nina shook me again, harder than before.

I tried. Really I did. But I just didn't have it in me. Instead, I closed my eyes and hoped when I opened them again, Mike would be sitting next to me.

Chapter Two

Erin

"She's better, Mad. At least I got her to eat something."

"Good. But I still can't believe you didn't call anyone."

Maddy and Nina were together, probably in the kitchen where we all tended to hang out whenever we came over. With long, full auburn hair, big brown eyes, and a killer body, Maddy was one of the hottest girls on campus. She'd never been stood up, much less dumped. As far as Nina and I were concerned, Maddy led a charmed life. Problems were just minor bumps in the road. Her saving grace that kept every girl on campus from hating her guts was that she was as nice as she was beautiful. Unless she got angry. Then she could be a real bitch. I figured I'd have the bitch side of her coming at me soon and giving me hell for what I'd almost done.

I rolled onto my back and stared at the ceiling of Nina's bedroom. Above her bed, she'd thumbtacked a poster of a stupid kitty holding on to the push-up bar. I wanted to reach up and yank the fucking cat off the bar and tell it not to "hang in there." What use did hanging in there do? It only delayed the inevitable fall.

And yet, I was still hanging on, too.

I hurt. My throat burned and my head pounded. But I didn't hurt anywhere as badly as I did in my heart.

I slicked my tongue over my grimy teeth, then licked the back of my hand and smelled it, catching the rank odor of my foul breath. How long had I been at Nina's? It could've been days or weeks for all I knew.

"I couldn't get her to tell me who to call and I didn't want to get her into trouble. Anyway, she's better now, right? Thanks for taking turns watching over her. I don't think I could've pulled this off without you."

"We're friends. What else would I do? But I still think she should see a professional. I mean, you don't do shit like that without something being off."

Off. Yes, I was *off.* Being *on* would've meant that I was still with Mike. I groaned and rolled onto my side. What was the point of even trying? What sane guy would want a fucked-up mess like me?

"We all have those times in our lives. And besides, she didn't do it."

"Only because you got there in time. At least Mike had the decency to call you. Even if he was douche enough to leave her alone."

"We don't know she would've done it. She hasn't for a long time now. Not since freshman year."

"There could've been more times we don't know about. But whatever, Nina. It was just too damn close this time."

Nina tried to placate Maddy. "You know how much she loved Mike. What'd you expect her to do? Throw a party?"

"I would've. Hell, I'd have thrown one for her. We tried to tell her he was an asshole, but she wouldn't listen. It wasn't as though she shouldn't have seen it coming."

"I know, but still—"

"But still, my ass. I know other people who've cut, but none of them have ever tried to kill themselves."

"She wasn't going to go there." Nina's voice wavered, the fear evident. "She only tried that one time way back when she was in high school."

"Once is all it takes."

"According to what I've read, cutting doesn't lead to suicide. At least, not most the time."

"No. In her case, it was the suicide attempt that led to her cutting."

"Damn, Maddy, keep your voice down. She'll hear you."

Their voices dropped to a lower pitch until I couldn't make out what they were saying. But I could guess how the rest of the conversation went.

Maddy was right. After my sister's death, I'd gone off the deep end. Too much guilt can drive a person to do the worst. I'd taken the classic suicide route, pilfering booze from my dad's den, then downing my mother's anti-depression pills with it. My father had found me just in time to haul my ass to the hospital and then on to the looney bin for a few months. I could still see the embarrassment and disgust in his eyes as he dumped me at Eternal Heights Recovery Center. The name had always sounded like a rehab for people who'd died and were trying to come back to life. I guess in a way it was.

But I was better. "Better" being a relative word. The Darkness that had enveloped me had loosened its hard grip long enough to allow other thoughts, not solely ones about Mike, to drift into my consciousness. It was finals week. I had to pull myself together or I'd have wasted all the damn money I owed.

Or were finals already over?

Crap. One more thing I fucked up.

My stomach growled. How long had it been since I'd eaten?

I remembered Nina hand-feeding me some kind of yucky soup, but I wasn't sure if it had happened yesterday or a few hours ago. The yummy scent of my favorite pizza wafted to me, urging my stomach to announce its need for nourishment once again.

The light from the small bedroom window filtered through the blinds to punish my eyes and my pounding head. Where there was Darkness, there was always Light. And, as it had happened before, The Darkness was beginning to give way to The Light.

Groaning, I rolled out of bed, stood up, then sat down when my head began to swim. I was weak, but finally ready to face life again.

Life *After Mike.*

My legs barely held me as I pushed off the edge of the bed and moved like a tottering old woman toward the door. Grabbing hold of the doorframe, I judged the distance from the bedroom to the living room to be a whole lot longer than it had ever been.

But pepperoni pizza with extra cheese was worth going the distance. Thankfully, the hall was narrow enough that I could put my hands against each wall and work my way toward my goal.

"Hey, she's up." Nina's bright blue eyes widened. Throwing her long red hair over her shoulder, she hurried past Maddy and slipped her arm around my waist. "How are you doing?"

"Okay. I think." With Nina supporting me, the trip from the hallway to the kitchen chair was over in a sec. "Hungry."

Maddy placed a plate with two pieces of pizza in front of me. "Take it easy. Your stomach's going to need time to adjust to spicy food."

Nina was back with a glass of cool water. I kind of wished I could pour it over my head. Instead, I chowed down on the first piece before looking them straight in the eyes. Like the good friends they were, they waited.

But I could only hide for so long. "I'm sorry." It wasn't enough by a long shot, but it was all I could offer.

Nina, in her usual forgiving way, shrugged. "It was no big deal."

Maddy, in her usual straight-at-you, taking-no-prisoners kind of way, glared at Nina, then leveled her guns at me. "The hell it wasn't."

Damn, but I hated it when she was right. Wasn't it enough that she was so fucking gorgeous? I wasn't by any means an ogre with my straight, mousy brown hair, puppy dog eyes, and ten pounds too heavy body, but I was no Maddy. Still, did she have to be right all the time, too? If she had a fault that was it. Righteous know-it-all-ness.

"Yeah. I know. I screwed up and I'm sorry." I shot her a smile, hoping it would get her to lay off. "But I didn't do it. Don't I get points for that?"

My joke fell flat.

"Not funny, Erin. We were worried sick about you."

I could handle Maddy's indignation better than the tears I saw in Nina's eyes.

Nina's lower lip trembled. "I know you've explained this to me before, but I just don't get it. Why would you want to hurt yourself? I mean, I know you loved—"

"Love. I *love* Mike." He'd hurt me, but that didn't mean I didn't still love him. I wished like hell I didn't, but unless they could tell me how to flip a switch and make me not care for him, I couldn't get over him so fast. Hell, I couldn't imagine ever getting over him.

"We get that." Maddy leaned forward and took my hand. "We really do. But it's over and you've got to start putting him in the past. Mike Rollingwood is an ass. We never thought he was good enough for you and he proved it. I say you got lucky he dumped you now instead of waiting until you had three kids and found out he was cheating on you."

I yanked my hand away. It was too soon to hear anyone attack him.

"Erin, please tell us you're all right."

"I'm all right." I'd do anything to satisfy them long enough to get food and coffee.

"No. I mean it. Tell us you won't ever try that again." Nina wiped away the tear sliding down her cheek. "I don't think I could handle seeing…" She shook her head, sending her red hair dancing over her shoulders. "Don't you get it? It just kills me to think of you hurting yourself."

She cringed at her choice of words. "That didn't come out right."

I hadn't thought about how much my actions could hurt others. Hadn't, in fact, thought of anyone other than Mike. That and how to rid myself of the pain still holding me hostage.

"I'm sorry." What else could I say? What'd they want from me? My right arm? I giggled, sounding a little cray-cray.

"Answer her question. Are you going to try that stupid shit again?" Maddy's stern expression stayed put, but the worry in her tone was enough for me to know how much I'd hurt her. She lowered her gaze as though she could see through the table to my ankles.

"No. I won't." My promise was a tenuous one at best. Still, I'd managed not to cut for a long time. Had, in fact, managed to keep The Darkness at bay without it. Maybe that's why it had finally gotten to me. I'd let my guard down and it had attacked.

"Promise?"

No one could make that promise and know they'd keep it. But Nina had to hear me say the words. "I just kind of lost it. It won't happen again. I promise."

Lost it. What a nice way to put it. Like I'd set my sanity down for a minute and forgotten where I'd left it. Yeah, I'd lost it, plain and simple. The problem, however, wasn't that I'd lost it because of a horrible breakup. The problem was the dark demon who still whispered in my mind. Whispering. Coaxing. Demanding I finally give in and do what it wanted. And if I didn't cut, it would grow stronger, meaner, ready to make me hurt myself as much as anyone ever could.

They waited longer, needing more than I'd given them. "Really. I won't. Besides, I didn't do anything."

I hadn't cut. I'd come close, but I'd wanted to save it for when the booze had gotten into my system and made everything nicer, floatier. Or better yet, gotten me drunk enough to ease some of the pain and keep me from cutting. Drinking was the first crutch. If it failed, then cutting came next. I didn't want to think about what might happen if the booze and the cutting didn't relieve the pressure.

"Only because Nina got there in time." Maddy wasn't backing off.

"Maybe. We'll never know for sure." Part of me wanted to argue while the other part of me wanted to hug her for sticking in there. But that was the thing. Sometimes I wanted someone to yell at me and make me stop. And other times, I wanted them to fuck off.

"Okay, it's over." Nina was the ever-hopeful one.

I went back to eating and avoiding their eyes. "Yeah."

"You missed all your finals, but I told your profs that you had the flu and couldn't get out of bed. They said you could take the make-up exams next week."

"Thanks, Nina." I risked looking at them again. "I really am sorry I caused you guys so much trouble. I don't know what I'd do without you." It was my turn to wipe away a tear.

"No problem. Just give it some time. Everything will get better. You'll see." Nina stood, holding out her hand for my plate. "Think you can handle a couple more?"

I gave it to her, thankful as always to have two great friends. Giving her a "seriously?" look, I tried to ease the tension with a joke. "Have we met? Hi, I'm Erin the endless pit."

She laughed, just as I'd hoped she would, and plopped two more pieces onto my plate.

Colter

"It's time. Hell, it's past time. You know that."

Back off, Burke.

That's what I wanted to say, but I didn't. I'm not stupid by any stretch of the imagination. Instead, I nodded, knowing he'd keep talking. He was more of a talker than most of us.

"Then you're doing the games, right?"

I nodded again. Supposedly, ninety-three percent of human communication was nonverbal. With us, it was more, unless we forced ourselves. Personally, I'd have made it a hundred percent whenever Burke was around.

He knew I didn't have a choice. Asking me was Burke's way

of being polite. He wasn't ordering, but that's what it amounted to. He was our alpha, and like the African lions that were a part of us, he demanded to be obeyed.

"They'll be getting the invitations soon."

"Was it as sappy as usual?"

His chuckle sounded a lot like his purr. "You know Roberta. Besides, girls like that kind of shit."

"Yeah, but the games aren't romantic. It's kind of a bait and switch." I'd said more than I should have.

"It works. That's all you need to know."

I kept back the growl rumbling up from my inner beast as it struggled to get free. Its need to run, to growl, seeped into my veins, daring me to hold it back. If I gave it what it wanted, then I'd risk having to fight Burke. Besides, it wouldn't do me any good to argue about the games, much less to bring the argument to fangs and claws.

"Colter. You're doing this."

A command. One that was definitely not hidden in a question.

I faced him, turning away from the green hillside of the North Carolina mountains to glower my frustration. "I went down to Chambers, didn't I? And I'll be at Fang's."

Burke's blue-silver eyes lost most of their blue, changing to iron in both color and intensity, signaling his beast's rising. "Don't give me any shit. This is the way it's always been and the way it's always going to be. You've put it off long enough."

I hated to admit it, but he was right. For over a hundred years, my people had used the same method to find their mates. They'd called it The Capture Games back then because that's exactly what it had been. A game, an adventure, and a rite of passage for the young males who'd just turned eighteen. Our ancestors hadn't tried to hide what they did with a challenge and the hopes of a reward.

Once a year, the males of the pride would find human women, capture them, then drag them back home and make them their mates. They'd taken "fresh blood" from human civilizations to keep the pride going. Burke was the one who'd changed the name and the games to what they were now. He'd made it so the girls who answered the invitation had a choice in their future. We didn't "capture" our mates any longer and it was our mates who really did the claiming. They'd choose the man or the money.

Pride, pack, gang, club. It didn't matter what we called ourselves. What mattered was that I'd come of age five years earlier and still hadn't taken a mate. I'd pushed the responsibility away, ignoring Burke and the others. But I couldn't delay it any longer.

"Cooperate." More silver sparked in Burke's eyes.

Cooperate. Another word I hate.

"I'm going through with it, aren't I?" *Lay off, Burke.* "You done?"

His lip lifted into a snarl. "Just see that you do." He relented a little, losing the snarl. "Come on, Colter, you know I've always cut you slack because of your mother, but I can't let you out of the games any longer."

The memory of my mother's face and scent had faded away years ago, but the pain still hit me dead center just like it always had. I didn't let it show on my face. I'd learned how to mask my feelings a long time ago. "Never said you needed to."

"I wouldn't have, except for my mate. You know Roberta has a soft spot for you."

Roberta and my mother had been best friends right up to

the end. I'd do almost anything for her. That meant, even though I didn't like him much, I'd do almost anything for Burke.

"I'll be there."

"Good." He eyed me hard. "Get on out of here. Shift and run it out."

He was right. I could use some time in my other skin. It'd been too long since I'd let my beast take over. I relaxed, giving it the go-ahead as I pulled off my clothes.

"Fuck, kid. Don't leave your clothes here."

I wondered if he caught my smile in the midst of my change. The world around me lost its myriad of hues and shifted to a metallic world where only shades of gray differentiated one thing from the other. I felt my animal rise as Burke opened the back door to the woods beyond Fang's.

Erin

"You're kidding. You got one, too?" I stared at the invitation Nina held.

"So did Maddy. I told her to come over so we can talk about it." Nina sipped on her soft drink.

Maddy burst into the apartment—Nina always left her front door unlocked—and held up the invitation before she finally noticed that we both had one. "Wait. Both of you?"

"Yeah. It's weird, right?"

We got together so we could examine each other's invitations. I read mine out loud as they silently read theirs, comparing them.

To Miss Erin Pierce,

This is your opportunity to fulfill all your dreams.

Do you yearn to capture a man's heart and have him capture yours? Do you dare to find a man who will treat you to your deepest desires, awaken your heart, and claim you for his own? Are you strong enough to find an extraordinary man?

If so, read on.

Congratulations, you are a semi-finalist in The Claiming Games. If selected, and if you make it through to the end of the games, you will be rewarded with your choice of two prizes. Will you choose an extraordinary man as your prize? Or will you choose $250,000 in cash? Survive the games and decide your future.

The Claiming Games are not for the weak. Your bravery, your stamina, and your courage will be tested. Danger is everywhere. Yet, in the end, you will have won everything your heart desires.

To accept this invitation, arrive at Fang's Bar and Grill in Cripple Creek, North Carolina on July 10th at 2:00 pm. An airplane ticket is enclosed.

Come and risk it all to gain the future of your dreams.

K.O.B. Corporation
Cripple Creek, NC

"Uh-huh. Mine's the same." Maddy turned her invitation over, checking both sides. "And there's the fine print at the bottom with the legal junk. You know. The usual warnings and stuff."

"Mine, too," added Nina.

"Do you think this is for real?" I twiddled with my hair and tried to keep my excitement contained. "I mean, it's has to be a joke, right? But who'd send us something like this? And to all three of us? How'd they get our names and addresses, anyway?"

I re-read the invitation and studied the expensive stationery, then checked the envelope. They looked genuine.

"The plane ticket's the key. If it's fake, then the whole thing's a scam," offered Maddy.

"Let's find out." After a quick search on my phone, I dialed Blue Skies Airlines.

The reservationist was very helpful and very certain. The ticket was real. The only problem was that it was for a one-way trip.

"One-way?" Nina made a face reflecting the squicky feeling in my gut.

But squicky feelings had never held me back. I'd done what no one had ever thought I'd do. Without anyone's help, I'd gotten the loans for my education and made it to college on my own. I wasn't the kind who was afraid of a challenge.

My fears came from within.

"One-way doesn't sound good." Maddy flopped back on the couch, still staring at her invitation. "But the fine print says we'll get money for a return trip if we don't want to be a part of it. Still, why not just buy a round trip ticket in the first place?"

"Maybe they don't expect us to come home."

Again, Nina was thinking the same way I was. "Yeah."

We sat on her couch, each of us lost in our thoughts for a moment.

"Maybe the one-way has something to do with the man. Like we'll stay if we find our *extraordinary* man. Not that I'd care." I wouldn't. Would I?

"Maybe they figure if you win the money, you can afford your own ticket home." Maddy shrugged. "Makes sense to me."

Her reasoning seemed okay. "So we choose between a man or a butt-load of cash? I'd take the cash in a heartbeat. I could pay off all my student loans with enough left over to help pay for law school."

A photo of one of the most prestigious law schools in the country was tacked to the pegboard in my apartment, reminding me every day that I'd have to figure out how to pay for it. One day, all the work and the mounting debt would be worth it.

Or would it? Every time I thought about being an attorney, I liked it a little less. But that's the path my parents wanted me to take and I owed it to them to follow it. Even becoming an attorney wouldn't absolve me of my guilt, but I was praying it would help. I'd make their dream take the place of my old one of love and family.

What had I read? I scanned the invitation again to find it. "Do you dare to find a man who will treat you to your deepest desires, awaken your heart, and claim you for his own?" I laughed. "Seriously? Like that kind of man exists."

I didn't bother to add that if a man like that did exist, he wouldn't want me. Mike had been pretty damn close to perfect and our relationship had crumbled as soon as he'd found out just how imperfect I was. Not only with my eyes being too close together, or my thin unkissable lips, or even my round stomach. Those were nothing compared to The Darkness, my internal imperfection, he'd finally found out about.

Thinking about Mike would only lead to pain. And pain led to...

No. Stop thinking like that.

"Erin's right. This sounds too good to be true. And you know what they say about things like that." Maddy tossed her invitation away. It floated to the floor.

I nodded. "It's crazy to take the invitation seriously. Why'd they call it The Claiming Games anyway? Because we'll find men who will claim our hearts?" Mike had already claimed mine and then broken it. I doubted it would ever be whole again.

"Probably because we're supposed to claim the man or the money," offered Maddy.

Nina held her invitation with both hands, studying it harder than I'd ever seen her study a textbook. "'Danger is everywhere.'" Her big eyes found mine. "That and the warnings in the fine print make it sound kind of scary."

"They probably just put that in there to cover their butts. Trust me, they'll make us sign a stack of releases, but nothing will happen. You know how it is." Maddy picked up her invitation. "Those kinds of warnings are everywhere. They're just trying to keep people from suing over the littlest thing. Like Caffeine Charlie's warnings about the coffee being hot. What moron doesn't already know hot coffee can burn you?"

I was ready to help Maddy along. "Yeah. Either that or they put it in to make the whole thing seem exciting. We could always go and check it out. Then, if things get shady, we'll leave."

I read the invitation yet again.

Are you strong enough to find an extraordinary man?

The butterflies went wild. It was a challenge and I needed a major diversion. A challenge sounded perfect. I'd prove to myself that I was okay. That I could finally beat The Darkness back into the deep recesses of my mind.

I'd go for the challenge and for the money. The love crap was just that. Crap.

"Okay, but I'm still wondering how they got our names and

addresses."

"Maddy's right. How'd they do it? From the school's records?" That's when I noticed how weird Nina was acting. Like she was holding out on us. "What did you do?"

"I didn't think it would really happen."

Aw, crap.

Nina had a tendency to jump into things, often taking us along with her. Like the time she enrolled us in drama club. Although she knew I hated doing anything in front of a crowd, she still managed to get me on stage. Or the time she signed us up for a ghost tour in Savannah, Georgia, even though Maddy was terrified of spooky things.

"You didn't think what would happen?" Maddy and I drew closer, backing her up until she plopped onto the couch.

Nina looked like she wanted to be anyplace else. But when Maddy wanted answers, she was like a bulldog with a bloody steak. "I got this email. At first, I was going to delete it, but then I saw that it was a challenge. You know. Like for one of those reality television shows."

Nina had always wanted to be on a reality show. "Go on." I edged closer.

"It's kind of a survival challenge mixed with a dating thing. Except they guarantee that, if you make it through The Claiming Games, you'll find the man of your dreams. Or win a lot of money. Which we all need, right? So...I kind of entered all three of our names."

She pulled a pillow in front of her. Like we'd ever hit her.

"No one can guarantee the man thing." Now it looked even more like a scam. One that played to both a girl's heart and her greed.

"She's right." Maddy took a swig of Nina's drink. "This is

total bullshit and you gave them our personal information. Haven't you ever heard of phishing? They lured you in and you took Erin and me down with you. What the hell were you thinking?"

"Easy, Mad. You sound like her mother." I sat down on one side of her while Maddy took the other. "And?"

There was a reason we'd nicknamed her Mad. More from the fact that her anger could go from zero to sixty than anything to do with her name. It was kind of funny when you considered that a nickname of Mad would've fit me better.

Nina's scowl wasn't scathing. Nothing she did could ever seem too mean. She was just too nice. "I know I should've deleted it, but it looked so real."

"Most of them do."

"Easy, Mad. Keep talking, Nina."

"It's sponsored by this company called K.O.B., the same one on the invitation. If you wanted to try for it, you sent in your name and some details."

"And you sent them all our names and addresses. Holy shit." Maddy groaned.

Nina hesitated to continue, then at my silent urging, she went ahead. "If you're chosen, you go somewhere in the woods of North Carolina. There's a set of physical and mental challenges, but once you get through them, you end up with either the man of your dreams or two hundred and fifty thousand dollars."

"So it's like an endurance course with a man and money for the prize?" Maddy laughed. "It's a joke, right? I mean, who puts on a contest like that?"

"Not the man *and* the money. You have to pick one or the other. *If* you make it to the end."

I skimmed the invitation for the hundredth time. The whole thing was ridiculous and maybe even dangerous. The best thing we could do was to throw the invitations away and hope we didn't get spammed or worse.

"So you saw this thing and just signed us up? Without even asking us?" Maddy stared at her invitation. "I still can't believe it."

Nina let out a big sigh. She may have messed up, but her heart was always in the right place. "I did it right after you-know-what. Erin was still in a bad way, so I didn't want to ask her for her permission. Then, once I'd entered hers and my information, I figured what the hell? Might as well get your info in, too. After all, we do everything together, right?" She glanced at me, then slumped back. "I figured I'd put us all in and never hear another word about it."

"I haven't heard anything about The Claiming Games before. I just hope that claiming doesn't mean we're going to get tied up and tortured." Maddy tossed her invitation on top of the coffee table. "You screwed up, Nina. Now we're going to get emails and junk mail from all kinds of freaks. Thanks a lot."

Common sense said Maddy was right. Yet I couldn't shake the feeling that I wanted to go. "But what if it's true? What if we do this thing and wind up with a great guy? Or, better yet, with the money? Is it two hundred and fifty thousand for everyone who wins? Or do the winners split the cash? Can there be more than one winner? I mean, if I won, I'd choose the money for sure. Think of what you could do with that kind of cash. Pay off school. Buy a new car. Take a vacation."

"And shoes. Think about all the shoes I could buy."

Maddy rolled her eyes, probably thinking the same thing I was. Nina was as obsessed with shoes as she was with reality shows. "You, girl, have a problem. Is there a support group for shoe addicts?"

"Never mind that. At least the plane ticket's real and it's paid for." I searched their faces, hoping to see the same eagerness I was feeling. "I say we go for it. How else are we going to pay off our school loans? Do you want to graduate and not have enough money to live? And what if we don't get a job right off the bat? I don't know about you, but I'm not going back home."

"She's right, Mad. We need the money. And if we can have some fun, too, then why not?"

"And maybe find the man of our dreams?" Maddy snorted, yet she made the sound seem cute. "Come on, Erin. You're just starting to get over Mike. Why throw yourself into a situation that's just begging for a letdown?"

Nina glanced between us, excitement dancing in her eyes. "If it's not something we want to do, we can always leave. If nothing else, at least we'll get a free trip out of it and maybe even a little excitement. And if it turns out to be a new reality show, then who knows? We could become famous."

That was Nina. The eternal optimist.

I hooked my arm in Nina's. For the first time since Mike had dumped me, I had something to look forward to. "Yeah, Mad. Let's take a chance. What can it hurt?"

"Oh, I don't know. Maybe nothing. Maybe everything." She shook her head. "It just feels wrong."

"So you'd rather spend the summer working for Old Man Luger?" Maddy had spent the past couple of summers working as an unpaid intern for a realtor. Although she liked the realty business and hoped to start her own brokerage one day, she couldn't stand her boss. He never missed a chance to hit on her whenever he asked her to work an open house with him.

"That's not fair, Erin."

"Life's not fair," I said, using one of my father's favorite phrases. "I sure as hell don't want to spend another summer working at the art supply store. Come on. We'll stick together so nothing bad can happen." I made a pouty face. "We don't want to do this without you. It's an adventure and just what I need to get my mind off you-know-who. Pu-lease, Maddy. For me?"

Again came Maddy's signature eye roll. "Fine. But when we get tied up and raped, don't go blaming me."

Erin

"This is cute, right?" Nina had her nose pressed to the cab's window.

"Doesn't look like much to me." Cripple Creek was easy to fault, especially for a city girl like Maddy.

I gave Cripple Creek another look. Okay, so it was a one-horse town with mom-and-pop shops. A lot of the stores looked like they'd been built back in the old frontier, but they were well-maintained and clean. Many of them had pots of colorful flowers dangling from hooks beside their front doors. The town had a coziness that appealed to me.

The cozy appeal was warped, however, by a line of Harley Davidson motorcycles parked along the street. Was Cripple Creek the home of a biker club?

"Hey, look." Nina pointed at one of the bikers coming out of the local pharmacy. "Didn't we see those guys in Chambers a while back? Yeah, I remember." She pointed at him again as though we hadn't seen her do it the first time. "Kings of Beasts MC. That was their name."

Kings of Beasts. I liked the name. At least it sounded better, maybe a little friendlier, than what most biker clubs were called.

"I think you're right." Maddy bumped her shoulder against mine. "You remember, don't you? The day we were outside Caffeine Charlie's with—" She stopped short, then made a face. "Sorry. Just forget I almost brought him up."

"Don't worry about it, Maddy." I was the one who needed to worry. Whenever I thought about how stupid I'd been with Mike, The Darkness would curl its claws around me, clutching at me, trying to pull me under.

"Erin, stick with us, okay? Keep on going. Stay safe. Remember?"

That had become our motto. Mainly for me, of course, but it worked in a lot of situations so we'd all started using it. Nina's hand on my shoulder brought me back. I smiled, pretending I was okay. "I will."

"Let's remember why we're here. Right, Erin?"

"Sure." I tilted my head at the cab driver. We were lucky the people putting on The Claiming Games had provided transportation. I doubted we could've found anyone else to drive us all the way from the tiny airport at the base of the mountains up to the secluded town. The place probably didn't even have a bus line.

"I'm starting to wonder about that." Maddy lifted her eyebrows, giving me one of *those* looks. "Again."

We'd discussed the invitations until we couldn't find anything more to say. And we'd all come to the same conclusion. It was risky, possibly even dangerous. But where there was risk, there was reward. Plus, we needed the money. If we could win enough to make paying for college a breeze, then how could we not try? We didn't say much about the angle of finding love, but I was certain it had helped get us on the plane.

I checked my friends, thankful they were there with me. I doubted any of us would've taken the chance if we'd had to do it alone. There was safety in numbers.

"I think it's nice looking."

Nina leaned forward, blocking my view out her passenger window. Somehow I'd gotten stuck sitting in the middle.

"I was afraid we were going to end up in the back woods of nowhere talking to a toothless Cousin Jeb."

Maddy and I smothered our laughs and grinned at each other. Nina could say the funniest things at times, and not even be aware of it. Often, she'd get ticked off if we laughed, thinking we were laughing at her, and we'd swear every time that we were laughing *with* her. The thing was, she believed us. She was just too good-hearted not to. It was mean, but, although I'd die before I admitted it to her, sometimes we *were* laughing at her.

I caught the cab driver's attention by way of the rearview mirror. "Is Fang's Bar and Grill on a side street? I don't see it."

He chuckled, then flicked the ashes of his cigarette out the window. "Girl, Cripple Creek ain't got but one street. The others are more like suggestions for roads. So no. Fang's ain't even in town."

A tickle of fear zipped up my spine. "Is it far?"

"Far enough."

What the hell did that mean? But when Maddy and Nina stayed quiet, I clammed up, too. Until he pulled the cab over to the side of the road.

"Why are we stopping?"

He twisted around, putting his arm on the back of his seat. His thinning hair, along with his hawkish nose, gave him a birdlike appearance. It wouldn't have surprised me if he'd pecked at me. "How you girls doin'?"

Maddy chimed up, taking the lead as she often did. "Why do you want to know?"

Oh, God. Don't start anything, Mad.

"Hey, don't go getting your hackles up. I'm just thinking you might want to hit the can before we get out of town."

"Why? Fang's isn't that far, is it?" We'd already spent a long time on the road.

"Nope. But Fang's don't have no toilet. Leastwise, not the kind you girls are used to." He shrugged and put his hands back on the wheel. "Ain't my problem. I'm just asking to be polite."

What kind of place could call itself a bar and grill and not have a decent toilet? What did it have? An outhouse?

"Okay, okay." Nina raised her hand. "I need to go. But where?"

He pointed at a tiny hole-in-the-wall diner. "Right there at CeeCee's. But don't take too long. I got to get back down the mountain before nightfall." He cocked his head to the side and looked up at the sky. "I don't like getting caught around these parts after dark."

Oh, shit. Maybe this was a bad idea after all.

"Why not?"

He met my gaze and, for a moment, I wasn't sure I wanted to hear his answer. "Nothing. I got things to do, is all." He waved his hand to get us moving. "Hurry up. Daylight's a-burnin'."

Nina pushed against me and I pushed against Maddy. We all piled out on Maddy's side, paused to check out the front of the diner, then headed inside. The usual conversation and chatter I'd expected to hear in a hometown diner died as soon as we crossed the threshold.

"Keep moving." Maddy pointed at the sign hung over a short hallway. A cartoon finger led the way to the restrooms. She opened the door marked Women's, then stopped. "There's only room for one of us in here. You'll have to wait your turns."

Nina let out a moan as I pulled her against the wall. One look back at the customers—*why are they still staring at us?*—had me wanting to keep her close.

"Is it just me—"

"No." She didn't have to finish her question.

"Erin, do you think we made a mistake? It's not too late to turn around and go home."

"No. We've gone back and forth too many times already." I wanted to show my friends that I was stronger than they thought I was. Hell, stronger than *I* thought I was. I needed a challenge and The Claiming Games had come at exactly the right time. I just hoped I hadn't screwed up. If I had, I'd dragged my two best friends into the shit along with me.

Maddy came out and let Nina go in. She leaned against the wall, taking Nina's place, then bent past me to smile at the people who were still staring at us. Lifting a hand in a wave, she did what I never would've had the nerve to do.

"Hey, everyone. Is there something you need to know? Are we hogging the bathroom?"

I cringed and hoped no one would take offence. Weren't small towns notorious for their distrust of outsiders? Why make it worse?

When the customers darted their attention away from us, I let out a sigh, then pressed close to the bathroom door. "Nina, are you about finished?" I hadn't had the urge to go before, but now I could hardly wait.

They were on us before I knew they were there, coming out of a room at the back. Two huge men, both dressed in black sleeveless vests, both with tattoos. One had the tat of the roaring lion's head on his left arm and the other had the same tat along the side of his neck.

"Well, look here, Hector. We've got some city girls in town." The older one with graying temples leaned toward Maddy.

I gave Maddy a hard look, silently asking her to stay calm. But I should've taken my own advice. I jumped when Hector took hold of a strand of my hair and twisted it around his finger.

"You're a pretty thing. Where you headed?"

He was kind of handsome, in a hard-life kind of way, with glossy black hair. His body was all muscles and ready to handle any situation. I just hoped that situation wouldn't include me. Should I tell him we were headed to The Claiming Games? Maybe he'd know about it. But I held back.

"It's none of your business," answered Maddy.

Hector ran his hungry gaze down my body, then back up. "Looks like yours is a feisty one, Blue. Mine's kind of skittish."

Blue? Did they call him that because his eyes were blue? But they both had the same blue-silver eyes. Where had I seen that color of eyes before? Thinking, however, was hard to do with Hector so close to me. I pushed as hard as I could against the wall behind me, but he kept inching closer.

"I like 'em with spunk, man."

My nerves jumped to an even higher level of alert. Hector had me trapped between his arms with nowhere to run. "Um, would you mind backing up?"

"Why? Am I bothering you?"

He was, but not in the way he was obviously hoping for. "You're in my personal space. So yeah. You are." Suddenly, I was more irritated than afraid.

"And so are you." Maddy proved she was braver than me by flattening her hands on Blue's chest and pushing him hard. Yet he barely moved.

In the next second, he had her back against the wall and pinned like me. A low mean sound rumbled out of him.

Had he just growled?

Hector put his face next to mine, then drew in a long breath. "Damn, you smell good." He turned my hair loose, then tracked his finger down my neck, getting his finger way too close to my breast. "Listen up, girl. You better get your friend in line before she gets you both into trouble. You understand?"

I swallowed and nodded my head. He was so close I could feel the warmth of his alcohol-laced breath on my skin. "Just leave us alone."

"What for? I like you."

What was I supposed to say? Great? Thanks? I hoped I wouldn't pee my pants. Yet, although I was afraid, I was getting even more fed up. "I'm sorry, but the feeling isn't mutual."

He pushed away fast and let out with a huge laugh, startling me again. "Damn, but I like your spirit. Too bad. I'd spend more time with you and make you learn to like me, but I gotta get moving. Come on, Blue. Burke's waiting."

When Blue didn't move, he grabbed his arm and pulled his friend away from Maddy. "I said come on."

"Get your fucking paws off me, man." Blue jerked away from him, winked at Maddy, then started toward the front door.

Hector twisted around and grinned at me. The pure lust I saw had me trembling in a very bad way. "Watch out for wild animals. You wouldn't want to get bit." He cocked his head to the side, then slid his tongue over his lip. "Or would you?"

I stared at him as he let out another big laugh and strode after his friend. "Oh, shit."

"You can say that again," whispered Maddy.

"Look at the back of their vests. It's the same motorcycle gang that came through Chambers. The Kings of Beasts MC. Same as their tats."

Maddy let out a hard breath. "You're right. What are they doing around here?"

"Let's hope they're just passing through." Although I wouldn't have minded seeing the lone rider I'd seen that day.

That's where I saw blue-silver eyes.

Finally Nina opened the door. "Who were you guys talking to?"

"Out of the way." I darted past her into the tiny restroom and shut the door. I held out my hands, saw how badly they were shaking, then clenched my fists.

Oh, shit. What have I gotten us into?

Colter

"They're here."

I gritted my teeth. The day had come too soon. I wasn't ready. I felt trapped and because I did, I wanted to run. Running, however, wasn't an option. Besides, I'd never leave my home in the mountains.

"Is everything in place?"

Roberta was almost as bad as Burke at pushing me since she'd taken on the role of surrogate mother to me. I'd never told her, but I'd kind of liked her having my back. At least, most of the time.

"Yes." I didn't bother telling her she'd already asked me three times.

We stood off to the side, hidden behind a row of trees behind Fang's Bar and Grill. Many of the candidates had already gone inside the bar and now four girls came together in the parking lot. Three of them had arrived in the same cab, their bodies moving alike as they stayed closed to one another. Like all the others, they weren't mature or prepared enough to be called women yet. The fourth one, with coal black hair, joined them, seeking safety in numbers.

I frowned, watching the tall, statuesque one with auburn hair and immediately discounted her. She was beautiful and curvy, yet the way she held her head high didn't boast confidence. To me, it signaled a stubbornness born out of fear. Fear of not being able to handle whatever life threw at her.

The red-haired one was interesting, but more timid than her friends. She needed to touch them, to take their arms, a sure sign she needed their support. I didn't want someone who'd cling to me.

The fourth one, the one who had joined the threesome, was more attractive. She'd arrived by herself, proving she had nerve. Or was it foolishness?

But it was the one with shoulder-length brown hair who grabbed my attention. I remembered her from the coffee shop. She didn't act too confident or too timid. Sure, I could feel her anxiety even from a distance, but it wouldn't have made sense for her not to be on guard. At least she wasn't foolish or stupid. At times, she seemed like she wanted to bolt. Then at other moments, she'd walk toward the front door only to reverse her direction and urge her friends to follow her.

Maybe it was because I couldn't get a firm hold on what she was like. Or maybe it was just that her profile with the slight bump in her nose intrigued me. She wasn't anything extraordinary, either in face or in body. Yet there was something about her that made me want to find out more.

I'd even had a few dreams about her. Dreams filled with raw, carnal sex.

"See one you like?"

Roberta would find out soon enough. I didn't need or want to say just yet. Instead, I shrugged, then stalked into the forest.

The beginning of the games was near and I'd find out about her soon enough. Once I got a good whiff of her, I'd know.

Erin

We fucked up.

Maddy, Nina, and I stood in the parking lot as the afternoon sun beat down on my neck. The woods around us were beautiful, like something out of an animated children's film. I wouldn't have been surprised if a bluebird had landed on my shoulder and sung a song just for me. But the idyllic beauty of the surrounding woods made what was in front of us look even worse.

Fang's Bar and Grill was a dump. Not just rundown. Not just a little shady. It was an all-out, shingles-falling-off-the-roof pit of a biker bar. The motorcycles were lined up two rows deep in the gravel pit of a parking lot.

This is so not good.

I was a fool to have thought the invitation would work out. I doubted anyone inside this shithole was going to give us money for our rides home, much less thousands of dollars. We'd get stuck forking over money we didn't have to buy plane tickets. That, along with losing an entire summer's paycheck, made it suck even more.

"Extraordinary man, my ass." I didn't want some long-haired, vest-wearing biker. As if. Most bikers I'd seen cruising the highway were older guys who'd been cool back before the gray hair and beer belly had taken over. Way back.

"I'm so sorry I got us into this." Nina tunneled her fingers through her tousled hair. "Don't bother, Mad. I'll say it before you do. You told me so."

Maddy was in a forgiving mood. "Don't worry about it. You didn't twist our arms. It was as much our decision as yours."

The idling sound of a car motor revving up had us whirling around, ready to jump back into the cab we'd just gotten out of. The driver had dumped our things and was already heading the cab out of the lot.

"No! Wait! Come back!" I ran after the cab like I could actually catch the damn thing.

"Fuck, fuck, fuck." Maddy tossed her purse to the ground in a huff. "Now we're really stuck."

Nina remained silent, looking forlorn and guilty.

"So you're not staying?"

I pivoted around to find a girl about my age standing near one of the motorcycles. Her raven black hair shone under the torturing sun and her green eyes sparkled as her attention jumped from one to the other of us. Her body was lean and trim with legs that stretched all the way to Mexico. If she was my competition for the man of my dreams, I was screwed. But then again, with Maddy around, I'd been screwed from the start. What was one more hot girl?

The man of my dreams. It was a lame idea. And yet, I found myself thinking about him all the time. Thinking about a fantasy man was helping me get over Mike faster. Was that a credit to my ability to bounce back? Or had I finally come out of it long enough to realize that he'd never been the guy I'd thought he was? I was ashamed to think I'd gone so close to the edge over losing him.

"Hi. I'm Mia Travers. Are you here for The Claiming Games? Did you guys get an invitation, too?"

"Yes. No." I dragged in a breath, steadying my frayed nerves before offering my hand. "Hi, I'm Erin Pierce."

Mia's laugh was light and airy, devoid of any of the anxiety tightening my neck. "O-kay. So which is it? Yes or no?"

"Yes. That's why we're here, but after getting a look at this place, we're ready to take a cab back to the airport." I scanned the area, but saw nothing except more motorcycles along with a few pickups that looked like they hadn't seen a carwash in years. "Did you come in a cab? Is it still around here somewhere?"

The cab ride back to the airport would cost a boatload of cash, even split between the three of us. But I wasn't worried about forking over a small fortune. Hell, I was ready to hop on a mule if I had to. As long as the mule knew the way back to the departure area for Blue Skies Airlines.

"Nope. I hitched my way up from Biloxi, Mississippi."

"You did? But why? Didn't they give you a plane ticket?" I noticed the backpack slung over Mia's shoulder. Her clothes were old, frayed, and a little dirty, too, but all in all, she didn't look half bad. Especially considering she'd hitched her way across several states. Her face and hair still looked like she'd just stepped away from a photo shoot.

"Yeah, they did. I cashed it in and gave the money to my mom. She's got seven other kids at home to clothe and feed. I'm hoping whoever sent it won't mind as long as I showed up on time."

I nodded as though I understood what going without new clothes and food was like. My parents hadn't been the greatest, but they'd kept me fed and clothed, and into a variety of recreational activities to keep me out of their hair.

"Wait. So you're saying you took rides from strangers to get here?" Maddy scrunched up her nose. "Damn, girl. Either you've got a ton of guts or you're just plain stupid."

"Maddy." Nina stared pointedly at her, then at Mia. "I'm sorry. She speaks her mind, but she's really a nice person."

"Nina's right." I lifted my hands to fend off Maddy's narrowed glare. "Hey, I'm agreeing that you're nice."

"Don't worry about it." Mia shifted the pack from one shoulder to the other. "I like people who say what they mean."

"I've got to ask. Do you think this is legit? And even if it is, why meet here? Why not at a local hotel? You know. Some place nicer than this." The bar wasn't getting any better-looking the more I studied it. "Some place that probably has a clean toilet."

"Aw, it doesn't look so bad to me." Nina tossed her long braid over her shoulder. "I'm Nina Winters and this is Maddy Wheller."

"Nice to meet you."

We kind of stood around awkwardly, unsure what to do

next. I figured I might as well lead the way. "Come on. Let's go inside and get this over with."

I bent and picked up my one suitcase. Thankfully, my purse was already stored inside it, freeing my other hand as well as keeping someone from stealing it. No one would want my battered old suitcase unless they were some pervert interested in women's underwear. I steeled myself for whatever I'd find inside and led the way.

Halfway there, I noticed that no one had followed me. I paced back. "We might as well find out what this is about. What else are you going to do? Hitchhike like Mia?"

"She's right. Let's do this."

I pivoted back toward the front entrance, now that I knew Maddy would come. Wherever Maddy led, Nina would follow.

It took my eyes a while to adjust to the darkness. Once they had, I wished I hadn't stepped over the threshold. The roaring lion's head logo with the Kings of Beasts MC written under it was everywhere. On their black vests, their black shirts, and their inked skin. Even on a sign hanging on a wall. "Look. It's them. The motorcycle guys."

Was it too late to back out? Yet, since I'd come that far, I figured I might as well go the rest of the way. Besides, the thought of seeing the gorgeous hunk with the blue-silver eyes gave me a thrill.

"Yep. Typical biker bar." Mia shrugged at me, then took the lead. "I've been inside a few."

"The girl definitely has guts," I whispered.

Mia strolled toward the center of the room, where one empty table remained next to several occupied tables. Thirty or so women, all around my age, appeared as nervous as I was. Some of them held invitations like ours.

I hurried after Mia, feeding off her courage, with Nina and Maddy at my heels. The men stood on the outskirts as though surrounding us, like a wolf pack ready to jump on its prey. Most of them didn't look like they were much older than me. Even if we were close in age, they were bigger, stronger than any of the guys I'd seen on campus, including the football players. These strong, virile guys were men, not boys, who looked like they could take a beating and get back on their feet kicking. They stared at us with hot looks that made me avert my gaze as a tingle skimmed over my skin. Yet not one of them spoke to any of the girls.

I could feel the heat of their looks warming me from the inside out. They were hungry and we were their meal.

"Oh, shit. We're going to get gang raped. Gang raped by bikers and left for dead in a ditch." Nina took hold of my arm with a sweaty hand.

"I say we run and don't look back. Every woman for herself."

"Thanks, Mad. Good to know you have my back."

But she was right. We should turn tail and get the hell out. But I couldn't. If the possibility that I could win money and wipe out my debt still existed, then I had to stick it out. At least for a little while longer.

I prayed I wouldn't get eaten alive.

We sat down at the table Mia had chosen. I tried to act like I had as much confidence as she did. The only way to keep my hands from shaking was to clasp them in my lap. I studied the girls seated at the other tables. Were they my competition? There were more girls than there were men. Did everyone have their own fantasy man to meet or would we be pitted against each other? Not wanting to, but unable to resist, I ranked them according to their beauty, style of dress, and confidence level.

As usual, I came in almost dead last.

Mia had them all beat as far as the confidence thing went. She was pretty, too, which put her above most of them. The majority of the girls had bodies I'd kill for and faces with full pouty lips and eyes sparkling with excitement. A few of them were dressed as conservatively as I was in jeans and T-shirts. Others had chosen to highlight their obvious physical attributes with shorty shorts and see-their-nipples tight shirts.

"This is degrading. It's like we're cows and they're picking out the ones they want to buy." Maddy's tone dripped with anger, but she didn't get up and leave.

I recognized life for what it was. A popularity contest with the best-looking people coming in first. As much as we tried to deny it, most girls spent a lot of their time trying to win the attention of a guy.

"You're right." Mia smiled, then reached out and patted Maddy's hand like a mother comforting her distraught child. With so many siblings, she'd probably done a lot of that. "But don't worry. We're sizing them up, too. They can't buy us, no matter how much they may want our milk."

How Nina and I managed to keep from laughing was beyond me. Maddy pulled her hand away, obviously thrown.

"Hey."

I twisted around toward the table to the right of ours. "Yes?"

A gorgeous blonde girl smiled, then pressed her large breasts against the back of her chair and leaned forward to whisper, "Hey, there. I'm Lucee Michelson. Are you here for The Claiming Games, too?"

"Uh-huh. I'm Erin and these are my friends, Nina, Maddy, and Mia." As far as I was concerned, Mia was one of us now.

"It's good to meet you." Lucee nodded toward her tablemate, who was too interested in watching the men to notice us. The girl's long black hair swayed as she moved her head back and forth, taking in one man, then the next.

"That's Juanita Reyas. She's a secretary from New Mexico and I'm an aspiring actress from Los Angeles. Where Hollywood is, you know?"

"Yeah. I know where Hollywood is." I edged closer to the buxom Lucee. "Have any of the men said anything?"

"Not a word."

"It's downright rude, if you ask me."

I shifted toward the voice, putting my body sideways so I could look at the two girls at the other table. Like the rest of us, I would've guessed them to be about my age.

The girl who'd spoken had a deep Southern accent with a touch of twang. She had short brunette hair with a smattering of freckles spanning her nose. Although she was plump, she wore her blouse tight, emphasizing her generous boobs. Boobs any man would love to motorboat.

"Hey, there. I'm Cassidy Hastings and my friend here is Angela Weston. I'm from Nashville. I'm a singer." She gave me a bright smile. "Or at least I'm trying to be. Angela's a big-time advertising executive all the way from New York City."

"Hey back at you." Meeting them was nice, but it didn't tell me anything I wanted to know. "So how long have you been here? Have you seen or heard anything about this? Have those men been standing there staring the whole time?" Are they silently judging us? Picking out their favorite for the gang rape?

"Lucee and Juanita were already seated by the time Angela and I got here. Almost all the tables were already filled by then. All in all, I'd say it's been like this for about fifteen minutes."

She pointed at an old circular metal clock on the wall behind the bar's counter. "It's just now two o'clock. Looks like everyone made it here on time."

If my guess was anywhere close to the correct number, there had to be at least twenty men in the bar to thirty or so girls. What were they planning on doing? Letting some men have more than one woman?

A shiver ran through me, urging me to get up and out of the place as fast as I could. And yet I couldn't make my legs move. The men were sexy as hell, their magnetism stronger than I would've thought possible. Dressed in their casual attire, they still gave off the confidence of a billionaire running a major corporation. As though they were the captains of industry who didn't need to dress the part.

"Shit."

"What is it, Maddy?" I followed her slight nod as she indicated the left side of the bar. "Oh, hell, no."

"Uh-huh. Looks like your friend is here."

"Bite your tongue. He's no friend of mine." Standing against the wall was Hector, the man who'd cornered me in CeeCee's. Lucky for Maddy, Blue wasn't with him. It was bad enough I'd seen him, but when he noticed me and sent me another one of his shit-eating grins, I wanted to crawl under the table. Instead, I got gutsy enough to glare at him. At least for a moment or two.

"Just ignore him." Maddy leaned closer. "Look to your right."

I did and caught a few of them sizing me up. Rattled, I darted my gaze away. But I couldn't keep it down for long. A tickle made the hair on my neck stand up as I gave into the urge to look again.

Holy hell. It's him.

My breath hitched in my throat as his eyes, that strange blue-silver, fixed on me. His dark hair teased the bottom of his earlobes. He was dressed all in black from the tips of his hard, black boots to the T-shirt that hugged his pecs, then emphasized the rolling abs of his six-pack. I wasn't sure about his age. He could've been in his early or mid-twenties. It didn't matter. A man like him wouldn't lose his sex appeal with age. He'd just get better, like an expensive fine wine.

There he was. The lone biker I'd seen following the rest of his group as they'd ridden past Caffeine Charlie's. Had it been a coincidence? Or had they come to Chambers on purpose?

He crossed his arms, never once blinking as his eyes narrowed. I tried to break the visual lock he had on me, but couldn't. My body was suddenly more alive than it had ever been, sending every inch of me on high alert. No one, not even Mike, had ever turned me on so fast or so hard.

I swallowed, my throat closing up as I realized exactly what he was. He was, by all definitions of the word, just what the invitation had promised. He was an extraordinary man.

At least physically.

It wasn't until the noise around them suddenly died down that he shifted his attention away. Someone pulled the plug on the jukebox, ending the music in a downward wind of a groan. All the men's attention riveted to the door at the back of the room.

"Oh, shit."

I couldn't have said it better than Maddy.

The man standing in the doorway of a dark hallway towered over everyone close to him. His shoulders were so broad they almost touched the walls on either side. He was dark, yet I didn't think he was African-American. Instead, his skin color came from a deep tan that had been burned into his flesh by year after year of long hours in the sun. The handlebar mustache he wore was as black as the hair slicked away from his forehead. He was so entrancing that I almost didn't see the woman standing behind him.

He strode into the bar like a king coming into his throne room, then in one graceful leap landed on top of the bar. The woman followed him into the room, her long, white hair showering her shoulders, and took a place in front of the bar directly under him. He spread his arms wide, like a Master of Ceremonies greeting his audience.

"Welcome, bitches, to The Claiming Games."

Chapter Three

Erin

Cheers and hoots erupted around the room, but only from the men. The girls remained silent, just as unsure as I was of how we were supposed to react.

Bitches? Why had he used that term?

I could've taken offense and knew Maddy had to be bristling at the name, but instead, I decided to give him a break. Maybe he hadn't meant it as a slam. Maybe it was just his way of talking. Like the way some guys said, "Yo, bitch" without meaning it in a bad way. What he'd called us was the least of my concerns.

The air thickened around me, forming a cocoon of testosterone and lust. I'd already felt like I was on display, but now I got the feeling that I was standing at the edge of a cliff, just waiting for the man with the incredible eyes to push me over. Would he grab me, capturing me within his strong arms? Or would he let me fall to the bottomless depths below?

The king, as I'd started thinking of the man on top the bar, lifted his arm, his hand clenched into a fist. Everyone grew silent and waited for him to speak.

"I'm Burke Ryder. I'm the leader of the pride."

The pride? Was that where they'd gotten the name Kings of Beasts? It made sense, though, considering they'd chosen a roaring lion as their mascot.

He scowled, then added, almost as though he hated saying it, but knew he had to. "If it's easier to understand, you can call me the leader of the pack."

Would a motorcycle gang call themselves a pack?

"What does he think he is? A wolf?"

Although Mia had spoken in a soft tone, her voice echoed around the room. Burke tilted his head, his hard gaze boring a hole through her.

"Aw, sweet thang. You got a problem with wolves? I don't blame you none, but let's get this straight. We aren't a bunch of mangy mutts."

"No. I mean—"

"We call ourselves a pack because we're a family. What happens to one of us happens to all of us. We work hard and we play hard. Pack, pride, clowder, family, gang. They're all the same thing. Whatever word you want to use doesn't matter none." He placed a fist on his chest. "What matters is what's in here. We've got each other's backs and we'll go down fighting until the very last one of us is dead."

Dead? Nina and I looked at each other. Was this one of those survivalist groups? Or an anti-government fringe element?

Burke tilted his head and arched one eyebrow. "Is that all right with you, sweet thang? Or do I need to stop and answer more of your questions first?"

Mia, for the first time showing signs of nerves, shook her head, then slumped lower in her chair. I wanted to reach out and pat her arm, but didn't want to draw his attention my way.

I gripped my jeans, then rubbed my sweaty palms on them. I'd wanted an adventure, a challenge, but had I bitten off more than I could chew? Had my dream of proving myself and winning money led me straight into trouble? One glance at Nina and Maddy told me they had the same misgivings.

Burke paused longer, then crossed his arms over his barrel chest. "I'm glad to see you ladies made it past the front door. It shows you've got grit, considering you didn't know what you'd be walking into." He paused again. "Either that or you're just plain stupid." He soaked up the chuckles of the men. "But don't you worry none. You're safe as long as you're in Fang's. Plus, if you're not lucky enough to get chosen, you'll get back home all right. You've got my word on that."

And the rest of them? If chosen, would those so-called lucky girls stay safe, too?

"Okay, let's get down to it." He accepted the mug of beer the bartender slid over to him. "I started The Claiming Games over twenty years ago and it'll more than likely continue long after I'm rotting in my grave."

Then why hadn't I heard of it? An Internet search had turned up nothing. I would've thought one of the television news magazines would've been all over the story of girls going to a biker-style bar hoping to meet the men of their dreams. Not to mention the chance to find love or win a ton of money.

Burke was hardly the kind of guy I should trust my future to. But I was already there, and too curious to leave. Besides, I wasn't about to stand up and draw his attention. Burke didn't seem like the kind of guy anyone wanted to irritate. But was this thing on the up-and-up? The jury was still out on that score.

I just wanted him to tell us about the money. I wouldn't be tempted with the whole falling in love thing. Been there and done that only to wind up miserable and alone. As far as I was concerned, money would buy me happiness.

The woman standing below Burke heaved a heavy sigh.

"Get to it, my mate."

Mate? I'd heard women refer to their significant other in many different ways, but mate seemed a bit odd. Still, I could think of worse things she could've called him.

Burke chuckled, his voice deepening as it rumbled out of his chest. He bent low to skim a hand lovingly along the long flow of her hair. "This mouthy bitch is my mate, Roberta. As the founder of the games, I was one of the first to claim my woman." He stood taller, straighter, and held his chin high. "Obviously, I got lucky."

"Get on with it, I said."

His pride-filled smile dropped into a scowl. "Even if she does chap my butt."

The other men chuckled along with Burke. Roberta sounded like she called the shots, but if she did, Burke and the other men didn't agree. If I'd had to guess, Roberta knew her limits and stuck to them.

Was that the kind of men these were? The kind who'd treat their women like possessions? Who'd boss them around like second-class citizens? If so, I had yet another reason to take the money and run.

Then again, every woman loved a forceful man. As long as he wasn't a brute.

"Roberta's right, as usual." He ignored her snort of derision. "Okay, then, here it is. Bitches, pay close attention. I'm not going to repeat myself. When I'm finished, you'll be asked one question and one question only." His piercing gaze scoured the women. "Will you join in The Claiming Games? Be prepared to answer. For right now, stay in your seats"—his grin was wicked—"no matter what."

Oh, fuck. This is going downhill fast.

The alarm bells in my head were going off full blast. I looked at my friends and knew they were thinking the same thing. If one of them took off, I'd be right behind her. But none of us did.

I lifted my gaze and found the delicious man still staring at me.

Then again, I've come this far already.

Burke jumped off the bar and moved into the sea of women like a cougar stalking its prey. I cast my gaze down, too unnerved to look directly into his eyes.

"Men, you're up. Stake your claim."

Stake their claim? Like we were objects to own? Slaves to buy? Had I walked into a real live version of a meat market? Or worse, into a sex slave trafficking gang? And what? Were we supposed to just accept whatever the men wanted to do to us?

Having them study us was one thing and accepting that we were on display for their pleasure was weird, but I could get over those two things. At least, until I could get out of there. But suddenly, it was a lot more. Was I ready to go with the flow no matter what that flow was like? Would Nina, Maddy, and Mia go along with it? Nina and I exchanged another look, but I wanted to see what would happen next.

I grew more anxious by the minute. If they tried to hurt me or take me away, I'd do my best to fight them. I doubted I could put up much of a fight against even one of them, but I'd do my best.

My nerves were jumping like crazy, and the sudden pounding in my head was a warning I shouldn't ignore. Yet every time I stole a glance at the hunk that had grabbed my attention and wouldn't let go, I couldn't move. Couldn't breathe right. Instead of listening to my gut, I took the coward's way out, shutting my eyes and hoping for the best.

I jumped and opened my eyes as the men who'd stayed so still, so motionless, came to life. They talked among themselves as they wove in between the tables. Four men headed toward our table, including the amazing man who'd kept his hungry gaze locked on me. The men were perfect specimens of male virility, each one as tall as the next, each one with muscles exuding power and strength. I pushed the legs of my jeans down and tugged my T-shirt higher to cover the swell of my breasts, making sure I didn't show too much skin.

Did I want to get chosen? Or did I want to go home? Again, I was torn.

The first two men came close, then hovered over me and...

Oh, shit. If he touches me, I'm going to scream. Please, don't touch me.

I leaned away just a little, shot him a fearful look, and hoped he wouldn't grab me. To my relief, both men eased past me, moving on to the next table.

Another couple of men, including the man I'd locked eyes with and a tall striking man with blond hair, stepped to either side of me. I tried not to run and tried not to squeak in fear when the blond bent over me. I could almost feel his hands travel between my breasts, then over to thumb a nipple.

Go away. Please.

I wanted my man to touch me.

My man?

I held my breath, then relaxed when the blond guy moved toward Mia. Yet when that sexy man who'd turned me on with just one look finally touched me, I startled, then swallowed and forced myself to keep my ass in my chair. His fingers trailed along my shoulder, then down my arm. Tensing, I waited. I wanted him to slide his hand lower and find the curve of my breast. Damn it. I wished I hadn't tugged my shirt higher.

Instead, he lifted the hair off my neck and put his face an inch from mine. "What's your name?"

His voice was a silky rich tone that made me want to puddle at his feet. Heat, driven by sexually-charged pheromones, drifted off him, searing into my flesh and sending my body temperature skyward. He was toned and charged with power that ran from the tip of his head down to his feet. He couldn't have been much older than me, and yet he exuded an amazing confidence. Not a cockiness, but a real inner strength.

"Erin. Pierce. Erin Pierce." I was surprised at how normal my voice sounded. Almost as though his being so near didn't affect me at all. Remaining as still as I could, I clasped my hands together and settled them in my lap.

"Erin Pierce, are you a virgin?"

If I hadn't already been sitting, I would've ended up on the floor.

What the hell, man? Who asks questions like that?

Even as unnerved as I was, I had to take a stand. Channeling my surprise and my irritation together, I spoke in my go-to-hell voice. "That's none of your business." I'd half expected him to get angry and had stiffened even more, waiting for him to tell me that I was the one going to hell. Or hit me. Or tell me to get out.

"Aw, now, that's no way to act."

His weird blue-silver eyes drew me in yet again. The intense sensation they gave me made me clench my teeth to keep from moaning.

Burke, the men at CeeCees', the hunk? They all had the same blue-silver eyes. But how?

"Don't worry." He brushed the hair away from my shoulder. "I'll find out soon enough."

I drew in a hard-won breath. Had he just said he was going to fuck me? That he'd be the one to take my virginity if it was still intact? I wanted to fire back, letting him know in no uncertain terms that, although I wasn't a virgin, I wasn't an easy lay. Did he think he could take whatever he wanted, including me?

When I'd finally gained enough courage to tell him, I froze at the sinful look in those blue-silver depths and I knew. Yes. He was a man who took what he wanted, whenever he wanted, and however he wanted. It wouldn't matter what I said.

He put his face close to my hair. I could feel his breath on my ear.

Oh, shit. Did he just sniff me?

What kind of man sniffed a girl? My gaze met Nina's as she watched, her mouth parted as though she'd started to speak, then had lost her voice.

I frowned and tried to identify the sound close to my ear. But what it sounded like was impossible. At least coming from a man. I would've sworn the delicious, sexy man had just purred.

Okay. I'm losing it big-time.

But if I was losing it, I was losing it in a very good way. My body tingled and he hadn't even touched me. Would he kiss me? Would I let him? The truth came to me as clear as anything ever had. I'd let this man do more than just touch me. More than just kiss me. If he'd wanted, he could've taken me outside and done whatever the hell he wanted to me. Sexually speaking, that is.

Mike had turned me on, but the way I felt with the gorgeous hunk of male in front of me was different. Way different. Where Mike had made me feel pretty, he made me feel sexy. Where Mike had gotten me moist between the legs, he made me flood with my juices. His very being tugged at me as though pulling something carnal and instinctively...*right*...out of me. There was no other word for it. I *craved* him. Like a good bottle of wine or a giant bar of my favorite chocolate. I shivered when I wasn't cold and ached when I wasn't in pain. All because of him.

I wanted him so much that I was no longer worried about what might happen. As long as he stayed close to me, I knew I'd be safe. At least, safe from the others. But safe from him? Not a chance.

Oh, hell, yeah.

How could any man, even someone like him, make me feel this way?

He straightened up and jerked his head at his friend who still hovered over Mia. Then, before I had a chance to react, they were gone, striding back to the side of the room. The men who'd surrounded Maddy shook their heads and moved to the next table to check out the other girls. More men surrounded us, each taking their time to study us like we were theirs for the taking. We'd tense with each new inspection, then let out a breath when they finally moved away.

The entire experience was both irritating and exhilarating.

Until, that is, a familiar voice took the pleasant feeling away, leaving only the irritation.

"Hey, girl."

I grimaced as Hector grabbed hold of the arms of my chair and put his face close to mine. Why did he have to get so fucking close?

I crossed my arms and glared at him. "Please get away from

me."

"Not until I get a good whiff of you." And he did. A long and disgustingly slow sniff. "Yep. Just as sweet smelling as I remember."

Asking him to leave wasn't working, so I tried a different approach. "Look, Hector, I'm sure you're a nice guy." I gave him a good once-over. "Underneath it all. But I'm not interested. Please leave me alone."

"Hector, get your ass back to the wall."

If anyone had told me I'd love hearing Burke's voice, I would've said they were crazy. But right then, he sounded like an angel.

Hector straightened up. "Talk to you soon, girl."

Not wanting to give him any reason to stay, I remained quiet and looked away. Then let out a hard breath once he was gone. When I looked up again, the amazing hunk was watching me, but he didn't look happy.

"What the hell was all that for?" Maddy made a face, then wiped off the expression just as Burke looked her way.

I almost laughed and was more thankful than ever to have brought Maddy and Nina along. "I have no idea. Did you feel like we were on the sale block? I felt like I had a sign painted across my forehead saying I was fifty percent off. All sales final." And yet it hadn't offended me. It had, in fact, made me feel sexy as hell. As though I was the only woman in the world who mattered. "I think the dark-haired one could tell what color my panties are." I followed his every move, trying not to be obvious, yet unable to stop.

"I know, right? That was pretty amazing. Don't look now, but he's staring at you again." Nina turned her head and pretended to watch the girls at the next table.

Yeah, I knew. He sent me a knowing smile, then jerked his head toward the bar, telling me to pay attention elsewhere.

I didn't want to, but pleasing him was more important than pleasing myself. I wasn't sure why. It just was.

A teenage boy came out of the hallway and stood next to Burke. After handing him a legal pad and pen, the boy hugged the clipboard holding a stack of small papers to his chest. His eyes were round as he studied the girls with obvious fascination.

One at a time, each man left his position next to the wall and spoke to Burke. They kept their voices low, their gazes shifting from one table of girls to the next. Burke nodded, then made check marks on the legal pad as the boy wrote something on a piece of paper then put that sheet on the bottom of his stack. Once most of the men had gone past him, Burke gave the boy a nod who then dashed back down the hallway. Burke strode to the center of the room.

"Quiet." He held up the pad. "Okay, bitches, listen up."

There it was again. Did he have to call us that? It was irritating, but again, not important enough that I'd make a fuss over it.

"If I call your name, you leave. No bitching. Roberta will meet you outside where she'll give you enough money to purchase your return trip home. Ask no questions before getting into one of the cabs outside. And remember this"—his expression went stone-cold—"do not speak of this to anyone. Not once you leave." His eyes narrowed. "Not ever."

He didn't have to give a reason to keep quiet. I could sense that anyone breaking his command would regret opening their mouth. I nodded, more than eager to do as he said.

"Aren't you going to tell us what this means or how this works? What is this K.O.B. Corporation? You've told us basically nothing. What happens during The Claiming Games? Are we chased and locked up? Claimed by these men? Is that the claiming part of it?" The girl who'd stood up turned to the rest of us. "Are all of you willing to do whatever he says? Don't you want to find out more information before letting them pick and choose us like we're puppies at the pound?"

She was right, of course. And yet, although I couldn't have explained why, we remained silent.

"What's your name, girl?"

The chill from his icy tone hit me, spreading through me like a wintry breeze. I would've hated to have been in her shoes.

"Eva."

He checked his list, then gave her one of those hard smiles before turning to one of the men. "She's out, Luke. Choose another."

"Fuck that. She's the one I want." Luke snarled, reminding me of a Doberman Pinscher about to attack. "Give me time. I'll teach her to keep her trap closed."

The collective gasp of the girls echoed around the room. And yet none of us got up. Instead, a cowed Eva took her seat.

"Don't go scaring them off, Burke." Roberta bit off the end of her nail, then spat it out.

"Fine." Burke went back to his list. "She can stay. For now. But she's your responsibility. Make sure she tows the line."

"Done," answered Luke, then followed it with a snarl.

A snarl. Like some wild animal.

The snarl didn't seem to bother Burke. "As for the rest of you, you'll find out more once we get rid of the losers."

Was I a loser or a winner if he called my name? If I stayed, would I find out the name of the man who even now stared at me like he hadn't eaten in a month and I was a four-course meal? Would it be worth going through with the games to find out? Whatever the hell the games were. And yet, to have come all that way only to turn around and go home really would make me feel like a loser. As though I wasn't good enough. As though, once again, I'd somehow failed to make the grade.

The idea that I might leave frightened me almost as much as the idea of staying did. I'd come to face a challenge, to prove I was stronger than everyone thought I was. To prove I was better than my past. That and the hope of meeting the mysterious, sexy man kept me in my chair.

"For those of you who aren't called, remain where you are. And keep your mouths shut."

"No. Eva's right. You need to tell us what's going on right now."

A girl with luxurious reddish-brown hair stood and lifted her hand. "I'm Cheryl Holland from Denver. Some of us have come a long way on a leap of faith that this thing's legit. From what the other girls have told me we're all desperate in one way or another." She glanced around her. "I'm sorry, but it's the truth. Either we're dying to find a man to love or we need the money. I don't know how you knew, but obviously, you played on our desperation to get us here. I think we deserve to know what this is all about. Especially after that weird thing the men just did."

Sit down. Please, sit down.

It didn't make sense for me to want her to be quiet, to not ask the questions whirling in my head, but I felt sorry for her. Not because she risked Burke's wrath, but because she might be one of the girls to be sent home. All at once, I knew without a doubt that I wanted to stay. I shifted my gaze toward the man who'd grabbed my interest.

For the money. Remember that.

"How can you guys afford to give away two hundred and fifty thousand dollars? You don't look like you could take me to dinner and pay for it." Dread mixed with fear on her face. She swallowed, then threw back her shoulders and kept going. "This is a fucking scam, isn't it? You got us here with the lure of money and love, but that's not what this is really about. Is this some kind of sex slave thing? Are you going to kidnap us and sell us to some pervert in another country?"

The girls started talking, most of them agreeing with her. And yet no one moved out of their chairs. It was almost as though the men had put us under a spell.

She has more nerve than I do. Or maybe a whole lot less brain power.

I think we assumed Burke would answer her, then toss her out. Instead, Roberta was by her side in a flash, taking Cheryl's wrist. The young girl yelped, but didn't try to yank her arm free.

"Listen up, little girl. You got the invitation and you decided to take the risk. No one forced you to come and no one's forcing you to stay. Leave if you can't handle it."

Cheryl's face turned pink. "I didn't say that. But we need more information if we're supposed to make the right choice. Tell us what's going on."

"This isn't any sex slave business. And as far as the money goes," Roberta gave her a smug grin, "I don't think you're going to have to worry about it."

Shit. There isn't any money.

My gaze darted to my man, searching him for an answer, and saw the hard way he looked at Cheryl. If there wasn't any money, then would I choose him?

Roberta drew closer and jabbed a finger against Cheryl's chest. "A lot of what's ahead of you is going to mean listening to your gut and trusting it. But I'll tell you this much. If you want a real man, a man who'll make you more of a woman than you've ever dreamed you could be, then you'll stay." Her smile was filled with derision. "*If* you're brave enough to find out."

I could see how hard Cheryl was trying to keep from crying and I felt even sorrier for her. But sorry enough to stand by her side? Not a chance.

"This is going to be rough." Roberta stepped back and waved her hand toward the guys who stood, some with their arms crossed and others leaning against the wall. But they all had one thing in common. They were getting a kick out of watching Roberta lay into Cheryl.

"These men want the toughest, sexiest women they can find. Life might be hard for you now"—she tossed Cheryl another smug smile—"but *if* you're chosen, then it's going to get a lot harder." She pointed at the poor girl. "Tell you what. I'll give you a hint. If you want flowers and champagne, then leave. If you want sweet words whispered in your ear, then leave. But if you want hardcore, animalistic sex that will blow your pussy to heaven and back, then stick around."

Animalistic sex?

I shouldn't have liked the sound of that, but I sure as hell did.

Animalistic. Hell, yeah.

"As for the money,"—Roberta sneered at us—"if you've already decided you want money over a good man, then you might as well leave. Don't let the door hit you in the ass. And I'll tell you one more thing."

Everyone hung on her next words.

"A hot man is a lot better to hold on to than a cold dollar."

A quiet murmur swept through the girls. We weren't sure if the prize of money was real or not. Yet no one got up to leave.

"Holy shit." Nina squirmed in her seat. "Do you think there's any money?"

I couldn't take my attention off Roberta. Not even to answer Nina. "I'm not sure."

"Are you staying?"

"Yes." Did I mean it? Yes. Yes, I did.

Roberta stalked around the room, weaving in between the tables. "Some of you girls—because you're not women yet no matter how many times you've spread your legs—won't make it. You'll cry and you'll beg to go home. If you do, you'll be sent packing. It's going to be rough, tough, and without the comforts you take for granted."

She whirled around, sweeping her arm wide. "This isn't some fucking day camp. I'm going to give it to you straight. You might wind up dead."

Dead? We could actually die?

Suddenly, everything had gotten real. Maybe too real. Shouldn't they have had us sign a butt-load of releases? Enough that would've sent us running before we'd even walked into Fang's?

"Yeah, you heard me. Some of you will be stupid and foolish and get yourself hurt. We don't have a doctor and we're not about to race you forty miles away to the nearest one." She paused, letting that sink in.

She studied us, then all at once, her demeanor changed, becoming less intense. Letting out a big breath, she put her hands on her hips and relaxed her stern expression, losing some of her hard-ass attitude.

"Look. I'm just trying to make sure you know what you're getting into. You're all good girls. You had to be or you wouldn't have gotten the invitation."

"Roberta—"

Her hand went up, index finger pointed toward the ceiling, silencing Burke.

Ooh, she told him. I kept back a giggle, sensing she'd turn back into Mamma Bitch if I laughed.

"Let me do this my way, mate." She lowered her hand and even put on something resembling a smile. "If you make it through the games, *and* if the man you've found is your future mate, then you'll end up with a man who will protect you, love you, and even die for you. How many of you can say you've had a man like that?"

Not one of us raised our hand. I sure as hell didn't.

She walked toward Cheryl. "That enough info for you, princess?"

Cheryl sat back down and Roberta kept on going right past her.

Burke cleared his throat, bringing our focus back to him. "Let's get on with it."

To my horror, Nina's hand went up. "Nina, what are you doing?"

She ignored me as Burke's gaze fell on her.

"What now?" His words sounded more like a growl than English.

"So…this isn't a reality television show?"

Other expectant, hopeful girls waited for Burke's answer. The men, however, found Nina's question hilarious and burst into laughter with hoots of derision.

Burke chuckled. "Sweet thang, do you see any cameras?

"No." Nina's response was so soft I barely heard it. But I could see that Burke had.

He arched an eyebrow at her as if to say "there you have it" then looked at his notepad. "Listen up."

The scene was surreal. Women from various backgrounds, ethnicities, and affluence waited, more questions unanswered than answered, to hear their names called. Waiting to see if they would stay or go.

I glanced around, wondering if any of them would finally opt out while they still could. Squirming in my chair, I prayed I wouldn't hear my name.

"The following bitches need to get the hell out."

Funny how his calling us the *B* word didn't bother me any longer.

Burke started calling out names. "Lilly Mathews."

A squeak of surprise came from one of the tables closest to the men. A beautiful blonde with the looks of a runway model gaped at him. "You can't be serious. You're not choosing me?" She sneered at the girls closest to her. "I'm better looking than all of these girls put together."

"No questions. No bitching." Roberta, who'd taken a position at the front door, pulled it open and lifted her eyebrows. Sunlight slashed into the room. "Get out."

"This is pure bullshit. I don't know who the hell you assholes think you are, but I'm glad you didn't pick me." She scanned the rest of us. "Are you all crazy? Are you going to sit there and let this reject tell you what to do? Come on. Are you all that desperate?"

Burke's smile was sinister, filled with that same iciness from before. "Get moving before we throw you out on your skinny ass."

Snatching her suitcase and purse, Lilly stomped to the door. "Like I said. This is pure bullshit."

Burke crossed his arms, his expression darkening even more as he waited for her to leave. He started reading again as soon as the door closed behind her, blocking out the light. "Wendy Schumer. Cynthia Willis." He ignored the gasp and disappointed moan of the two women and kept reading. "Davida Harroll, Alicia Black."

I waited, my heart in my throat as murmurs erupted around me. Each woman whose name was called stood and left the bar, some of them obviously relieved and others fighting back tears of disappointment. One by one they were gone and still I remained.

"Juanita Reyas. Charlotte Zeia."

Juanita? No. I hadn't talked to Juanita, but she'd become one of the small group of girls I'd met. And now she was leaving. I lifted my hand in farewell and received a slight shrug before Juanita hefted her duffel bag over her shoulder and walked, head down, toward the outside.

Burke's voice droned on, and although I listened for my name, I let the other girls come and go without a sound, like wind drifting through my hair. As long as Nina, Maddy, and Mia stayed, I'd be all right. That and the possibility of being with the sexy man with the mesmerizing eyes kept me in my seat.

Was I crazy? Was I going to go through with this and not be guaranteed the money? Was I really willing to risk physical injury to find a guy? And yet, I knew. He wasn't just any man.

Funny how I'd never thought of Mike as a man. He and all my previous boyfriends had been boys and nothing more. Why hadn't I understood that before now?

I mentally shook my head, wiping away thoughts of romance. I'd learned my lesson. I'd choose the money.

At last, Burke lowered the pad and brought his attention to those of us who remained. "Congratulations, bitches. You've been chosen."

Chapter Four

Erin

A few of the other women cheered, but most of them, me included, were too busy wondering if it was a good thing that we'd made the cut. I glanced at my Mr. Tall Dark and Blue-Silver Eyes and decided that, yeah, it was a good thing. At least, so far.

"Listen up. Here's how it's going to go down." Burke sauntered to the center of the room, too close to my table for my comfort. "One or more of the men have decided that you're the woman they want. You should consider yourself lucky."

I dragged in a breath. If it was the man I wanted, then, yeah, I was lucky. Wait. One or more of the men? Did some women get chosen by more than one man?

"It's up to you to decide to continue." He turned around, his arm outstretched. "These guys aren't ordinary men. They're not the weak-willed, soft-handed college boys you're used to screwing." His chuckle was filled with derision. "Naw, bitches, these men are more than just human. They're fucking animals."

I wasn't sure what he meant, but I wasn't about to raise my hand and ask. Instead, I kept my attention locked onto Burke and fought to keep from looking at the men. Especially that one particular man.

Burke stalked to the side, grabbed one of the guys by the

back of the neck, and turned him around. He pointed at the lion emblem on the back of his shirt. "You wanted to know what K.O.B. stands for? Well, here you go. We are the Kings of Beasts. We're more than some damn motorcycle club, we're a family, a pride. If you decide to go through with the games, if you make it through the challenge, you'll have the honor of becoming one of us. Or you can take the money instead." He shrugged, dismissively. "If you take the cash, then you weren't good enough for us anyway."

I could join the Kings of Beasts MC? How would that go over with my college professors? I imagined riding up to the head of the English department, stuffy Old Man Haskle, on the back of my sexy man's Harley, and almost laughed. Like that would ever happen.

I could take the money and pay off loans, or hang with a motorcycle club. It was a no-brainer for me, no matter what the man looked like or how much he turned me on.

Burke smiled like a benevolent king welcoming his subjects to the lion's den. "The man, or men, who have chosen you will take you outside and tell you what to do next. Your body, your mind and your guts are going to be tested. He'll tell you where to go, but wherever it is, you'd damn sure better get there before nightfall. If you don't, you're out."

"Once you're there, you'll have two nights to survive on your own. Your man might show up and he might not. It's up to him. But he can't give you supplies, water or food, or you're out. Got it?"

If he didn't show up, when would I get the chance to meet him? How could they expect me to choose a man without getting to know him first?

"It won't be easy. If you're weak, if you can't handle

yourself"—did he look straight at me?—"you're fucked. There will be obstacles along the way, from traps to animals. It'll be up to you to overcome them."

Nina gasped. She didn't like the wilderness or the animals living in it. Yet we'd talked enough about this, so she shouldn't have been surprised. We were, after all, in the mountains. I shot her a look telling her that, if there was any way for me to help her along, I would.

"So it's like a survivalist training course?" Maddy met his gaze.

Oh, shit. I just prayed she wouldn't regret speaking up.

Burke's expression didn't change. "Yes and no. We don't care about whipping you into shape. Either you're strong enough or you're not." He moved closer still, zeroing in on our table again.

"We live on the outskirts of civilization, off the grid as much as possible. If you hope to stay with your man and become one of us, you'll have to fit in. We don't make any allowances for the weak. It's survival of the fittest and only the best among you will make it to her destination and back. If you don't, then you get kicked to the curb. If you can't make it on your own steam, don't expect us to drag your ass home. You understand?"

Maddy nodded, subdued for one of the first times I'd ever seen.

"If you do get through the challenge, you'll have the ultimate choice to make. Keep the man or keep the money." He laughed, then pointed at us, moving his arm from one side of the room to the other. "And just so you know, you can't choose the money, then meet up with the man later. We'll know and you'll both regret it."

The air bristled with excitement at the mention of the prize money. I had a feeling most of the women had come hoping to win the money. I doubted any of us were thinking we'd claim the money, then hook up with the man later.

"So we have to fight for our man?"

Maddy was usually a lot tougher than I was, but talking back to Burke was pushing it, even for her. It was a cowardly thing to do, but I slumped down in my chair and, hopefully, out of Burke's visual line of fire.

"If he's the man for you, then that's what you'll do. If you don't, then it wasn't meant to be." Burke eased up close and personal next to Maddy. "It's the challenge that'll either bring you together or split you apart."

Oh, shit.

To her credit, she leaned back only a little. I would've turned tail and hauled my not-so-small ass out of there.

"So you're saying it's fate? That just because some guy *chooses*—" Maddy stood up and planted her feet apart.

Aw, crap, Mad. Don't add the air quotes.

"—me I'm supposed to just go along with it and believe he's my soul mate? Like we're in some stupid romance book?" Maddy laughed. Right. In. His. Face.

I glanced around. Had someone passed around drugs or booze? Maddy had to be high because I knew she wasn't foolish.

"I don't believe in soul mates," she added.

He got closer and—*oh, my God*—growled. I don't know how it was possible, but the quiet of the room suddenly got even quieter.

Burke's eyes glowed as the silver became brighter. An intensity that was both frightening and exciting burned from them. I only had enough time to wonder how his eyes could change before his words swept the question away. "I'm not talking about soul mates or love at first sight or any of that other bullshit. This is better. Stronger. Now sit the fuck down and let me finish."

All the courage left Maddy in one rush of air. She sat down with a thump.

"That's it, ladies." Burke made *ladies* sound like an insult. Even more than calling us *bitches*.

Another girl spoke up. "All we have to do is make it to our destinations, stay a couple of nights, then get back here and tell you which prize we want? It's that easy?"

"There's a lot that can happen along the way, but yeah. That's it."

Then why did his smile make it seem like it was anything but easy?

He turned around, slowly, taking in all of us. "Anyone want out? Now's your time to do it."

We remained quiet, rooted to our spots. And then the noise of chairs scraping over the hardwood floor broke the silence as girls around the room stood up, grabbed their belongings and scurried like rats off a sinking ship. Burke didn't appear surprised when most of the girls practically ran out the door.

I glanced at my friends and waited for them to stand. But they stayed where they were.

Burke crossed his arms over his broad chest, surveyed the small group of ten girls who had remained, then nodded. "Good to see some of you have the guts to give it a try. Okay, then, leave your suitcases, purses, and whatever the hell else you brought. Roberta will watch over them until you return. Or contact your next of kin if you don't."

He had to be kidding. We'd assumed the gloomy talk about

getting hurt was just a scare tactic. To get rid of the girls who shouldn't have come in the first place. And yet, one look at the men's faces told me it wasn't a joke. So we could actually get injured? Maybe even die? Was it worth it? Was I willing to risk literally everything to find the man of my dreams? No, nix that. Finding a man was not why I'd do this thing.

The image of Mike's angry face hit me. I'd risked my life for less.

"The man, or men, who decided you're worth a chance will come to you outside." He nodded at the group of men. They left the room at a leisurely pace as though they were headed home after an afternoon bending their elbow with their buddies. The dark-haired man that had ignited a flame inside me got to the exit, glanced my way once, then followed the rest of them.

Did he choose me? Was I ready to find out? Burke didn't give me any time to think.

"Time's up, bitches. Get moving."

"This is unbelievable." Maddy mumbled a few curse words, then stood as Nina, Mia, and I got to our feet. She took one more look around, then grabbed the handle of her suitcase. "I'm out of here."

"No, Mad, you can't go." But I was damned if I knew why she couldn't. Not when I was tempted to follow her.

"Please, Maddy, don't go." Nina took her arm, keeping her with us.

"I'm sorry, but I can't do this. A wilderness challenge? Some guy choosing me? It's just too freaky. How do we know they won't get us out in the woods and kill us? After they do whatever they want to us?"

"If they wanted to hurt us, they could've already done it." I waved my arm around, mimicking Burke's earlier gesture.

"Right here in the comfort of Fang's." I was only half kidding. And maybe trying to convince myself.

"Like I said. I'm sorry, but I'm not staying." Maddy spun around and headed for the door. Nina, Mia, and I followed after her like puppies chasing after their mother. Bitches? Yeah, I guess we kind of were.

I squinted against the sunlight, then cupped my hand over my eyes for shade. The four of us stood like deer in headlights as we grew accustomed to the bright light. The other girls didn't fare much better. We'd been herded from the bar to the parking lot while the men formed a semi-circle in front of us, blocking us from going to the cabs that waited by the side of the road. I didn't see any of the girls who'd left earlier and assumed that they were already on their way back down the mountain.

Burke strode past us, stirring the air in a way that made me think his body contained a personal tornado whirling inside it. One I didn't want to get caught up in.

"Well, all right. What the fuck are you waiting for, guys? Claim your mates."

Claim your mates? He sounded like he'd just told them to pick out their steak for dinner.

The men started coming toward us, making me feel like that poor deer again. But this time, the hunter was moving in, ready to put a bullet in my heart and mount me on his wall.

A huge man with blond tousled hair took Nina's arm and tugged her away from our small group. She yelped, but he didn't pay any attention as he led her off to the right. Fear framed her face, and yet I saw another emotion there.

Was my sweet friend, one of the shyest girls I'd ever known, turned on? I mean, not just excited like I'd seen her before with other guys, but turned on big-time? Like she wouldn't ask any questions if he ripped off her clothes and flung her to the ground? When she didn't call for help, I knew she didn't expect me to rescue her.

Yeah. As if I could.

"Erin, are you coming with me or not?" Maddy still clung to her suitcase and had already taken several steps toward the waiting cabs when she'd turned around to ask.

"I…" Answering was too hard. Common sense dictated that I leave with her, but how could we go without Nina? Besides, something about the mesmerizing man was keeping me there. Whatever that something was I didn't know, but it was strong and unyielding. I looked to my new friend for guidance.

Mia shrugged. "Do what you want, but I didn't come all this way to hitch a ride back home."

In the next moment, however, she didn't have to worry about hitching anywhere. The man who took her arm was just as big as all the others. His blond hair feathered around his ears and his strong masculine face was stern. He cocked his eyebrow at her and that was it. Mia shot us an "oh-shit" look and walked away with him.

"Erin?"

I checked both Nina and Mia. Both of them were quiet, listening intently to the men who'd snagged them. "Mad, I don't know. I think it's for real. And if it is, if I can win the money, then I've got to give it a shot. Seriously, we're in North Carolina, not the Amazon." I smiled, trying to believe what I was telling her. "How hard can it be?"

"Listen to me." She came back to me, keeping her voice down. "This is crazy. You know it is. Let's get out of here before it's too late. Are you coming with me or not?"

"Not."

Maddy's eyes widened. She hadn't expected my answer, but, then again, I hadn't expected to give it. She started to argue, then widened her eyes even more at something behind me. I spun around and ran into a brick wall of human flesh. A rush of air escaped me as a swirl of sinful need twisted in my stomach.

It's him.

Had I said that out loud? He was tall, several inches over six feet. His black hair was exactly the way I liked it, long enough to hold on to and pull his face to mine. The sleek strands curled around his earlobes, then waved to touch the curve of his jaw. Dark stubble covered his square jaw and made a path around his upper lip. His blue-silver eyes held a glint that mixed both amusement and challenge.

His plain black T-shirt stretched tightly across his chest. The muscles in his arms stood out as though they were ready to flex into action at a moment's notice. I looked down, needing to get away from the magical hold his gaze had on me to try and think, only to end up staring at his crotch. The bulge in his jeans didn't come from an erection. I'm not sure how I knew that, but it didn't. And if that was true, then it meant the bulge came from a non-erect cock.

As my dearly departed granny would've said, *Oh, my lord.*

I lingered far too long over that mound of material before drifting my way down the long legs and ending up at the worn black boots. I studied him as I made my way back up, determined to find an imperfection. Everyone had at least one imperfection and I was a master at finding them. After all, I practiced on myself every day. And yet, I found none.

I felt him lean toward me a second before I realized he was doing it. My body tensed, but it was the good kind of tension that had my libido dancing.

Breathing became more difficult when he pushed my hair behind my ear. I felt the tip of his lips brush my skin. The slight touch was enough to send a tremor streaking down from my head to the tips of my toes. His warm breath teased my flesh.

The wait was deliciously long and tortuous. But at last, he spoke.

"Stay."

Was it a command or a request? I no longer cared. I turned back and found Maddy still waiting for me. Although I didn't say a word, she knew my answer.

"It's okay. Just be careful. I'll be with you in spirit every step of the way. And let me know how it goes, okay?" She whirled around, put her head up high, and strode toward the nearest cab. She paused once, turned back to me, and said, "Keep on going. Stay safe." It was our slogan, Nina's, Maddy's, and mine, but most often, it was their way of telling me to stay strong, to not give in to The Darkness.

"Maddy, please stay."

"Let her go."

The tone of his voice was easy-going, yet the sensuality of it made it seem like he'd said the most important thing in the world. I wanted to wallow in the texture of it, to sigh, and to ask him to speak again. Read a textbook. Whatever.

But I had to think. Even when it suddenly got a lot harder.

"She's my friend."

The silver in his eyes brightened, but how? Was the strange eye color driving me to distraction? Was it making me think about how yummy he'd be in bed? How great it felt whenever he leveled his penetrating gaze at me? "We're your friends now. If you make it through."

Okay. Hunk or no hunk, his comment hit me the wrong

THE CAPTURED HEART   87

way. "Are you asking me to pick you over her? Because if you are, then I'll get my suitcase and leave with Maddy. I won't push my friends aside for you or for anyone else."

I hadn't done it for Mike, who'd often complained about how much time I spent with Nina and Maddy. And I sure as hell wouldn't do it for some guy I didn't know. No matter how much I wanted to push him to the ground and hop on top of his face.

He chucked me under the chin, then dove into me with those amazing eyes. "I'm not telling you to do a fucking thing. Got it? You'll learn soon enough that you're leaving your old world behind. If you choose to go on."

"What does that mean?"

His face hardened and my stomach clenched. I didn't want to be a pushover, but I didn't want him angry at me. Anger was the last thing I wanted from him.

"Are you going through with the challenge or not? Tell me now and I'll leave you alone."

I looked over my shoulder. Nina and Mia were still listening to their men, but Maddy was nowhere in sight. She must've gotten into a cab and gone. When I faced him again, I was ready to stand my ground. "Yes."

"Okay, then know this. I can't help you. You're on your own, not matter what. Do you understand?" His hand closed around the back of my neck and tugged me to him.

"I think—"

He caught me off-guard when his mouth met mine. I didn't have time to take in a breath, much less to think about kissing him back. Instinct mixed with my natural sex drive and I came back at him, giving as good as I got.

He was even more masterful than I'd assumed he'd be.

Bringing my body against his, he cupped my breast, then deepened the kiss. My body flamed to life, scorching every inch of me. Mike's kisses had been nothing like this. His had been weak imitations of the real thing.

Could I get my body closer? I wanted to, but it wasn't possible. The world, Nina, Mia, and even Maddy were pushed away, gone in the turmoil of emotions and sensations that made my legs shake and my heart pound.

He devoured my lips, licking, and biting at the corners, then sliding his tongue in and out, teasing me until I groaned. If he'd wanted me to, I would've wrapped my legs around him in front of all the others, and let him do as he wished. As I'd always dreamed a man would do.

I'd been right. He was around my age, but he was no college boy. He was, by any standard, a magnificent man who would consume me.

Life is a fucking strange thing. In such a short time, I'd gone from diving into complete despair to wondering what life would be like with a complete stranger. Not any stranger, of course, but the incredible man who was all bronzed flesh and hard muscled steel.

And he wants me.

Oh, my lord.

Just after the thought came and went, he turned me loose. Although I was thankful to be able to take a full breath of air, I felt the loss of his body close to mine.

"Tell me your name again."

Was he asking or commanding me? Either way was fine, though. Just as long as he didn't let go of my arm.

"Erin Emily Pierce." I cringed at the formality of how I'd said it. "Erin. Call me Erin."

His mouth crooked upward. "Erin Emily Pierce, you're my chosen one."

Although I didn't know what "chosen one" meant, I was thrilled. "Which means?"

"It means that, if you want to do this, and if you make it through the next three days, then you're my woman."

His woman. Just like that. No asking me if I wanted to be his woman. No asking me if I'd choose the money over him.

I fought back the stupid grin from showing on my face. It wouldn't have lasted long anyway. Not when the wild tumble of thoughts started running through my head.

Why does he want me? I'm not the prettiest one here. Am I his second, maybe even third choice? Is this all a big scam? A way for these guys to get their laughs?

The Darkness tried to snake its way back in. Whispers slithered in telling me I was too plain, too dumb, too everything. I shoved them aside, but just barely.

"And what if I don't want to be your woman?" I did my best to look at him in a critical manner. As if I'd find anything wrong with his delectable body.

He stepped back. "Then choose the money."

The money. I'd almost forgotten about the money. What I could do with all that money hit me again. Pay off my maxed out credit cards. Pay off student loans. Buy a decent car. The possibilities made my head swim. How could I let simple sexual chemistry get in the way? Yet what I felt between us was anything but simple.

"Is there a way to have both?" I smiled a little, afraid I should've kept the question to myself. I didn't want to seem greedy, even if I was. Burke had said it couldn't happen, but who could blame a girl for asking?

He didn't return the smile. In fact, he clenched his jaw, the muscle twitching. "No."

The way he looked at me made my stomach do a sickening flip-flop. Had I just blown my chance with him?

"Go on. Get in a cab. You don't belong with us."

He turned on his heel and was stalking away before I could do anything more than open my mouth. "Wait."

He kept going.

"Wait." I hurried after him, running to catch up with his long strides, and snagged his arm. "I want to do it."

He took his time, studying me, sizing me up. "Fine. Then pay attention."

Relief powered into me. If he'd said no, I'm not sure what I would've done. "Okay."

"You have until nightfall to make it to your destination."

"My destination?"

His finger pressed against my lips quieted me. "Listen. Don't talk."

I nodded, determined not to press my luck.

"Once you've gone a mile up the road, then go into the forest on your right. Look for an old burned-out tree. You'll find a map with your name tacked to it. Take the map and follow it to a cabin about eight miles into the forest."

"A cabin?" One hard look had me snapping my mouth shut.

Goose bumps danced over my skin. I waited for more instructions.

"Be sure you get there before the sun goes down."

Eight miles before night came? That didn't seem so hard. I wasn't in the greatest shape, but some people ran more than that every day. Surely, I could walk it by the time the sun set.

He pointed toward the road where the girls were already

trudging up the hill. "Get going. But remember. You can talk to them going up the hill, but once you're in the woods, you're on your own. You can't help each other."

"So that's all there is to it? All I have to do is walk to a cabin? For two hundred and fifty thousand dollars?" When he tilted his head to the side, I hurried to add, "Or you."

It seemed too good to be true, which made me nervous. Eight miles to be with the man who turned me inside out? Eight miles to claim two hundred and fifty thousand dollars? The skeptic in me was screaming "bullshit." But the other side of me wanted nothing more than to believe.

"You're forgetting about finding food and water."

Yeah, I had.

Those blue-silver eyes pierced me yet again. "This isn't a stroll around the mall. Be careful. I want you at the cabin in one piece."

"So you're going to meet me at the cabin?"

"Maybe."

Pulling information out of him was harder than trying to catch lightning bugs. Once I caught one, I had to open my hand to see it. But then it'd fly away. "I thought you weren't supposed to help me."

"I never said I would."

I studied the other girls and wondered if they'd gotten more information than he'd given me. Nina and Mia were already starting up the hill. If I could catch up to them, then we could do the challenge together. Who'd ever know?

"Just as in life, each woman has her own path to take."

Had he guessed what I'd been thinking? "So we can't team up?"

"If you did, then only one of you would make it to her

destination on time."

I twisted back toward the road. Only one cab remained, but I wasn't going back. The life I'd led at college seemed so far in the past. Mike. Classes. They'd been reduced to images, memories that didn't fit in the surroundings of Cripple Creek, North Carolina.

Had Maddy really gone home? I already felt lonely without her by my side.

I couldn't help but think she might have missed her chance. Even if she hadn't wanted to find out which man had chosen her, why had she given up the money so easily? And what had happened to the man who'd wanted her? Did he pick some other girl? I searched the area.

Shit.

Hector rested against one of the motorcycles, still sporting that awful grin. I didn't smile back. At least I hadn't seen him go up to Burke. Which meant, I hoped, that he hadn't wanted to claim me.

Thank God.

"What's with that Hector guy?"

He glanced at Hector. "Why do you want to know?"

Hector started up his bike then pulled out of the parking lot. Thankfully, he drove away from the girls.

"No real reason. Except that he's not with a girl."

His expression darkened. "Are you interested in him?"

"Oh, hell no. Just curious."

"Hector wasn't supposed to be here at all. He's not allowed in the games."

"Why?"

He tilted his head at me. "No more questions. You need to get going."

I ignored him and kept searching for Maddy. If she'd rejected one of them, had he left disappointed?

"Did you see my friend? Did she leave?"

Yet when I turned back, my man was gone. I whirled around, thinking I'd find him. If I'd had sense enough to ask him his name, I would've called for him. Instead, the only thing left for me to do was to start walking.

Chapter Five

Colter

I stood off to the side of Fang's and watched Erin hurry to catch up with her friends. Even now my heart beat wildly. My mind whirled, overwhelmed with the sensations I'd picked up from her. Overwhelmed that the day had finally come.

I wouldn't have wanted to admit it, but Roberta and Burke had been right all along. I'd found my mate. Not every man did, so I was lucky. I'd stayed away from participating in the games for several years, unready to find her. Maybe even a little afraid that I wouldn't find her. Yet when I'd stayed away from the games, I'd always felt a knot in my gut. An empty place that, with each passing year, became stronger and more painful. Now I was glad I'd waited. Once I'd taken a deep breath of Erin, I'd known. Still I'd resisted, unable to believe it. Then, when I closed my eyes and concentrated on her, letting her fragrance seep into me, any doubt I'd had washed away.

"Quaid, she's not the one for you."

I swallowed back a groan. Shayna Tamlyn slid her palm along my shoulder, then slunk next to me, pressing her body close to mine. Trying to move away, or worse, getting her to move wouldn't happen. Fuck knows I'd tried often enough.

"I picked up her scent."

"You're wrong. Don't let Burke and Roberta force you into

this." Her voice purred against my neck a moment before her tongue slid along my skin.

"I'm not desperate. It's time and I found the one."

I didn't flinch when her claws dug into my shoulder.

"She's weak. She'll never be the mate you deserve. She'll never be me."

"If that's true, then she won't make it back."

"She won't."

I shot her a questioning look. Was she hinting at something?

It was an old story, one we both knew well. But at least I recognized that the story was over. Shayna, however, still clung to it.

We'd grown up in the mountains together, our families living close enough for us to make the quick run to each other's houses without our parents' watchful eyes. We'd played together, at first roughhousing like two boys. But when Shayna started changing from a tomboy into a teenager with all the curves and sensuality of a mate-to-be, I'd taken notice. I'd been wrong to do so, but I was, after all, still a male with a male's needs. We'd lain together under the trees of the forest and had joined our sex sounds to those of the animals around us.

Then we'd declared our love.

The problem was that Shayna still loved me, but I'd never really been in love with her. Like a lot of young boys, I'd lied.

Now I was paying for my mistake.

Irritation, more at myself than at her, broke free. I felt the change take me and let it ride high, almost making it to the end. Fangs ripped out of my gums, replacing my teeth, and claws pierced the ends of my fingers. I whirled on her, saw the fear flash across her face, and enjoyed the powerful feeling it brought.

"Back off. I took her scent."

Shayna's eyes glinted with her own anger. She was beautiful, with long, black hair I'd wrapped around my finger. But that had been then, not now.

"I don't care. You can smell all of them if you want. But until you've driven your fangs into her, until she knows what—"

"I am?" I lifted my lip in a snarl. "That's the way it is. But it doesn't change things between us."

"She'll run. I saw her. She's too timid. She'll never accept you."

"I took her scent. I dragged it inside me." Taking my future mate's scent was the first step toward mating.

"So? You took my scent at one time. You took mine first."

I couldn't tell her I'd lied. I'd only pretended to take her scent to get between her legs. As a grown man, I felt like a jerk for having done so, but I couldn't change the past. It had been years since we'd been together. How could she not know I didn't love her?

Pushing her back, I steeled myself against what I had to do. I hated treating her badly, but she had to understand. I couldn't let her keep thinking she had a chance with me. Maybe if I'd never found my mate, we could've tried to make it work. But I had found her. It was that simple.

"She's my mate. Deal with it."

"Bullshit. You're one of the Kings of Beasts and I'm your woman. You want me. You know you do." Shayna took hold of the collar of her black T-shirt and tore it apart, ripping it down the front to expose her naked breasts.

She was beautiful. She always had been, but beauty had very

little to do with choosing a woman. Choosing a mate was more important than just raw sex. Although, if I were truthful, the way my mate looked was part of it for me. The scent I'd picked up from Erin was different than any other woman's. Including Shayna's. It had taken hold of my inner lion's craving and sent it flying.

If I'd wanted to claim Shayna, if I hadn't taken in Erin's scent, I might have finally accepted her. The other men who'd seen their women off stared at her, lusting after her full, luscious breasts, as any man would. Yet they wouldn't make a move on her. Not after finding their mates.

"Cover yourself."

"Are you telling me you don't want me? You're rejecting me?" The realization of what I was doing hit her as she took in the watching crowd. Anger turned to fury. "We've already fucked and it was amazing. We belong together. Fuck the games. I'm the one you want."

She was my friend. The last thing I wanted to do was to make her unhappy.

Yet what choice did I have? Refusing to tear the rest of her clothes from her, then claim her, would shame her in front of all the others. But I couldn't, wouldn't choose her over Erin. Hating that she'd forced me into it, I heeled around and stalked off in the opposite direction. No one, not even Shayna, would misinterpret my actions.

The other men stood silent, casting their gazes away from her and the shame that would follow her. I heard her growl, her refusal to accept what was. But the soft whimper she made next stabbed at my heart and threatened to tear it open.

Feeling sorry for her didn't come easily. She was one of the strongest females in the pride and could have found a human mate without a problem. Maybe even one of the males in the pride, although those matings rarely worked out. But now she'd ruined her chances. No one would want to be her second choice.

I glanced over my shoulder and caught her furiously glaring at me. I'd never seen such intense hatred. Knowing Shayna, I realized this wouldn't be the end of it.

Erin

"Damn. I knew I was out of shape, but I didn't think I was this much out of shape."

Nina's puffing was almost as loud as mine. "Where's Maddy?"

"She left."

Nina pulled up short, but Mia and I kept walking toward the top of the hill. If I stopped before I reached the top, I wasn't sure I'd get going again.

"She did? Really? I know she said she was leaving, but I didn't really think she would."

"You heard her. She didn't want to do the challenge."

I resisted the urge to turn around and look back at Fang's, although I could sense Nina still searching for Maddy. "But she didn't even say goodbye."

That was part of it, but just because she'd told me good-bye didn't mean I felt any better. "It was her choice. You know Maddy. Once Burke called us bitches, she got pissed off." I waved for her to catch up. "So what did your guy say?"

Mia was the only one of us who wasn't having a tough time doing the incline. "I didn't know what to expect, but I sure as hell didn't think some guy would lean over and sniff me."

"You too, huh? Yeah. That was really weird." And sexy as hell. But I'd let someone else put it out there.

Nina made it back to my side. "Mine, too. But you know what? I kind of liked it."

At least I wasn't the only one who'd liked getting sniffed.

"I guess they all took whiffs of the girls." Mia shrugged, keeping her attention on the road ahead. "Mine told me thanks for liking his hair."

"His hair?"

"He wears it kind of long. A little shaggy. And the color went well with his eyes."

"Were they blue with silver?"

"Yeah. And yours?"

"Same thing. Freaky, huh?"

"And mine, too," added Nina.

We walked on, lost for a moment as we wondered how all of them could have the same eye color. I couldn't offer any ideas and neither did they.

Mia was the first to reach the rise of the road. She pointed to the left side. "He told me to go into the woods here and find a map and directions stuck to a tree."

"Did he tell you his name? My guy didn't." Hopefully, it wasn't a bad sign. I'd been too caught up in the excitement to think to ask.

"No."

Nina frowned, giving her answer before she spoke. "Mine, either. Okay, this is getting scary."

"He told me to do the same thing. Except to go to the right side." A few of the other girls were venturing into the woods.

"We should go home."

Nina had read my mind. "We should."

The three of us stared at each other.

"Then why aren't we?" Nina bit her lower lip, a sure sign that her nerves were on the fray.

"Money," answered Mia.

The man. And yet I couldn't bring myself to say so. Besides, I'd still choose the money. I didn't have a choice. "Yeah. The money."

"But what if they want us in the woods so they can do horrible things to us?" Nina would bring blood to her lip if she didn't stop gnawing at it.

The dark side of me leapt to the forefront, daring me to find out what those horrible things might be. "Like I said before. If they'd wanted to rape us and leave us for dead, they've already had plenty of time to do it."

"Maybe they'd rather play cat and mouse first."

I hadn't thought about that. Lots of serial killers toyed with their victims. "Maybe. But if you really think so, then why don't we get the hell out of here? Why are all these girls taking this risk? It can't be only about the money."

We stood together, our little huddle, and watched as another girl stepped into the shade of the tall pine trees. My nerves were jumping like crazy.

"We came this far." Mia shifted from one foot to the other, then stared at the road ahead. "I came because I need the money and because I've always dreamed of an adventure like this. I want to try my luck at being alone, out on my own, instead of trapped inside a tiny house filled with all my brothers and sisters. Or where my father…" Her body shook as though she'd just been touched by an evil spirit. "This is the most exciting thing to ever happen to me."

I smiled at the way Mia had phrased it. When we'd first met, she'd seemed so sure of herself, making me think of her as older than me. Yet, hearing her talk made her sound so much younger. So eager to live her life.

"I could say the same thing." I didn't add the whole truth of it and knew Nina would never expose my secrets. I kept the real reasons to myself, affirming them. Maybe trying to talk myself into staying.

I'd come to earn the money I needed to keep going with my education. And to prove I could do something this amazing. To prove I was finally strong enough to fight The Darkness. To get my friends to stop worrying about me. To get me to stop worrying about me. And yet, now that I'd spoken to my extraordinary man, I found my reasons for staying changing.

Could he be the man who'd love me in spite of The Darkness? It was so simple, and yet so complicated. Just like the rest of my world, my reasons were filled with both dark and light, changing and growing.

Taking Nina's hand, I tried to ease her anxiety. "You don't have to keep going. I wouldn't think any less of you." I laughed at how silly I sounded. Knowing what I'd done and what I was still struggling with, she was the one who should've thought less of me. And yet, she never had.

She lifted her head, thrusting out her chin. "No. I want to do this. I came for the money and out of curiosity. But now that I'm here, I want to keep going to test myself." She squeezed my hand, then turned it loose. "I'm stronger than most people give me credit for."

"Yes, you are. Way stronger than me."

"No, I'm not." Her gaze dropped to my feet—and my scarred ankles. "You're a lot stronger than you think you are.

Sometimes I think you're the strongest person I know."

I shot her an incredulous look. "Then you must not know very many people."

"I know enough." She grinned, looking like the Nina who loved to joke around. "Besides, how can I not go? Did you see my guy? He's freakin' hot."

"Not as hot as mine." I glanced down the road, but Fang's was too far in the distance to pick him out of the crowd.

"Okay then, I guess this is goodbye. For now." Nina fell against me, her arms enclosing me. "You take care of yourself, okay? Keep on going. Stay safe. Don't do anything—" She stopped, remembering that Mia didn't know about my problem.

As much as I loved my friend for worrying about me, having them mention my cutting, even in a remote way, sometimes made me want to do it again. But I wouldn't. That was my first real challenge.

"You, too. And you, too, Mia."

Mia lifted a hand in a farewell salute, then turned on her heel and started walking down the other side of the hill. "See you back at Fang's to claim the money." She spun around and wiggled her eyebrows. "Or the man."

"I just wish we could keep both." But then it wouldn't be much of a choice to make, would it? A sexy man and a load of cash? That was too good to happen.

Nina and I stayed together, our arms around each other's waists. I didn't want to let her go, but time was running out. It had taken us far too long to make it up the damn hill. If the rest of the journey was as difficult, then I might not make it to the cabin before nightfall. I'd forfeit the games without getting a real chance.

Nina hugged me again, then stepped away. "Like I said. Keep on going. Stay safe."

I could almost hear the words "and don't hurt yourself," but only nodded. She drew in a long, slow breath, then stepped over the small rut in the road and onto the grass leading into the dense forest.

I was the only one left and I was afraid. Yet, strangely, I felt more alive than I had in a long, long time.

Colter

I watched Erin from the edge of the woods. She needed to get moving before she ran out of time. Having her claim the money instead of me was an outcome I was ready to accept. But to have her not make it to the cabin before nightfall, thus tossing away both the money and me was unacceptable. The others would laugh their asses off, taunting me for choosing such a lazy and weak woman for my mate. They'd make staying with the pride difficult. I never wanted to leave the mountains where I'd been born and raised, but living with the others knowing how my mate had failed would be tough.

I'd accepted her scent. When it had happened, I'd been thrown. Finding my mate was the last thing I'd expected. It had been my plan to tell Burke that none of the girls were for me. That I'd have to wait yet another year. And then I'd sniffed her and known.

Finally, she was moving. It felt like it took her forever to get from the road to the edge of the trees. Then, after another hesitation, she pushed aside the branches and stepped into the shadows.

Into the darkness.

I couldn't get a grip on it, but I'd felt a sadness surrounding her, like an invisible mist enveloping her, keeping her down. Everyone had both good and bad inside them, and although I didn't sense that she was evil, there was something inside her, tearing away at the woman she wanted to be.

The fact that she fought against it made me feel better. But not by much.

She'd walked far enough into the forest for me to begin following her. Even if I hadn't been able to track her, I would've heard her. The noise she made could have awakened the dead.

She'd learn better soon enough. Once she was changed.

Erin

This isn't so bad.

I'd found the map, one of the pieces of paper the teenage boy had taken with him, without a problem. The old burned-out tree wasn't very far from the road and stood out from the rest of the healthier trees. How it had become scorched when the others hadn't wasn't clear.

The map was hand drawn, but it was easy enough to follow. All I had to do was to keep going in the same direction and stay on the path I was on now. Then I'd pass over a creek or a river—I was hoping for a small creek or "crick" as most people in the area called it—through a clearing and on to the cabin.

Easy enough. Or at least, I hoped so.

The biggest problem was to keep from getting scratched up. But I was used to scratches. Maybe not all over my body, but enough. I kept walking, thankful that the trees formed a canopy above me and kept the heat down. Even in the mountains, summer could get really warm. A fair-skinned girl like me could get one hell of a burn. Too bad I hadn't thought to bring along suntan lotion as well as a spray to repel ticks. But how could I have known I'd end up hiking through the woods? I made a promise to strip and check for ticks once I reached the cabin.

Would the cabin be livable? Or would it be an old hunting shack that wasn't much better than sleeping on the ground? Would it have electricity? How about running water? Maybe even warm running water?

According to my man—damn, I wish I'd gotten his name— as well as the brief notes on the map, I was supposed to stay in the place for two nights. Depending on the way the cabin was decked out, I'd either get a good rest or end up pacing instead of sleeping.

Unless he showed up. He'd said he might.

I licked my lips, both from the need for water and from the memory of his lips on mine. If I was supposed to sleep with him, all the better. From the moment I'd started up the road from Fang's, I'd had an almost painful need to see him again. To feel his hands on me. If and when I did, I'd make damn sure to do more than kiss him back.

I'm not the kind of girl who hops into bed fast. It had taken Mike months before I'd let him pull my jeans off. Not that I was a prude or anything, but once the jeans were off, then I'd have to lie and tell him the story about the wire. That or do my best to always keep the lights off so he wouldn't see. Keeping my secret was hard enough with my girlfriends, but with a guy I was interested in? Way harder. Mike had been the first I'd told the truth to. But then again, he'd been the first I'd fallen in love with. The first I'd trusted to understand.

And I'd paid for it.

I shook off the thoughts about Mike. If I let them seep too far inside, they'd take over. And once they took over, it was hell getting them out. I'd almost given in completely after Mike had thrown me out.

But I was stronger now.

I'm stronger.

That became my mantra as I continued deeper into the forest.

Challenge, my ass. This isn't so bad.

When my legs started hurting, I knew I should've gone to the gym with Maddy and Nina more often. Or at least done more than sit on the stationary bike next to them and play a game on my phone. But it was too late now. Still, I'd make it to the cabin one way or another.

The snap that came from behind me jerked me out of my zoned-out mindset. I stopped, then did a slow circle around, but I couldn't see very far with all the bushes, leaves, and branches forming the thick underbrush.

"Hello?"

Nothing. Not one little sound. Was that normal for the woods? Hell if I knew.

"Is anyone there?" I figured it might be one of the other girls. We weren't supposed to help one another, but did that include just talking?

"It's okay. I won't tell anyone if you want to talk." I waited again and got nothing. A creepy feeling stiffened my spine and I wiped away a drop of sweat from my forehead.

Another snapping sound came and I whirled around again, searching. "Is anyone there?" Was I talking to no one? Or was I talking to an animal? I'd done enough research about the area to know the forests had all kinds of animals in it. Like raccoons, squirrels, rabbits, deer and more. Including bears.

Oh, shit. I forgot about the bears.

I couldn't remember what to do if a bear attacked. Stand still and hope it wasn't hungry? Grin and bear it? Drop and roll? No, that was if I caught on fire. Run like hell? How fast could a bear run anyway? No doubt a lot fast than I could.

The sound came again, tightening my throat. I had to fight to drag in a breath. I stood still, listening, but when the sound didn't come again, I decided to keep moving.

Sticking to the path, I tried to get the stiffness out of my legs. They'd already started hurting, but it was as though they'd gotten sealed in concrete. It was a struggle to bend my knees.

The noise came again. This time I didn't turn around. Instead, I sped up, my breaths coming out in hard, short blasts.

Please don't let it be a bear.

A low, mean growl put me into a dead run. If the bear tried to catch me, at least I wouldn't see it before it ripped my head off.

The whimpers I heard came from me. I ran harder.

I hit the ground face first before I even knew I'd fallen. Letting out a small cry of despair, I flipped over onto my back and looked back down the path.

It wasn't a bear.

Chapter Six

Erin

The large cat pounded to a stop, sending pebbles and dirt flying into the air. It was huge, far bigger than I'd read mountain lions could be. I stared at it, suddenly wondering why it looked more like an African lion than a cougar. But that was impossible. Lions didn't live in North Carolina. It had to be a cougar. A very large, very angry cougar.

The yellow fur was dappled from the sunlight filtering through the trees and its muscles flexed as it dug first one front paw then the other into the dirt, clenching and releasing its dagger-like claws. Dipping lower, it put its ears flat and pulled its mouth into a snarl. Fangs, long and viciously sharp, dripped with saliva. But it was the eyes that compelled me. Its silver gaze fixed on me, ridding me of any impulse to get away.

For what had to be a full minute, we watched each other. I'm not sure why, but it struck me as being a she. She hunched even lower, a prelude to her leap, and still I didn't move. I had no control over my body. Panic had overtaken me, rendering me incapable of action.

The cat took a couple of steps closer. That propelled me back onto my feet. I searched around and found what I hoped would save my ass.

Snatching up the fallen branch, I lifted it over my shoulder like a baseball bat and got ready to swing. If I was lucky, maybe I could scare her away. Failing that, I hoped I'd land at least one decent blow before she sank her jaws into me.

Fuck, fuck, fuck.

Holding my makeshift bat tighter, I kept my gaze locked to hers. If I went down, if no one ever found my mangled and half-eaten body, it'd be okay. Just as long as I got one good blow in.

A strange calmness swept over me. I stood taller and smiled. "Come on, bitch. Show me what you've got."

I would've sworn she laughed at me in a cat kind of way.

"Erin."

Both the cat and I shifted our focus to the man standing just beyond the break in the trees. A shock of his dark hair fell over his forehead and he was naked from the waist up.

"You." If only I knew his name.

He glanced at me and that's when I noticed it. His eyes were the same color as the cat's. Stone-colored silver that rivaled the brilliance of sterling.

A cat and a man had the same eye color. Was my mind rebelling, fear locking onto that small detail and distorting it? Was it an illusion caused by the light in the forest? Maybe my eyes looked silvery, too.

"Erin, when I say run, then run as fast as you can. And don't look back."

"I'm not sure I can. My legs—"

He scowled. "You can and you will."

He eased out of the forest and strode, slowly and carefully, toward the cat. Stunned, I could do no more than watch. Why didn't he grab a weapon? Even my pitiful branch was better than nothing.

The cat spun to face him, her tail moving back and forth, like a soldier waving a flag on the battlefield. But she didn't pounce, only growled. She dug her claws into the ground, but didn't move closer. As he came nearer, she backed up.

Her growl didn't sound as threatening as her earlier ones had. She sounded almost fearful. Yet why would any cat that large be afraid of a man without a weapon? But she was afraid. My own fear started slowing down.

"You can't do this."

Who can't? The cat? I could understand talking to the animal, perhaps using the sternness of his voice to make it appear that he wasn't afraid, but what he'd said didn't make sense. She was big enough, powerful enough to do almost anything she wanted.

The cat's low, throaty growl came again. Along with another step backward.

Stunned, yet excited, I lowered the branch, then dropped it to the ground. I was mesmerized as he moved closer to the dangerous beast.

He scowled at the animal. "Stay back," ordered Colter.

She snarled, the sound rose in pitch then fell to a low moan. But she wasn't giving up. She growled and turned toward me again. As though she'd decided he wasn't a threat any longer.

"Erin. Run!" he shouted, startling me, awakening every muscle in my body. When he shifted his silvery gaze my way, I was ready before the order came again. "Run. Now!"

I didn't hesitate, didn't even think. The instinct to obey him took over. Whirling around, I ran as fast and as hard as I could. Looking back wasn't an option. If I had, I might've fallen and landed face down in the dirt again.

Exhilaration mixed with relief as I ran on. My breath

hitched in my throat and my heart pounded. I'd survive the cat attack, but would he?

I ran as long as I could, which wasn't very far before the hitch in my side and the rasping of my breath brought me to a stop. Bent over, I craned my neck around to look back the way I'd come. Was he all right? Should I go back and find out? But if he wasn't, what could I do? Tell the mountain lion to "scat" then use my shirt to bandage his wounds?

Shit.

I couldn't help him. I knew I couldn't, but I had to try. Sure, he'd ordered me to run, but I couldn't just leave him there. Gathering what little was left of my courage and my stamina, I started back down the trail.

I hadn't gone more than a few yards when I let out a shriek of delight. He was running up the path like a Sunday jogger going to pick up his morning coffee. Rushing toward him, I threw my arms wide and wrapped them around his waist.

"Oh, my God, I'm so glad you're okay." He felt so good, so right, and so uninjured. I leaned back to give him a good once over and was still astonished to realize he really was unharmed. "How'd you get away? What happened to the cat?"

His expression was unreadable, but when he pulled me back into his arms I knew everything I needed to know. I clutched him, eager to have his body next to mine, yearning to have his hands slide over me.

The relief I'd felt earlier was nothing compared to the relief that he wanted me in his arms. His strong arms enclosed me, binding me to him. My body, already desperate for oxygen, clamored for more, pain searing through me as I tried to drag in a breath. I might never take in fresh air again, but it didn't matter. Feeling his hard chest against mine, his crotch pushing against my stomach, was all I needed. The trembling of my body might have started out of fear, but now I trembled for a different reason.

I needed this man, more than I needed anything else. I craved him like an alcoholic craves whiskey. I ached for him in a way that didn't make sense. After all, we'd met only hours earlier.

But I didn't care. My body thrilled at his touch, burned for him to touch me everywhere. If I'd have thought begging him to take me would've worked, I would've gotten down on my knees.

When he pushed me away, I cried out, a combination of a plea and a complaint. "No."

"Are you all right?"

I smiled, liking the question. He cared. Even if his concern was only for my safety just as he would've been concerned for any other girl's safety, I didn't care. It was a start. A start to what, I didn't know. Not yet anyway.

"Answer."

There it was again. A one-word sentence. He wasn't a talkative man, but I'd more than make up for it. "I'm fine. Are you?"

"Sure." His hard chest heaved up and down. My fingers skimmed along the lion tattoo with the name *Kings of Beasts MC* written underneath it.

The two lines of muscles on his abdomen kept my gaze there. His jeans hung low, not far enough to see the curly hair below, yet far enough to show that he wore no underwear.

"Do you want to go on? You can give up and quit."

I jerked my head up and found his eyes. Eyes no longer drowned in silver. The blue took most of the silver away, but flecks still remained. They sparkled at me, drawing me in.

"Answer."

I forced myself to pay attention instead of getting lost in the blue. "Do I want to go on to the cabin? Yes."

"Are you sure? It's dangerous in the woods."

He was getting downright chatty. "No shit. But yeah. I'm sure. I mean, the cat won't try and get me again, will it? It was just bad luck running into it. How'd you get away from it?"

"I just did."

"But how? I thought you were dead meat."

His smiled. "You were wrong."

The temptation to touch him again was too much. I lifted my hand to run my fingers over the dark stubble on his chin, but he grabbed my arm and pushed it away.

"If I hadn't been—" He paused, blinked, then continued. "You'd be dead."

Dead? The cat was gone, and with it, my fear. "No. It would've run off after I hit it with the branch." It was total bullshit, but he didn't have to know it.

But, of course, he did.

"She wouldn't have stopped because you threatened her with a stick. Believe it. You would've died."

I swallowed, all at once unsure of whether I wanted to continue. "I have to keep going."

"Because of the money?"

No. "Yes. Why else? I mean, we just met. Why would anyone trade that much money for a man she just met? Even one like you?"

The silver in his eyes shone brighter. I glanced up, expecting to see an opening in the tree cover and the sunlight on his face, and found none.

"Things are only going to get harder from here on out."

"Should I expect a pack of wolves to attack next?"

"Don't joke. This isn't a college campus where everything's safe and secure."

He must not have visited many colleges lately. They weren't very safe any longer. Not for the hearts of girls like me.

"Do you want me to leave? If you do, you should've just said so from the beginning."

"I don't—" The muscle danced in his jaw. "That's not what I'm saying. It's dangerous."

"Yeah. Like I said. I know." But the cat was a fluke. Lots of people hiked in the woods and never got hurt. With the cat gone, I'd have no problem getting to the cabin. "I want to win this."

He gripped my head, taking it between his hands. "Which would you choose, Erin? Tell me. If you had to make the choice right now, which would you choose?"

I couldn't say I'd pick him. Not when I didn't even know his name. Not even when the word *you* was on the tip of my tongue. "The money. I need the money."

"Why?"

He frowned. Had I hurt him? Really hurt him or had I just bruised his ego? "Because you can't count on love."

My answer seemed to confuse him even more. "Love's the only thing you can count on."

"I can't. And even if I thought so, I couldn't trust it to last."

"When it's right, you can."

He skimmed his thumb over my lips, his gaze falling there, then coming back to meet mine. "Let me prove it to you."

He pulled me into his arms, then shoved his hand under my shirt and bra and found my breast. His groan melted into my mouth, filling me with his need as well as my own. Our tongues dueled, mine taking control as much as his. A quick tug sent my jeans flooding to my ankles and I kicked my shoes off, daring to bring one leg out. I kept the other leg in my jeans just in case I needed to pull them up fast. My shirt and bra soon followed in a wild whirl of our hands, both of us working to free me of them. The fever spun into a frenzy between us as he took me to the ground.

At first I stiffened, remembering the last time I'd had sex. I'd thought it had been making love, but I'd been so wrong. Would I be wrong again?

He had me on my back on a pile of leaves, straddling my legs, and stared at me. My hair spread out behind me and I prayed he liked what he saw. If I could believe the look in his eyes, then he found me sexy, desirable, everything I'd ever wanted to be.

I reached for the top of his jeans. He sat still, his hands on his thighs, and watched me pop the button, then slide the zipper down. His cock pushed the flaps away, giving it freedom to burst out of its confines.

At first, I couldn't believe what I saw. Granted, I'd been with only a handful of men, but none of them could've compared to the length and width of him. Even in the shade under the forest canopy, I could see the tip of his bulbous cap glistening with pre-cum. At once, my hands became useless.

His intense focus held me as he shoved the denim over the rise of his butt. He lifted one leg and his jeans were gone. I hadn't noticed before that he wore no shoes.

At that moment, nothing else existed. Not the games, not the big cat, not even the pain hiding inside me, demanding to be released.

His large hands covered my breasts, but still his gaze stayed with mine. Massaging them, he played his thumbs over my hardening nipples, then squeezed. I arched, shoving my breasts against his palms, aching to have him press harder. Yet he was the one in control.

"Please."

His tongue darted over his lip, his only answer.

I closed my eyes, savoring the sensation of his skin against mine. The way he held them was reverent, respectful, and yet so sinful. Both relaxing and exciting.

At last he bent, took my nipple into his mouth, and fondled the other one. I tunneled my fingers into his hair, daring to snare the soft strands and hold him close. Without letting go, he moved his body lower, then brought his legs between mine.

I let my hands fall to his wide shoulders to feel the movement of his muscles. How a man could feel so soft yet so hard was beyond my understanding. The same would hold true of his cock. His kisses feathered my shoulders, then circled my breasts, teasing me until, once more, he snared my nipple between his teeth.

Without warning, he groaned and pulled back. "We have to stop."

I didn't answer because I didn't agree. How could anything that felt so right be wrong? Instead, I reached for him, silently begging him.

Thankfully, he didn't stop. If he had, he would've torn me apart from the inside out.

He kissed his way downward from between my breasts and over the small rise of my stomach. I tried to suck it in, hating myself again for not losing the weight, but lost those awful thoughts when his tongue found my belly button.

He moaned, his palms covering my breasts, as he flicked his tongue around the circle, then dipped it inside. I bucked, surprised at the flash of added lust the simple action gave me. Again, I begged him.

"Please."

And again, he didn't answer.

He kissed my stomach, then nibbled at the soft mound. He lifted his head, his eyes sparkling against his tanned face and the dark hair falling forward, and lowered his body farther down between my legs.

My gaze found the tops of the trees and the sunlight coming through the small breaks in the foliage. I gasped when he pushed my pussy lips apart and pressed his mouth to me. He held me down, snaring my legs as he wrapped his arms under them, then flattened his hands on my pelvis. I thrust my hips upward, not on purpose, but in an instinctual consent, giving him permission.

I was lost in this new world. Lost in a time and place where everything else was forgotten. My heart beat a quick rhythm, matched only by the throbbing between my legs. The birds sang above us as we added our own music to theirs with each sigh and moan. He was a master of desire and I was his slave, willing to give my body and my life to please him.

He sucked on my clit, pulling it into his mouth then releasing it to dive his tongue into my pussy. I bucked, trying to get away even though that was the last thing I really wanted to do. But I couldn't help myself.

Digging my fingers into the ground beneath me, I lifted up to see his dark hair, then his eyes just above my mound. He licked me, over and around my clit, then down to my pussy. My body responded to his touch as though made just for him.

He sucked, nibbled, then lashed me until the need to have him grew higher, stronger.

I wanted to beg him to fuck me, but couldn't catch my breath. He ate at me, feverishly, lapping up the juices that flowed out of me and over the cheeks of my ass.

Again and again, the surge of need flooded me. Again and again, he brought me high, then let me plunge down, only to bring me higher still. In and out his tongue went, driving as deep as he could go as he pulled my pussy folds apart. Just when I thought I couldn't take any more, he'd leave my clit to sweep around my flesh, kissing then biting just hard enough to drive me crazy.

It had been too long, perhaps never, since my body had been possessed so completely. I gave in to him, no longer pleading, but simply reveling in his caresses.

Fingers were added to the blissful torment of his tongue, pumping into me as his wicked mouth came back to capture my clit. The sounds of his pleasure echoed my own. I reached out to him, aching to touch him, to skim my hands over his body, to feel the movement of his muscles as they worked to pleasure me.

My body writhed under his hands and tongue. Shudders raced through me as, once more, he caught my throbbing clit between his teeth. Delicious torture had me whimpering, begging him to relieve my agony.

Yet as much as I yearned for his touch, not once did he demand I give him anything. I would've given him everything if he'd asked. My body took over, answering him as his fingers searched for the spot that would send me flying toward the trees and the sun above us.

He played me. He knew exactly where to skim his fingers

lightly over my skin without giving me the release I needed. Instead, his fingers and mouth kept me on the edge and, just as I was about to jump off, he pulled back, adding more painful delight.

At last, I found my voice. "Please."

His chuckle was his answer.

When he found my sweet spot, my reaction hit me hard and fast, driving into me like an invasion of sexual warriors. I tensed, then tensed more, until I had to come or break into pieces. For one moment, he lifted his head, smiled that knowing smile of his, then crushed his mouth to me again.

The explosion of my climax tore through me, throwing back my head in a silent scream as my body shuddered through the thundering waves of my climax. My clit pulsed, shooting out the release. And still he kept his mouth to me, demanding more.

I screamed again, tears rolling down my face. Bucking against him, it was as though my body wanted to be set free, yet my mind shouted for me to stay close, to never let him go. The line between pleasure and pain grew thinner.

I was still crying when he pulled his body alongside mine, his huge erect cock pressing hard against my leg.

"Quiet. You don't want the world to hear."

But I did want the world to hear. I'd never understood the thing about shouting your love from the rooftops, but now I did. He deserved recognition for such an amazing performance.

And now it was my turn.

I tugged my jeans on, then turned toward him, ready to give him the same kind of satisfaction. He pushed me back and shook his head, both crushing and confusing me. "You don't want me suck your cock?" I glanced down at his long, thick erection.

He groaned an agonized sound. "Fuck, yeah. But we've been here too long."

He was on his feet faster than I would've liked. He was the first man I'd been with after Mike and I wanted to savor the experience. The difference between their lovemaking was beyond what I could've put into words.

"What's your name? You never told me."

He studied me as though telling me his name was a secret he never wanted exposed. "Colter Quaid."

"Nice to meet you, Colter." As if getting laid in the woods happened to me every day.

I pulled my other clothes together as he grabbed his jeans, then he gave me his hand and helped me onto my feet. He tugged his jeans up.

"Um, not that I'm complaining, but where are the rest of your clothes? Or do you always run around the forest in your bare feet and no shirt?"

He glanced down at his feet as though only now realizing he didn't have any shoes on. "I'll explain later. Right now, you've got to know that this wasn't right."

"What wasn't?" Did he already regret what we'd done? But we hadn't done enough, as far as I was concerned.

"I fucked up. I've broken the rules and helped you. If Burke or the others find out, whether you complete the challenge or not won't matter."

His hair was mussed and I was desperate to run my fingers through it. Instead, I stuck my hands in my pockets to keep from doing so.

"I shouldn't have touched you. If I hadn't stopped…"

The old thoughts came back, telling me the real reason he was backing away from me. I was too ugly. Too fat. Too average.

Too damaged.

Had he seen what I'd tried so hard to keep hidden? I got ready to lie.

"Are you saying I shouldn't keep going?"

"No." He let out a tortured breath. "I'm not."

I was sure he'd reach out and he almost did. It tore me apart when, instead, he stepped past me and went to the edge of the forest.

"Just be careful. Keep your eyes open."

He'd backed up until the bushes pressed against his shoulders. Was another man leaving me? Had he seen the scars and changed his mind?

"Wait, Colter. Don't go." But it was too late. He'd already disappeared into the forest.

Suddenly, I wasn't sure about my decision to go on. Was this all a setup? A real game where the girls were lured into sex? I couldn't be sure the prize money existed, much less the choice of keeping Colter. What if I kept walking only to find out that there wasn't any cabin?

Fear wasn't my only companion as I decided to keep going. Doubt took over, ridding me of the wonderful afterglow of being with him.

Chapter Seven

Colter

I wasn't sure what had come over me. Seeing Erin ready to take on Shayna in her cat form had left me with no other option except to come to her defense. At least that part of my actions made sense even if I'd known I was breaking the rule about helping my mate.

But the rest of it was a total fuck-up. After keeping her safe, I should've taken off. Instead, I'd stuck around and put my face and fingers where they shouldn't have gone. We were allowed to be with our mate—up to a point. Intercourse wasn't allowed until the girl made it to her destination. To play around before that was okay, but it was inviting trouble. If I hadn't been able to stop, I might've fucked her and lost control. I might've bitten her, claiming her before she'd completed the games. If that happened, I wasn't sure what the pride would do. No one had ever broken that rule. At least, no one that I knew of.

Her scent was now deeply imbedded in me. After our first kiss outside Fang's, my gut had burned for her. I'd done my best to ignore it, but she'd taken control of my hunger, a hunger I'd kept at bay for years. With that first kiss, she'd pulled me in like a fish dangling from a hook.

Fuck.

I was lucky she hadn't kept on with the questions about my

shirt and shoes. I'd chucked them when I'd seen Shayna advancing on her and only when I was halfway into a shift did I remember that changing was a bad idea. After reversing the shift, I was already on the path before I'd realized I only had my jeans on.

I couldn't let Erin see me in my lion form. The rules forbade us from revealing what we were until after our mates had chosen us.

Damn, Shayna. Didn't I make it clear enough?

Any chance of our mating was over after my refusal outside Fang's.

It was harder for the females of our group and I felt sorry for them. They sometimes fell in love with males already in the pride, but those relationships rarely worked out. Instead, they had to seek out a human mate and make them their own. Even worse, human males didn't accept what we were as easily as human females did. Maybe it was their natural tendency, like ours, to be the one in charge. To be the dominant one.

Shayna shouldn't have attacked Erin, even if our laws said she had a right to. A female of the pride could try and get rid of an intended mate during the games in any way she could, including killing her. Although it was allowed, very few had ever tried. To do so was seen as being disrespectful to the male as well as to the spirit of the games. However, if she did attempt it, the only time she could do so was during the games. Once the intended mate completed the challenge and said she wanted the man over the money, then the female shifter's chance was lost.

The actual claiming wasn't completed until the man bit his new mate and transformed her into a lioness, but her choosing him at the end of the games was considered the same thing. Like an unbreakable contract that would soon be fulfilled. No one had ever tried to run off a mate, much less kill her, after she'd accepted the man.

But that wasn't my biggest concern. If she wanted to, Shayna could tell Burke and the others that I'd interfered. If she did, then Erin would be disqualified and sent home. And I'd risk being exiled from the pride, sent away to live alone in the mountains, blocked from living with either my people or humans. The consequences of breaking our laws were often harsh, but our life was a difficult one.

I hated to think how lonely that life would be.

All I could do was hope Shayna wouldn't want to tell the others. I doubted she would, especially since she'd failed. Failing, along with my public refusal to mate with her, would make her lose even more of the other members' respect.

Still, I'd done wrong. I'd broken the rules by helping Erin. And I'd wanted to fuck her. Thankfully, somehow I'd come to my senses and had kept from shoving my cock inside her.

But damn, she'd tasted good.

Even now, as I ran through the forest, loping over the ground, I could still smell her on me, still had her flavors lingering on the tip of my tongue. I ran, determined to keep away from her until we met at the cabin. Yet whenever I let my mind wander, I'd find myself turning back to run in a parallel path with her, staying hidden by the forest. No matter how hard I tried to keep away, no matter how many times I told myself I was flirting with danger, I couldn't go too far from her.

The truth was difficult to believe, but there it was. She'd already captured my heart.

Erin

The path grew harder, more rugged the farther I traveled. My breathing was labored and my legs were sore. My body was scratched both by branches and my fall. After Colter had gone, I'd thought about trying to follow him, but after going a few feet into the trees, I knew it was impossible. He'd gone too fast, leaving nothing to show that he'd been there.

I put my fingers to my mouth, remembering the way his lips had felt against mine. He'd stirred a hunger inside me that Mike had never done.

Colter had given of himself, making me feel special. Unlike Mike who'd given me all the promises I'd wanted to hear, Colter had said nothing about the future, except to finish the games. And yet, he hadn't needed to. His touch, his licks, his nibbles were enough.

I stopped, listening to the sounds around me as animals scurried through the underbrush. Being one with nature had never been my thing. To me, roughing it was sitting on a white, sandy beach with a waiter standing nearby to fetch drink after umbrella-festooned drink. But for some strange reason, I was suddenly into it.

Weird.

The noise of rustling drew my attention to the left and I squinted. Was it Colter? Or was the large cat stalking me, following me until she was ready to pounce? I listened again, even trying to keep my breathing shallow.

There it is again.

I ducked behind a tree, hugging my body as close to it as I

could. If danger was near, I wanted to see it coming.

A flash of red hair caught my attention, then was gone. I eased around the tree and searched for it. Was that Nina?

The rustling kept on, the noise coming from nearby, but just where, I couldn't be sure. I started moving, going as fast as I dared on the uneven path while glancing to my left every so often. Again, I caught a flash of color.

"Nina! Is that you? It's me. Erin."

Whoever or whatever it was kept moving. Either she hadn't heard me or it wasn't Nina. I wondered if it was an animal, but didn't think many animals had red fur.

It didn't help that I was trying to run uphill. The ache in my legs intensified and the stitch was back in my side.

Again, I saw a quick peek of red.

If it was Nina, then she didn't have a problem getting up the hill. I wasn't even sure there was a path for her to take. She'd had a rough time walking on the road. How could she be going so fast now?

The pain in my side struck harder, taking away what little breath I had. I stopped, put my hands on my knees, and sucked in as much air as I could. Checking ahead of the last spot where I'd seen red, I tried to find the splash of color again, but couldn't. We weren't allowed to help each other, but I wanted to see Nina so badly that I was ready to take the risk. Besides, Colter and I had already broken the rules. If no one found out, what did it matter?

Taking several minutes to regain my breath and wait for the ache in my legs and side to ease gave me time to think. How far had I already gone? How much farther did I have to go? I pulled into a standing position and lifted my face to the sky. It was getting later. Time was running out.

I started again, taking it at a slower pace and no longer looking for the red color. If I was lucky, maybe Nina's destination was close enough to mine for me to know she was all right.

Thankfully, I'd worn my favorite pair of running shoes. I'd seen other girls with clogs and even heels. I'd bet they were in a world of hurt by now.

Sweat trickled down my spine and along my brow. That damn cabin better have a good shower. I'd take a long, slow one before I let Colter touch me again.

Assuming he wanted to touch me again. Although what we'd done had been wonderful, I wanted more. I had to have his cock inside me. Needed to feel it pushing my walls as he ran his hands over my body.

I trudged on, keeping my mind focused on Colter. Of course, I'd still have to choose the money once the games were over. I had to. But if I could convince Colter that we didn't have to follow the rules once the decision was made and the money was in my bank account, I'd consider myself a real winner. I doubted he'd go along with it, but it was nice thinking he might.

It's amazing how much time I had to think about things. I kept putting one foot in front of the other. At times, the path disappeared into a thicket, but I kept going, working my way through the branches while trying to keep them from slashing my face and arms. I tried not to like the feeling the slashes gave me. All that was part of my past.

Letting my mind go into the past could be dangerous. Like opening a portal to another world, one filled with regret, pain, and self-doubt, I could lose control and wind up exactly where I didn't want to go.

I wonder what Mike's doing.

And yet, there I went.

Had Mike ever really loved me? Or had I fit into the mold of what he wanted as a girlfriend? Pliable. Easy to cheat on. Stupid. The list could go on.

Had I ever really loved him? I didn't think so now. I'd been searching for someone to make me feel better about myself and I'd found it in him. At least for a while.

I stumbled, bringing me out of my thoughts. Pulling out the map, I checked to make sure I hadn't missed something. But it seemed easy enough. Just stay on the path until I found the creek and then the clearing. The cabin wouldn't be much farther. But I was hot, tired, and getting hungry. If only I'd brought along some water, it would've given me more strength to go on.

A scream split the air, catching me off-guard. Lasting only a short time, I waited to see if another one would follow. When it didn't, I was torn between relief and fear that whoever had screamed couldn't scream again.

I ran. Faster, harder, than I should've. But I couldn't bring myself to stop.

The next scream came from me. Down I went, not landing on my face, but on my side. I kept moving, rolling downward. A swirl of images flipped past me, as dirt, leaves, and other debris flew into the air. My mouth filled with the stuff. Pain splintered into me from all sides, then collided together in one large jolt that sent me spinning into the air. I landed again, once more on my side, rolled a little more, then finally, blissfully, came to a stop.

I groaned, not daring to move. My entire body hurt. My hand felt something run over it, but I couldn't force myself to jerk it away. If I did, I was afraid I'd hurt even more.

"Shit."

I lay there looking up at the breaks in the trees. Hadn't I done the same thing earlier? But now was different. Colter wasn't by my side. Instead of joy, I wanted to scream, to shout, to curse at the world.

I'd ended up in a deep rut. If I'd been paying closer attention to the path, I might've noticed how it ended without warning. Instead, I'd dropped into the pit like some dumb animal being herded for slaughter.

Closing my eyes, I tried not to cry. I couldn't go on. Didn't want to go on.

Colter's face came to me. Then I heard Maddy's and Nina's voices.

"Keep on going. Stay safe."

When I opened my eyes again, I blinked several times before I realized I couldn't see well. My vision was blurred, my head aching.

"Get up. Keep on going. Stay safe." Again, their voices drifted through my head.

Stay safe? I giggled. *So much for staying safe.*

But I couldn't just lie there.

Mike had lied. All his promises had been lies.

But I'd lied, too.

Maybe we were both to blame.

My mind wouldn't focus no matter how many times I tried to make it. Like a slot machine, images and thoughts spun around and around in a dizzying whirl of colors. Every once in a while, they'd stop, teasing me to take hold and make them stay still. Then they'd start again.

Start again. Every day's a new day.

No. That's another lie.

Every day was just a continuation of the day before. Same old problems. Same old pain. Same old lies.

I rolled onto my side, then tried to get up. But I didn't make it very far. Didn't even get my bottom half off the ground. Groaning, I lay back down as my head started going through another slot machine ride.

As it had done before, the whirlwind slowed down until my mind cleared. I had to move before another spin came.

Keep on going. Stay safe.

At least now it was my own voice in my head. I'd blown the *stay safe* part of it to hell and back, but I was determined not to do the same to the first. I'd keep on going. Safe or not.

Gritting my teeth, I pushed up again. My cry of victory when I managed to ease my body into a sitting position echoed around me.

Would Nina hear me? Would Colter?

The trench I sat in ran lengthwise on either side of me. It had been a small creek before, probably the one on the map, but now it was as dry as the desert.

I had to get out of there. Not only because of the huge spider web near me—had it been a spider that had scurried over my hand?—but because I still didn't know how far I had to go to reach the cabin. I picked up a stick and flicked a spider the size of a quarter back toward the nest. If he left me alone, I'd leave him alone.

"Shit, shit, shit."

My mother had been wrong. Cussing did help.

I took it nice and slow as I eased myself onto my feet. The spin threatened to take over again and I wobbled. I counted it a win when I kept from slipping back onto my butt and instead, leaned against the same hilly slide I'd ridden on my way down.

But how the hell was I going to get out of there?

I could follow the creek bed, but that would lead me away from the cabin. Then what would have been the point of everything I'd gone through? Hopefully, Colter was waiting there. Thoughts of him and the idea of two hundred and fifty thousand dollars in my bank account got me to shove away from the wall.

I studied the opposite wall. Branch limbs broke through the rock and dirt barrier. If I could use them to climb out, then I might just be able to make it.

Wiping the dirt and grime off my face, I paused, expecting my mind to give me another blurry ride. When it didn't, I counted it as a good sign. Taking care to pull on the branches to check how much support they'd give me, I put one foot on a lower branch, then gripped another one as far up as I could reach.

Keep on going.

Yeah, I was determined to do just that.

I tightened my hold and pulled myself up. And found out all too soon that my handholds weren't as strong as I'd thought they were.

Branches crumbled out of the dirt wall and I fell again, landing right in the middle of the spider web. If no one had heard my screams before, they had to have heard the one I screamed then. I scrambled away, my body no longer too tired to move, brushing my hands over my clothes and body.

"Shit, shit, shit."

Anger surged through me. Anger at Mike. Anger at trusting some motorcycle gang. Anger at getting myself in a mess I couldn't get out of.

I threw myself at the wall again, taking hold of different branches. My body complained, telling me it had had enough, but I didn't listen. One branch led to the next, then the next. I laughed, a kind of hysterical sound, then took hold of the highest branch.

I was almost out of the ditch when I lost my grip. Just as I started to fall backward, a hand gripped my wrist.

Chapter Eight

Erin

Colter.

Even if he hadn't helped me get out of the ditch, I would've still thrilled at seeing him. The expression on his face, however, wasn't the one I would've liked to have seen. He was pissed off and not bothering to hide it.

The man was strong, stronger than anyone I'd ever known. He pulled me out of the dried up creek without a problem. One minute I was falling backward, then his hand was around my wrist, and he was bringing me into his strong arms. I stayed quiet, happy I was no longer trapped, and excited to see him again.

He didn't speak and didn't lessen his hold on me. Once again, I was transported to a world where only we existed. I closed my eyes and prayed we could stay that way forever.

His heart thumped against my ear, perhaps a little faster than was normal. He had his shirt on and I clutched the fabric, curling my hands into fists. His crotch pressed against my stomach as we melded our bodies together. Maybe it was my imagination, but I would've sworn his cock grew, lifting his jeans in a tell-tale kind of way.

He wanted me. And God knew I wanted him.

"Erin." His voice was deep and filled with emotion. "Are

you all right?"

Aside from a little spinning in my head. "I'm fine."

"Damn it. This is wrong."

I wanted to keep my eyes closed. Wanted to ignore him. I didn't answer and wouldn't until I had to.

"Erin?"

A question this time, but one I couldn't answer. I wouldn't risk losing the tenuous hold we had.

He slid his hands to my wrists and brought my arms down. I didn't fight him, but my hands remained fisted even after losing hold of his shirt.

"Stop saying that." I wanted to shout at him, but managed to keep my voice low.

"Stop saying what?"

"Stop saying this is wrong. As far as I'm concerned, it's right. Very right."

"No. It's not. You don't understand. We can't—"

I was on him then, uncaring if I seemed desperate. My body craved his and I was damn well going to have him. Taking him by his hair, I brought his mouth to mine.

At first he didn't kiss me back, but then he did. Intensely. Needy. Consuming me as I wanted to consume him.

He took me under the arms and yanked me closer. Taking hold of my hair as fiercely as I'd taken his, he yanked my head back, then broke the kiss and put his mouth against the curve of my neck.

I whimpered, begging him to take me. I shivered as his teeth skated along my skin, bringing every nerve ending alive. I could almost feel his teeth sinking into me, tearing my flesh, and letting my blood slide down his throat. It was a strange feeling, an instinct I didn't understand, but I didn't care. If he bit me,

I'd treasure the wound. None of that made sense, and yet it did. More sense than anything ever had.

I burned for him, my need overwhelming me until another kind of dizziness swept over me. His hands explored every inch of me, tugging my jeans aside to dip his fingers between my legs. I grew wet with his caresses and throbbed for more. He wrapped my leg around his and pushed my shirt aside as his tongue explored the hollow of my neck.

"Colter, fuck me." I didn't care how. As long as he took me right then and there.

His moan, a low, dangerous sound that was more like a growl, rumbled out of his chest, against my palm, then traveled up my arm. I leaned back, letting him support me, and pushed my pelvis against him, wordlessly urging him to do more, to take more.

When he suddenly broke away from me and staggered back, I was left stunned, confused, and angry. "Colter, don't. I need you."

His own lust darkened his face. "Erin, no. I can't be with you. Not until you've made it to the cabin."

"Why? What's so special about this damn cabin? There or here on the ground. It doesn't matter to me."

"That's the way the games work."

"Fuck the games."

A quick small smile came and went. "And I can't keep helping you."

"Why not?"

"You know why. It's against the rules."

"We've already broken the stupid rules, so what's the problem?" I glanced around. "Besides, who's going to see us?"

He was amazing, hot, strong, commanding, everything a

man should be. And I was just…me. No one special. And yet, I could see how much he wanted me.

"That's not the point." He turned me loose and stepped away. "It's my fault. I shouldn't have interfered." He ran a hand over the back of his neck and shook his head. "I just can't seem to help myself."

My body still hurt from the fall, but those aches weren't half as painful as his sudden refusal to make love to me. "Then just do it. Unless, of course, I'm too much trouble."

"What? Hell, no. You know I want you." He arched an eyebrow, then lowered his gaze to his still-bulging crotch. "I want to fuck you so much it's fucking painful."

I tried a different approach, straightening my body and thrusting out my breasts. "Of course you do. What sane man wouldn't?" I waved my hands over my body, showing him exactly what he'd get.

But this time he didn't smile.

"This is serious, Erin." His pained expression turned into a scowl.

"If you want me like you say you do, then great. No one's going to see, so what's the problem?"

"Erin, we call these The Claiming Games, but it's really not a game. This is how we find the women who will become our mates. If you make it to your destination and through the next two nights, then back down to Fang's, then we'll know you can handle becoming one of us."

"So far it doesn't seem so hard. I can handle it. Trust me."

"Not hard? You've had a big cat try to eat you and then you fell into a dry river. You'd still be stuck down there if I hadn't pulled you out. Plus, you've got scratches all over you."

"But I can do this. Don't you think I can?"

"Yeah, I do."

That got me. How often had I heard anyone say that? Knowing he believed in me gave me a surge of confidence I'd rarely felt. "And I won't let you down. I promise."

No matter what The Darkness tried to do, I'd do it for him. Most of all, I'd do it for me.

He backed up even more, slicing me to the core. "Good. But I have to stop helping you. If I don't, we won't know if you have what it takes to withstand our kind of life. It's better to find out now than later."

I moved toward him, but didn't get very far. The spinning came back, blurring my vision. I reached out, needing something, someone to hold on to, and felt him save me again.

"You lied." Surprise and irritation filled his tone. "You are hurt."

He helped me to the ground, then brushed my hair from my forehead. I blinked, willing my vision to clear and the dizziness to go away. He skimmed his palms along my arms, murmuring words that comforted me even when I didn't understand their meaning.

"I'm okay." My voice sounded like it had left my body and hovered in the air above me.

"The fuck you are."

"Fuck." I giggled, remembering the last time he'd put me on the ground. "Yes, please."

But when his hands started traveling down my legs, I kicked and brushed them away. "I said I was fine."

"Are you sure about that?"

I saw him better and with a clearer head. "Yes. I'm feeling okay now. Seriously."

He gave me a suspicious look. "Just try to keep from falling into dried-up creeks."

"I'll try, but I'm not the woodsy kind of girl. I'm more the luxury resort kind." I grinned. "Or at least, I'd like to be. But trees, bugs, and big cats? Not so much."

"Then you won't make it as one of us. This is our home and that's not going to change."

It was hard to read him. But I wasn't about to let him throw me a curve. "Are you trying to talk me out of this?"

"No."

"People adapt. I can adapt." I was getting ticked off. So it was all his way or the highway?

"I'm just telling you how it is."

"Yeah. I get it." I pulled my shoulders back and jutted out my chin. I'd show him, Mike, and everyone else who'd ever doubted me. Me included. "I'll make it."

I knew it was awful, but I couldn't help it. "Don't worry about me making the grade. Besides, you won't be losing anything if I don't. Because once I do, I'm taking the money anyway." I regretted it as soon as I opened my mouth, but by then, it was too late.

He reacted as though I'd sucker-punched him. But hadn't I told him before? And yet, I couldn't help but take a small bit of delight in the way I'd affected him. Even if it hurt me as much as it did him.

I didn't try to reach out to him. He shot me a glare that seared over my flesh. Without another word, he pushed through the bushes and was gone.

"Colter, come back." I'd messed up again. "Colter, please."

To my surprise, he returned, carrying a long plank. He set one end of it on the ground, then let it fall across the ditch to form a makeshift bridge. "For the walk back."

"Thank you." All my irritation was gone as though it had never existed.

He placed a foot on the board, then walked across it as though he'd done it all his life. When he turned toward me again, he hadn't lost the scowl. "That's the last time I'm helping you. If you want the fucking money, then you're going to have to earn it on your own."

Why'd he have to say that? "Like I said before. I will."

Colter

I kept moving away from Erin, away from my overwhelming need to have her. When I'd had my teeth at her throat, I'd almost claimed her. I never should've watched over her, but the fear of losing her, especially after Shayna's attack, ate at me.

I'd been compelled to help her just as my father had helped my mother during the games. He'd regretted it later and so would I. If only someone could've stopped her that final day, then maybe she'd still be with us. With me.

But Erin was not my mother. She'd been attacked and she was clumsy, not suicidal.

She had to make it on her own. Testing a woman's strength was the very foundation of the games. I'd already screwed that up as much as I dared. And yet, when she'd needed me, I hadn't been able to stop myself.

The growl flowed up my throat as my inner beast clawed to get free. Traveling alongside her, watching over her took its toll on me. Even after shifting, I wouldn't be able to shake the need to keep her safe.

The growl of another shifter drifted on the air. Was it one

of the other men? Or was Shayna still around? If she was, then I'd have no choice but to stay close by.

We didn't think like our human counterparts while in our cat bodies. Instead, the world and everyone in it came to our senses in waves of images and memories. I'd remember Erin in my lion form. Shayna had remembered her just from watching Erin as she'd left Fang's. But the feelings, the memories we held came from two very different places.

Shayna's memory of Erin came from hate, envy, and a willingness to rip Erin's throat open and watch her life's blood flow out of her. It wasn't personal. At least not in the way most people thought. For Shayna, it came from a place of survival, of the instinct to possess the mate she wanted. My refusal to take her as my mate wouldn't stop her from killing the woman she saw as her competition.

My memory of Erin came from an emotion I'd never experienced. At first, I hadn't even known what the emotion was. And then, it had hit me.

My memory of Erin came from love.

I growled again, hating how fast and hard I'd fallen. Love didn't have anything to do with the games. Taking a mate was solely for the continuation of our kind. If a male fell in love with his mate, then even better. But it wasn't necessary.

I lifted my head and sniffed, drawing in a myriad of scents. Even with all the other aromas tantalizing my nostrils, I could still pick out Erin's scent from the rest. Her fragrance was buried in my psyche, becoming a part of me that would last a lifetime, regardless of the outcome of the games. I shucked my clothes as fast as I could, planning on coming back later to retrieve them.

My body burned both with the physical pain of the shift, as

well as the overwhelming need to turn my lion free. The change devoured me, ripping tendons, breaking bones, then reforming them. My skin tingled as fur spread over it. Teeth grew longer, sharper. Claws erupted from fingernails. Dropping to all fours, I moved like a frenzied fire over dried grassland.

The world shifted, colors fading until, at last, everything was a mix of blacks, grays, and the ever-present silver. My paws struck the ground without a sound as I stretched out my legs and sent soft clouds of dust swirling around my feet.

Picking up speed, I ran as hard as I could. I'd end up going around her several times, making a large loop that would take me away from her at its farthest point, but would always bring me back. To go at her slow pace would've driven me crazy.

I ran harder, faster. Free at last. Free to pound out the strange new feeling. Her name and face echoed in my cat's mind. I lengthened my stride as though I could outrun the images, the feelings for her, leaving behind the way she twisted my gut and made my cock grow strong. My mind focused on her and her alone.

And then I was hit, thrown off my feet, rolling over twice before I came back on all four paws, claws extended. I snarled a warning as I whirled toward my attacker.

Shayna.

She struck out with her paw, swiping across my flank. I reared back, standing up on two legs and hissing at her to stop. She came again, pressing the fight. I jumped into the air, unwilling to let her attack me any longer, and landed on top of her. Her snarls grew more strident as she fought to get me off her. Although she was large for a female, she had no chance against me.

I bent and closed my jaws over her throat. A whine escaped

her as she went still, submitting to me. Holding her, I was torn.
If I turned her loose, she could cause more trouble. She could
expose the wrongs I'd done. She could go after Erin again. But
if I killed her, I'd commit a crime against the pride. Lions did
not kill lions. Worse, I'd have the stain of her blood on my life,
a guilt that would never go away.

I turned her loose, growled, and jumped out of her reach. I
stayed in my lion body, shook my mane, and waited for her
next move.

She lowered her belly to the ground, bowing to my
authority. Once I was sure it wasn't a trick, I shifted back into
my human body. She did the same.

"Go home, Shayna."

"No. You're mine. I won't give you up."

"You're not the one."

"You thought I was once."

Again, my lie came back to bite me. Sex with her had meant
nothing more than that. Just sex. But now that I'd taken in
Erin's aroma, I no longer wanted anyone else. No one would
ever satisfy me the way she would.

"Damn it, Shayna, you have to stop." She had to let me go.
If she didn't, then all kinds of trouble would break out.

"And if I don't?" She slunk over to me, her fingers trailing
over my chest, then over the lion tattoo, and down to flick over
my cock.

"You will. You have to." I brushed her hand away.

"Not if the human bitch doesn't make it to the cabin in
time. Or if she doesn't survive."

My hand was around her throat before the thought to do so
registered in my mind. She gasped, fear glinting in her eyes and
washing the color from her face. "I'm warning you. Back off. If

you go near her again, I'll protect her. No matter what."

I thrust her back, then stalked away. If I didn't put some distance between us, there was no telling what might happen.

Erin

"Shit." I swatted a flying something-or-other away from my face. I had to be getting close, but I was moving slowly.

It was just because I was out of shape. No surprise there. Plus, I was using a rocky, uneven path to go up a damn hill. I was a girl who liked spending the day shopping, then meeting up with friends at a party. Not climbing a mountain.

I met Mike at a frat party.

Screw parties from now on.

And yet, even as I allowed the thoughts to come, I realized the hurt that usually twisted my gut wasn't as bad as it used to be. It was still there, more like a regret than a heartache, but I could breathe through it. More filled with anger than with pained rejection. Somehow, along the way, my feelings toward Mike had taken a definite shift.

Was it because of Colter? And if it was, was I simply shifting my obsession, my attraction to another? To one who might hurt me just as much? Maybe even more?

"Don't be stupid." I swatted at the damn bug again. Another one landed on my arm. I squashed it, cringed, then wiped dead bug gunk off me. "You're doing this for the money. Not for some wilderness biker dude, no matter how good he uses his tongue and hands."

I kept moving, trying to ignore my thirst and the hunger gnawing at my ribcage. Had anyone said if there'd be food or water at the cabin? I couldn't remember.

I wondered where Colter was. We'd parted in a not-so-good way. Would I still see him once I reached the cabin? Or had he had enough of me and my big mouth?

Too damn bad. His loss, right?

If he wanted me as more than just a fuck then he'd have to get used to handling me. I was who I was and I wasn't about to change for a man. Not like I'd done for Mike.

The Claiming Games had morphed into my way of regaining my life. If I lost both the man and the money, I'd still come out of it as a winner. As long as I finished.

And if I didn't? Roberta's words came back, spurring me on.

"You'll cry and you'll beg to go home. If you do, you'll be sent packing."

She wouldn't send me packing. I was going to make it. After all, aside from almost getting attacked by a fucking big cat, then falling into a hole with a web of fucking big spiders, and knocking my head, it hadn't been so tough.

All I needed now was to run into a grizzly bear who'd give me a great, big, old bear hug. No biggie.

A sound, much like the one I'd heard before, had me whirling around, checking the forest behind me. Was I being paranoid? Or had I really heard something? I hoped with all my heart that it was Colter.

But it wasn't. Instead, the man stepping out of the forest was the one man I never wanted to see again.

"Hector, what are you doing here?"

"Just out for a stroll, girl."

He kept walking toward me. I looked around and, not finding a stick to use, picked up a large rock. "Yeah, right. Don't get any closer."

He stopped, frowning at me. "Hey, relax. I'm not here to bother you. Why would I do that? You're going to be one of us, right? At least, that's what I thought."

"You thought wrong." I knew I was supposed to make it on my own, but I still scanned the trees, hoping to see Colter come to my rescue again.

I hated Hector's smile. He was handsome enough, but I couldn't get past the *ick* factor with him. Especially now that I'd been with Colter.

He took another step my way. "It's Erin, right? Don't get all worked up. Look, I'm sorry about how I acted at CeeCee's. I acted like a jerk and you have a right to whack me one." He lifted his hands up, warding off my possible attack. "Not that I want you to." He glanced around, then dipped his head and gave me a conspiratorial wink. "If you want, I could help you get to the cabin."

"I don't need your help."

He acted like he was impressed, but I could tell it was all fake. "Okay, okay. But there's no harm in my tagging along to make sure you make it in one piece, is there?"

Was he out here for me? Or was he playing me? "No thanks. I like going it on my own."

"No problem. Just offering, is all."

I waited for him to leave, but he didn't move. "Okay then. I've got to get going." I held the rock up a little higher. It was getting heavy. "You're not going to follow me, right?"

"Nope."

"Good." I didn't drop the rock as I turned around. A quick look over my shoulder showed me he was still in the same place. And yet, I couldn't shake the impression that I needed to get away from him as fast as I could. That he was playing with me, like a cat with a mouse.

I kept my attention on him and started walking. And walking faster, careless of the branches slashing me. And then I started running.

His laughter followed me.

I'm not sure how long I ran. At last, however, I had to stop. I waited a minute or so, heard and saw nothing, then started walking again. As far as I could tell, he'd been true to his word and hadn't followed me.

I trudged on, the incline growing so steep I had to bend over. My head was down, my gaze on the ground. If nothing else, I wouldn't fall into any more dried-up creek beds.

I was going to do it. On my own, without Colter or anyone else. Pride surged in me, and yet I knew from so many past experiences that pride sucks wind against the black recesses of my mind. I walked, and walked, and kept on walking.

A while later, I'd had it. I couldn't take another step.

"I'll take a little break and then get right back at it."

At least the bugs had finally decided I wasn't worth chomping on. I stepped off the path and sat down against a large tree, resting my back against its rough bark.

The forest was more beautiful than I'd imagined. My father had taken me out for walks in a nearby wooded area, but that was nothing compared to the majestic splendor surrounding me. Since I was no longer concentrating on keeping one foot in front of the other, I could enjoy the rustling sounds of unseen creatures. Birds chirped and a rabbit scurried past me, caught in the corner of my eye as a flash of brown blending into white.

The light grew dimmer as I sat there, taking it all in, studying the way the leaves in the trees above me swayed with the high breeze. I lifted my hair off my neck and waved my hand, trying to create my own breeze, but it was a pitiful second best.

I needed to get moving again. As it was, I wasn't sure I'd make it to the cabin in time. They'd said I had to make it to the cabin before nightfall. But how would they know?

Keep on going. Stay safe.

One of these days, I'd put our slogan on a T-shirt with my face under the words.

Staying put any longer wasn't a good idea. Walking at night in a forest without a flashlight wasn't a bright idea. Even I knew that much.

Groaning, I pushed against the tree and tried to get to my feet. The stab of needles and pins in my legs had me crying out and plopping back on the ground.

"Damn." I rubbed my legs, then tried moving them to get the blood flowing. Little by little, the feeling came back. I tried again to get up. The light filtering through the tops of the trees had grown a little less bright.

Wiping my dry lips with the back of my hand, I started forward again, my head down and my gaze locked on the path. I walked, stumbling at times over stones. The heat of the day was easing, warning me of the failing sunlight. It would be dark soon and I would've blown my chance at either Colter or the money.

A thicket of bushes lay sprawled across the road, blocking my way. Going slower than I had before, I took care to keep the branches off me. I was already scratched up enough from the other times I'd pushed through the limbs and I didn't want to add any more marks. I'd started the challenge with enough of my own.

The branches pulled at my hair and clothes, but I walked

slowly, easing ahead one step at time. The light appeared brighter at the other end of the thicket. If I could make it through, I'd be all right. I'd just untangled my hair from a branch when I felt something move over my foot. I froze, then dared to look down.

Oh, shit.

I let out a squeal, kicked the snake off my foot and started running, heedless of the stings of the branches as they whipped against my skin. Suddenly, throwing my body toward the light, I broke through the barrier and into a small clearing. I stayed on my feet, jumping and kicking to make sure the snake hadn't wrapped itself around my foot.

The terror gripping me washed away as I slumped onto the green grass. The softness felt good after walking on the hard-packed ground for so long. Laughing my relief at having escaped the snake, I slumped down, going to my back, flinging my arms outward. Thankfully, it was nowhere to be found.

This was where Colter and I should've had sex. Although, strictly speaking, I guess we hadn't had real sex. At least not intercourse. But what we had done was enough to give me an idea of how hot the sex would be once we went all the way.

The sound of someone running, breaking through the underbrush, caught my attention.

Colter? Oh, damn, please don't let it be Hector.

At first glance, I didn't see anything. And then I saw her.

Nina.

She was running across the clearing, going away from me, her red hair flying behind her. I doubt she saw me. Right behind her was the man that had talked to her outside Fang's. I lifted my hand, ready to signal to her, then stopped. Shading my face, I squinted, trying to see if Nina was running because she was afraid or because she was having fun, perhaps caught up in a game of chase. No matter how hard I looked, I couldn't tell.

I brought my arm down and watched as she disappeared into the forest. What if he wasn't helping her? What if she was running to get away from him? Maybe even running for her life?

I had to help her. Fuck the rules and the game. She was my best friend.

Ignoring my protesting legs, I took off running as hard as I could. The man entered the forest and was gone before I made it across the clearing.

Should I call out to her? Could I draw his attention to me? Or would it be better to chase after them without giving myself away and losing the element of surprise?

I hauled ass, bursting into the tree cover again. Although I kept moving, I wasn't sure I was going in the right direction. A path didn't exist, but at least the trees were farther between, making running easier.

I'm not sure how far or how long I ran. Soon, with my strength gone, I had no choice but to stop. I'd lost them.

"Nina!" I tried calling her name in between gasps of air, then twice more, but heard nothing. "Damn." I hoped she was okay.

Turning back the way I'd come, I walked a few feet and then stopped as cold, hard realization hit me.

I was lost.

Chapter Nine

Erin

I am so screwed.

Taking a deep breath, I pivoted around, then around again. Nothing looked familiar, but why should it? Trees were trees, as far as I was concerned. One didn't look much different from the next one. Without a path to follow, I had no way of knowing which way to go, especially after turning around a couple of times.

"Don't panic." That would become my new mantra. The best I could do was to guess which way to go, but by then, doing eeny-meeny-miny-moe was as effective a way to choose as any other.

"Nina!" I figured she was out of earshot by now, but it was worth a try. But I got nothing in return.

Taking my best guess, I started walking. If I could find where the light came into the forest a little brighter, then I might be able to find the clearing. Once at the clearing, I'd look for the path on the other side of the grassy area just as it was drawn on the map.

I'd gone several minutes, fighting back the rising panic. But it was no use. I'd headed in the wrong direction.

All I had to do was to turn around and go back to where I'd first realized I was lost. Then I'd try another direction. If that wasn't the right one, then I'd go back to my starting position and try another direction.

No problem. I'd just repeat the process until I got it right.

I pulled the map out of my pocket, but without the path to lead me, it didn't help. My plan would work only if I found the clearing.

What felt like a long time came and went. I was on my third attempt at finding my way back. The sweat had plastered my shirt to my skin and the knot in my stomach had gotten bigger and tighter.

"Please." I paused, searched the forest, and wished like crazy for Colter to once again break the rules. Hell, by then I would've welcomed the appearance of Big Foot. Or at least a more civilized human version of the Missing Link. Maybe even Hector.

I was exhausted, fed up, angry, hungry, and scared. Why had I agreed to this? I needed money just like everyone else, but not enough to risk my life. And yet I'd done just that.

Hell, I wasn't even sure they had the money to give me once I finished the challenge. Instead, all this could turn out to be one messed-up dating experiment with a bunch of lion-loving bikers.

And I'd dragged my friend into it. Sure, Nina had given them our names, but I was certain she'd agreed to do the games partly because she thought she'd be helping me get over Mike. I should've come alone. If anything happened to Nina, I'd never forgive myself.

Or Maddy.

Where had she gone, anyway? Hopefully, back home? Maddy had always been the smart one of our group and she'd proven it again.

Fighting the battle to keep back the tears, I slumped against a large tree, went to my butt, and gave in to the need to cry. Just as Roberta had predicted, all I wanted was to go home. Or to find the cabin. But to spend the night lost in the woods was terrifying.

Didn't I have enough problems? I'd already been to hell and back. And my constant companion, The Darkness, was still with me, ready and willing to come to my aid. It whispered to me, urging me to give into it. It swirled inside me, growing the need for me to find release before it pushed me too far. To find a sharp stick and release the demons rising to the surface, threatening to tear me apart.

I hugged my knees to my chest, crossed my arms over them, and put my head down. I'd promised Maddy and Nina that I'd never hurt myself again in any way, but I wasn't sure I could keep my promise.

My sobs grew louder as the light in the woods kept fading.

Colter

She's lost.

I slid behind one of the trees, getting even closer. Breaking the rules had never been hard for me, but since meeting Erin, I'd broken more rules than even I was used to doing.

My gut told me I was making a mistake by again coming to her aid. The Claiming Games came about for a purpose. If a woman wasn't able to finish on her own, then she wasn't likely to survive the hard life of my people. It was a test, plain and simple, and she was failing it.

And yet I was back, watching, trying to figure out how to

help her.

I shifted enough to bring out the sensitive hearing of my animal. A couple of the girls had made it far enough for me to pick up their scents. Their cries drifted on the wind, their aromas, so different from everything that existed in the woods, flared my nostrils.

Fuck it. She was a part of me now, and I'd do whatever I had to do to get her back to Fang's safe and sound.

The hairs on my neck stood up, sensing another shifter close by. I couldn't decide if it was Shayna or one of the others. Many of the males would stick close to their chosen mates, but wouldn't let them know they were there. It could even be Burke or Roberta, checking on how things were going. If they saw me helping Erin, then they'd disqualify her and send her packing. As long as a woman hadn't seen any of us transform, she was allowed to leave. If, however, she'd found out what we were, then she'd face a different outcome.

That was a part of the games no one had told the girls. A man couldn't reveal himself to his mate until she'd chosen him. If a woman saw one of us shift before making her decision, then her options were gone. She had to stay with the pride whether she wanted to or not. We couldn't have her telling the outside world about us. Too many curious people, including the media, would come to our mountain and threaten our way of life. After she became one of us, she wouldn't want to leave.

I couldn't remember it ever happening. But just in case, Roberta made sure they chose girls who weren't close to their families. Even if someone did come looking for them, they wouldn't get very far. The townspeople of Cripple Creek knew better than to talk.

Erin's sobs had broken my heart. Soon after, she'd fallen

asleep, exhausted. But I couldn't leave her alone. If I did, she might sleep through the night and never make it to the cabin. Breaking the rules was one thing, but hiding the fact that she'd never made it to her destination was too much to try and slip by them.

I moved closer, then felt the hair on the back of my neck stand up. Someone was near. But who? I was torn between waking her and taking a chance of getting caught, or letting her sleep and risk her not getting to the cabin on time.

But I had to do something. My only chance was to try and wake her up without getting caught.

I edged closer still, keeping my body as far in the shadows as I could. Her arms, face, and neck were marred with slashes of red where the sharp branches had raked over her skin. I wanted to lick her wounds to make her feel better. Once I'd driven my fangs into her, claiming and changing her, the healing power of my kind would take over and her wounds would heal quickly. Until then she'd have to heal the human way.

Taking a long stick, I poked her in the back. She grumbled in her sleep, but didn't wake up.

Damn it. Come on. Wake up.

I poked her again, this time harder.

She squirmed and moaned. And stayed asleep.

Erin. Wake the hell up.

I stabbed her again, aiming for the curve of her breast peeking out from under her arm. She jerked her head up, gasping as she whipped her head back and forth, scanning the area around her.

"Erin, don't turn around." Whispering, trying to stay undetected, was a difficult thing for us to do. We weren't used to hiding in our human forms and, as a shifter, we tended to get away as fast as we could. Sticking around to hide wasn't in our genetic makeup.

She straightened up, but to her credit, she kept looking directly in front of her. Remaining quiet, she did her best not to let on that she'd heard me.

"When you talk, whisper very softly. Are you all right?"

"Y-yes." Her whisper was too loud. Any shifter could've pick up the sound.

"Softer. You're lost?"

She hesitated, the pride I'd seen before rising to the surface again. Pride would help her once she became one of us, but she needed to learn that all her emotions, including that one, had to be controlled.

"Yes."

Her whisper was barely a sound I'm sure she thought no one could hear. But if one of my people was around and in their shifter form, they would've heard it.

"Don't worry. You'll get out of this, but you've got to start walking. It's getting late."

"I know." She squirmed and, for a moment, I thought she'd turn and look for me. Once she'd settled down, I allowed myself to breathe again.

"I want to go home."

That hurt. Smack in the middle of my chest. "Why?"

"This is too hard." A sob racked her body.

"Hush. Be quiet. There are others around. If they hear you or me, then we're both in trouble. Now keep calm and tell me why you want to go home."

"I told you. It's too hard. My whole body hurts and I'm hungry, thirsty, and tired. I don't even know why I'm doing this any longer."

If she already wanted to give up, then maybe she didn't have the stamina to do what would be expected as my mate. We led a closed life, away from most humans. Being part lion was difficult, having to restrain our inner beasts as much as possible. Our lives were hard because of the inner turmoil between the human and the beast. Our laws were strict and demanded that each of us give all we could to the pride. Consequences were often harsh and even brutal.

If she couldn't handle the games, then she'd never be able to handle being part lioness. If I was smart, I'd let her quit. Yet I found it hard to breathe, just thinking about her leaving.

Hadn't she felt anything when we were together? I didn't expect her to love me, not yet, not until we were mated, but I'd sensed her attraction. She'd been wet and hot when my fingers had found her pussy. I couldn't let her go home. For her sake and my own.

"You're going to go to the cabin and you're going to stay the two nights. Then you'll go back down to Fang's and collect your money." *Or me.*

"Will the others be at the cabin? Will my friend, Nina, be there?"

"No. I told you. They have to make it to their own destinations. This is my cabin. We're the only ones who'll be there." I wanted to shake her, to make her understand that she had to stay. That she had to choose me over the fucking money.

"Your cabin?"

"Yes. It's where I was born."

"Then your family lives there? Does your mother live there?"

She had so much to learn, but she had a lifetime to do it. "Not any longer. She's dead."

"I'm sorry. Did she die in childbirth? I mean, having a baby and not being in a hospital can be risky. Even dangerous." She bit her bottom lip. "I'm sorry. I don't know why I said that."

The old sorrow, the heartbreaking pain I'd shoved down until I could live a day without feeling the torment or seeing her lying on the bed, came back. The force of it struck me, making me unsteady. I hadn't seen it coming. Had, in fact, rarely talked about it since the day she'd died. And I still wasn't ready. We didn't have time, anyway.

"Erin, you have to get going."

"I told you." She heaved a huge sigh. "I want to go home. Tell me which way to go."

Anger swept over me. How could she give up so easily?

"Didn't you feel anything?" What was I? Some pussy-whipped shithead who had to beg a girl to stay with him? Yet if I had to bare my feelings to get her to go on, I would.

"You mean…"

"Yes. When we were together." I glanced around and listened. They were still close, but not too close. At least I hoped they weren't.

"I'm not sure what you mean."

That was bullshit. She wanted me to spit it out. Like waiting until the other person in the relationship said the word *love* first.

"You know what I mean. Not just physical, but like a feeling. Like we could mean something great to each other." I sounded like one of those guys in the daytime drama Roberta loved to watch.

"I'm not sure."

Why was she lying? Was she afraid to admit it? Or had she really felt nothing more than carnal lust? I didn't want to believe it.

"Please, Colter. Help me." Although she spoke softly, the panic was thick in her voice.

"Listen to me. Do exactly as I say."

"Why?"

I'd had enough. Adding a touch of my lion to my human voice, I commanded her. "Enough talking. Do as I say."

I didn't speak any louder than before, but the thickness, the primal strength of my voice would do the trick. I had to get her to stop freaking out. It would take up precious time, but I had to distract her, had to make her listen. If she didn't, she'd quit. But if she followed my orders, it would bring us closer and give her the strength, the yearning for me that she needed to keep going. Her primal instincts would kick in and rid her of her fear. "Put your hand on your breast."

"What? Now?"

I growled, letting the sound roll over her. She swallowed, then did as I'd told her.

"Under your shirt and bra. Do it. Now."

Her lips parted as she slipped her hand under the material. Her breathing picked up and I sensed her heart rate spike.

"Pinch your nipple. No. Not too hard." My cock came alive, pressing hard against the zipper. I undid my button, then turned my cock free. My hand encircled my shaft.

"Rub yourself, baby." It was the first time I'd called her that, but if I had it my way—and I would—it wouldn't be the last. I slid my palm to the tip of my cock, then back again, closing my eyes for a moment to savor the feeling.

"Do you like that? It's me who's caressing you. Your hand is my hand. I control what you do and when you do it. Can you feel my hand on your skin?"

She closed her eyes, her chest rising faster. "Yes."

I smiled, unwilling to think about where we were, the approaching night and the time slipping by. This was more than just sex. This was her listening to my voice, heeding my lion's call to her. If she did as I said under these conditions, then she wouldn't give up. But she had to learn to listen to me and follow my directions. "Good. Now put your other hand, my other hand, between your legs."

I was proud of her when she didn't hesitate. She wasn't the only one I was taking on a seductive ride. My hand quickened and I licked my lips. I remembered how she tasted. Sweet and tangy. I remembered her sweet cream spreading over my tongue.

"Ohhh." Her hand moved up and down.

"Quiet. That's it. Play with yourself. Tell me what it's like. Are you hot, baby? Are you wet?"

"Uh-huh."

I stroked harder. "I'm pinching your clit. Making you burn for me. Do you feel how hard your button got for me? I'm rubbing harder now and dipping my fingers into your pussy. Tell me how good it feels."

"It feels so good. Amazing." She opened her legs wider, scooting down to give her more access. "I love your fingers inside me."

"I know, baby. Squeeze your tit. Rub harder."

She moaned, her hands doing my bidding. Moving her hips back and forth, she grew more frantic, needier, desperate to come.

"More, baby. Yeah. Is my hand wet with your juices?"

"Yes. Oh, God, I'm going to come."

"Not yet. Not until I say you can." I closed my eyes,

increasing the speed of my hand around my cock. I'd never come to the end so fast. I gritted my teeth, centered my attention on her, and fought to keep from letting go.

She lowered herself until she was lying on the ground. Her jeans were around her hips and her knees bent as her hand moved. Her shirt had risen above her bra, thrust out of the way. She fondled her breast, capturing her nipple between her fingers.

The beast inside me roared to life, demanding I take her. I'd fuck her until she screamed my name and then sink my fangs into her shoulder, claiming her as mine.

I fought back. It was too soon.

"Listen to me, baby." I had to tell her. If I didn't, she might still want to leave. "You're mine. I know that. And you know it, too. Just listen. You can hear it. You can feel it. You know it."

She threw her head back, her eyes still closed, her mouth opened wider. Did she hear me?

"Say it, baby. Tell me you know it's true."

"I-I don't..." Her moans changed to whimpers. "Please, I can't hold on any longer. Please, let me come."

The world turned to grays and blacks with the silver undertone. If I didn't end this soon, I'd shift. "Come for me, baby. Now."

She cried out, much too loudly, and I winced. "Quiet. Cover your mouth."

At once, she took the hand from her breast and slapped it over her mouth. Her body bucked as the climax rode through her, powering outward in shudders.

I couldn't hold back any longer. Putting my forehead against the tree, I climaxed, keeping my roar smothered behind clenched teeth. Teeth that were quickly changing into fangs.

The struggle to stay human splintered me. Everything I was screamed for me to shift, but I had to think of Erin. She still needed me.

By the time my own body had calmed down, she was breathing easier, but still lying on her back.

"Erin, tell me that you felt nothing for me. Try and tell me it was just a sex thing." It was stupid of me. I should've ordered her to get on her feet and leave. But I had to know. "Did you feel something or not? Tell me the truth."

She got to her feet, using the tree for support. I smiled at how unsteady she was. Once we were finally and truly together, she wouldn't be able to get out of our bed until her strength came back.

"I felt…"

I held my breath. Something? Nothing?

"I'm not sure what I felt."

The snarl came before I could hold it back. Her eyes widened at the sound. She turned toward me, staring straight at me, but I doubted she could see me. "Yes, I felt something. I was… I'm not sure how to explain it, but I want to find out what it was. I want to keep going to the cabin."

My body shuddered from the tension leaving me. "Good. If you do, you'll find out what we can really mean to each other. If you don't, we'll both regret it for the rest of our lives."

I wasn't telling her the whole truth, but it was close enough. Now that I'd chosen her, if I couldn't have her, I'd end up miserable and alone. No one could take her place and I needed to believe it would be the same for her.

"You're close. Less than a mile to go." I gritted my teeth and added, "Remember the mountain lion? I think she's still in the area." Fear was always a good motivational tool.

"Why can't you come out so we can go together?"

"You know why."

She did. The acceptance was on her face. "Fine. Which way do I go?"

"Turn to your right." She did. "Now start walking. Once you make it back to the clearing, the path will start again on the other side. Hurry. You don't have much time left."

She turned her head my way. Not far enough to see me, but enough. "You'll really be there?"

I'd stayed near her all this time. Why wouldn't I meet her when it was all right to do so? "Yes. Now go."

She started walking, pushing through the foliage.

Erin

I am fucking nuts.

It wasn't the first time I'd ever had the thought, but not about anything involving sex. But was it a good or bad kind of insanity?

Colter had a hold on me. Just hearing his voice had thrown gasoline on the burning need inside me. I'd had no way to resist him. Truth was, I hadn't wanted to try. His voice was so commanding, like a king who could rule the world and think nothing of the weight of responsibility. It wasn't so much his words as the tone and texture of his voice. Like a physical entity flowing over my body, seducing me to let it inside and take over. Ridiculous as it seemed, I would've sworn I felt his hands on me, his mouth layering kiss after kiss along my skin. It had been his hand on my breast, his hand between my legs.

Insane, maybe, but damn, it was also fucking hot.

Afterward, I had to continue, as though the sex with him had given me strength, driving away my weariness and pain. I had to reach the cabin and see him again. Each time I was with him, I became more alive, filled with a yearning to get more and more of him.

I walked on, at times hearing others in the woods, but I didn't attempt to find them. Nothing would get in my way of reaching the cabin. I glanced up, noted the darkening sky, and picked up my pace. If I didn't make it before nightfall, I'd keep going even in the dark.

Colter was amazing. I never would've believed anyone like him would find me attractive. If I could've recorded what he'd said to me, I would've. Then I'd play it back again and again.

He'd talked about the future. Not in a direct way like if we'd got married. About how many kids we'd have. Or what kind of dog we'd get. The typical suburban couple, right? As though he could ever be a typical anything.

Colter in the middle of a city didn't feel right. He struck me as being too wild, too raw, too free to live anywhere other than in the mountains. He exuded a power that didn't come from any macho kind of ego. His was more natural, reminding me of an animal, a wolf. No. Better. He reminded me of a lion.

"Kings of Beasts." The more I got to know Colter, the more their club name made sense. And to me, he was the king of all of them.

I wiped the sweat from my forehead, then rubbed my palms against my jeans. If I got lucky, the cabin would have a tub or a shower. If not, Colter wouldn't want to touch my stinky body.

Then again, he didn't have to touch me to make me come. I smiled, letting the memory of his invisible hands rubbing me to a climax make me even hotter than I already was. At least, that kind of heat was the good kind.

I'd gotten so absorbed in thinking about him, of reliving the amazing sex under the tree that I was at the cabin before realizing it. I let out a yelp of joy and started running toward the front door.

The cabin wasn't large, but it looked solid. And it was old. Really old. The porch was wide and deep enough for the two rockers on it. Four steps led up to the porch. The windows were uncovered and the wood wasn't painted. It had a weathered, beaten look I liked. My gaze slid to the side even as the sun's orange glow settled across the small yard. Another very small wooden building backed up to the tree line. My heart sank.

"Oh, hell. It's an outhouse."

I would've bet those things no longer existed. Unfortunately, I was wrong. Which meant the cabin probably didn't have running water, either.

There goes my bath.

I looked the other way, expecting, yet hoping I wouldn't see a well. But there it was, a few yards away from the cabin. A shingled roof covered the opening while a long rope was attached to a wooden bucket. I could already imagine lowering it then cranking the lever to bring the filled bucket up to the top. Provided the well still had water in it.

"This is so not good."

I tried to think of where, if any place, I could get clean. If nothing else, I could ask Colter to dump a few buckets over my head. Cold well water flooding over me didn't seem so bad. At this point, *any* water would feel good. Especially if both Colter and I were naked while taking turns washing each other's filthy bodies. Fun, lust-filled ideas popped into my head.

Yeah. I'm a dirty, dirty girl.

Still, if I was lucky, maybe I'd find another way to get water inside the cabin. I started up the steps, hoping to find Colter waiting for me. Yet my hopes were dashed when I saw the note on the door.

Mate—

There was that word again. *Mate.* Not girlfriend. Not friend with benefits. Not simply Erin. I tried the door handle, one of those old curved iron ones, but a padlock secured it in place.

Mate.

As long as the note was meant for me, then I was okay. Hell, if it was meant for me, then I was more than okay. I'd get him to tell me why they used such an old-fashioned word later. Until then, I was ready to get inside. The night was crawling closer, the shadows on the ground inching toward me.

Mate—

Find the key to the padlock to enter the cabin. Do it before it's too late.

Too late? Why would it be too late? I'd made it to the cabin even if I was stuck outside it. I tore the note off the door. Why couldn't he have just left it open? It wasn't like he wasn't expecting me. I started reading again from the beginning.

Mate—

Find the key to the padlock to enter the cabin. Do it before it's too late.

Look at the tall tree near the well. It's up to you to figure out how to reach the key. If you can't get the key and get inside before night comes, you fail.

"Aw, come on." I groaned, listened to the sound echo around me, then stomped back down the steps and over to the well. Hanging from a slender rope from the large tree was a metal key with elaborate carvings. It looked like it should've fit the front door of a nineteenth century Victorian home instead of a cabin in the middle of the North Carolina woods.

But it was hanging from a high branch. Still, if I could grab the rope—which, thankfully, didn't look very secure—or hit it with something, it might come down like a piñata at a birthday party. Too bad I didn't have a bat.

"How the hell am I supposed to get it?"

The wall of the well wasn't tall enough to use. Even if I somehow got on top of the well's small roof, I doubted it would hold me. Falling into the well would end my chances for sure. Scanning the yard again, I searched for anything I could use. A ladder would've been terrific, but I didn't see one.

Instead, the only thing I saw that might have a chance of working was a long branch. I strode over to it, then picked it up. It weighed more than I would've thought it would, but I could still carry it. Lifting it high enough to snag the rope with the key wasn't going to be easy.

I leaned the branch against my shoulder and studied the key. Too bad it wasn't windy. A good stiff wind might've knocked it out of the tree. But nothing about my journey so far had been easy and this wasn't going to be any different. The only good thing about trekking up the hill had been getting to know Colter on a more intimate level.

But I wanted to get to know him even better. And not just his body, but his mind, his beliefs, and what made him tick.

The money or the man. My decision had grown harder since getting to know him, but I'd still have to choose the money. I had too many debts for there to be any other choice. And if I chose the man over the money and he turned out to be as big an ass as Mike? I'd be left with nothing.

Yet my gut told me he was nothing like Mike.

I cried out, pushing the branch away from me and slapping at my shoulder. Several red ants scurried along my shoulder and down my arm, biting me as they ran. I couldn't hold still and slapped at them again and again. Their bites felt like a hundred tiny needles sticking into my skin. Off came my shirt, jerking it around as hard as I could. I bent over, shaking my head to get rid of any bugs in my hair. After dancing around, brushing my arms, face, and neck, I finally settled down enough to check my shirt. One last flick sent the remaining ant flying.

"Shit."

I checked one last time before tugging the shirt over my head. Kicking the branch to rid it of more ants, I timidly picked it up and hefted in my hands to get used to its weight. I lifted it as high as I could, barely making it to the place where the key was tied to the rope.

Trying to use the branch like a bat didn't work. Every time I swung at the key, I lost control of the branch. It whizzed past the key, the weight of it unbalancing me and taking me to the ground. Time and time again, I pulled it up for another try. And failed every time.

"Fuck!" After the last attempt, I whirled back to face the woods where I'd come from. "Colter? Where are you? Why don't you help me?"

The approaching night and silence answered me. I was on my own.

I studied the key and rope again, and saw something I hadn't noticed before. The key was suspended by one rope, but the rope had been looped. Maybe it had been the breeze from the branch every time it had fallen past the rope, but a gap had opened up between the two strands. If I could push the branch between the strands, one of two things would happen. Either the branch would get stuck and hang on top of the key, trapped between the two strands, or the weight of the branch would put enough strain on the rope to break it free and drop the key. I had to hope the heavy branch weighed enough.

All I needed to do was to get my aim right.

Yeah. Easy peasy.

I held the branch in front of me with one end dug into the ground and leaned it toward the key. Closing one eye, I lined the branch up with the gap between the rope strands, then let it go. The tree fell, but only struck the side of the key, sending it rocking from side to side.

I groaned. I'd just made it harder. Now I had to hit a moving object.

The exhaustion that had cornered me before was back, but I was too close to ending the first part of the challenge to give up. The sun was setting, barely peeking over the tops of the trees. I picked the branch up and tried again, judging when the key would swing into range again. Trying again, I let the branch go and, once more, missed.

I closed my eyes and fought back the urge to scream. Then I picked up the damn branch and tried yet again. And again. And another three times.

Lifting the branch was getting harder. Taking a deep breath and letting it out steadied my nerves and, with yet another try, I turned the branch free.

When the branch fell dead center into the loop between the rope's strands, I whooped in victory and spun around. I'd done it. Now all I had to do was to grab the key and open the door.

Except for one thing.

My fear had come true. The branch hung suspended between the strands.

"No, no, no. This is so not happening."

I sank to the ground, defeated and ready to be sent home. I'd failed not only myself, but Colter, too.

In only a few minutes, night would come and, without a flashlight or even the glow from a cell phone, I wouldn't be able to see much. The moon was full, but I couldn't count on it giving me enough light to find my way through the forest and back down the hill.

Cuts and slashes from my journey decorated my arms. They were red, but not bleeding much. I closed my eyes, trying to keep my mind on the task.

Yet as hard as I fought, another type of darkness, one that was far too familiar, seeped into me. The Darkness reached out to take hold, swirling outward from my gut, its wickedness bringing along its promise of release. I knew it all too well, but I no longer wanted its company.

Or did I?

Why was I trying to be something I wasn't? I wasn't brave or strong. I didn't deserve anyone, much less a man like Colter.

I wiped away a tear. It was stupid of me to think I was strong enough to handle the games. Stupid of me to think I could overcome my past. Stupid of me to think I was worthy of winning any money. And worse yet, I was beyond stupid to think I could ever have a real family and the future that would come along with it.

"I should just do it and get it over with. Get rid of the pain." I whispered, much like the voice inside my head did.

"Just do it."

The sticks at my feet would do the trick. They weren't clean, but that had never stopped me. The scratches on my arms could testify that the fallen twigs would do a good job.

I picked one up and studied it. All it would take would be a few swipes. Breaking the skin and seeing the blood would relieve the real agony. No one would ever know. Especially not since my arms were already covered with slashes from battling my way through the underbrush. I'd always kept my cuts confined to places I could keep hidden with clothes or socks. I'd never done it on my arms. What would it feel like? Would it be better? Would it bring me more relief? I took one of the sticks and pressed it against my skin.

"Go on. You know you want to. You need to," whispered The Darkness.

I swallowed. I'd promised Maddy and Nina I'd stopped. But more than that, I'd promised myself.

My mind fought back.

Keep on going. Stay safe.

But, oh, how I wanted it. I put the twig to my flesh.

"Just do it."

No. I don't want to.

"Liar."

People had it wrong. It wasn't a devil on one shoulder and an angel on the other taking turns to whisper in my ear. The Darkness was a wicked blend of both, teasing me with a little light and hope before tearing it away. Like the frail human being I was, it contained both sides of my personality, evil and good swirling together, each side shouting to be heard above the other.

A tear slid down my face. I was so tired. Not just from the

journey, but emotionally, mentally. It would be so easy to just let go.

I closed my eyes, struggling to win another battle. But would I ever win the war?

The look in Nina's eyes the day she'd rescued me from Mike's came back, haunting me.

I had to fight it. I'd won the fight before and I'd win again.

"Why suffer? Just do it. No one will ever know."

No. I can't. I won't.

I felt myself getting stronger, fighting against it. I was winning.

I stood, walked over to the tree, and glared at it. "I am not giving up."

Putting my foot on the branch, I jumped up, using all my weight against it. For a moment, I was sure nothing would happen.

The crack of the branch snapping in two startled me as it fell to the ground, taking the rope and key along with it. I looked at the key, then back at the twig lying only a few feet away. The battle was over. For now.

Yanking the key free, I ran to the front door. I was going to make it.

Chapter Ten

Erin

Damn it. It doesn't work.

I fumbled, once more sticking the key into the padlock and getting nowhere. I tried again, struggling to see in the dimming light. It had to work. If it didn't, then I was stuck sleeping on the porch and hoping Colter would show up.

It was a sweet feeling when the key finally slid into the hole and turned without a problem. I tore off the lock and shoved the door wide, eager to see what was inside.

In the next moment, I was off my feet and being carried over the threshold. My heart jumped to my throat then fell back to center in my stomach.

Colter hurried over to the bed and placed me on top of a frayed blanket. I gazed up at him and hated it when he straightened up and moved away from me.

"You scared the hell out of me."

He towered over me. His expression wasn't the one I'd hoped for, especially with the descending darkness shadowing his face. Taking the matches from the table next to the bed, he struck one, then put the flame to the candles resting on the table and along the windowsill on the right side of the cabin. He continued, lighting other candles around the room as well as turning on oil lanterns.

Had he planned them? Had he put the candles and lanterns around to give the room a romantic feeling? Or was that what he always used for light? I didn't see any lamps or overhead lighting.

The flicker of the flames danced over the walls as he returned to me. "I'd like to use the fireplace, but it's already too hot in here. And we'll leave the door open a while for some air. The windows don't open."

I nodded and hoped one day I could come back when it was colder. With him, of course.

My gaze darted to the windows. They were older windows, most of them with dirt and grime accumulated on them. Even if they'd been clean, I couldn't have seen through them any better. They were the kind of antique windows that had waves in them. But they were clear enough to see that night had finally come.

"You almost didn't make it."

"But I did. No thanks to you." I was kidding, but the startled way he looked at me said he hadn't caught on to my sense of humor.

"You're fucking kidding me. If it weren't for me—"

I grabbed his hand and tugged on it. "If it weren't for you, I wouldn't be here. It was a joke. Trust me. I know how much you've helped me. I'm just not sure why." I had my hopes, but hopes were too often squashed.

"I told you why. Earlier on the trail."

He had, but I still couldn't let myself believe what he'd said. "I guess."

"You guess?" He sat on the edge of the bed, taking one of my arms. "Damn it, Erin. Those scratches need to be cleaned."

"I'm okay. It doesn't hurt much." Not like I'd been hurt in the past. Physical pain was nothing compared to the pain I often felt inside. But someone like him wouldn't understand and, with him near, I could forget about the pain.

He went over to the tiny kitchen, which was only a strip of wooden countertop holding a sink and a portable stovetop. It was built for function and not aesthetics.

The interior wasn't much to look at. A beat-up old sofa sat in front of the stone fireplace. The fabric was torn in several places and the cushions made me think that sitting on the floor might be more comfortable. The walls were as old as those on the outside, although not as weathered. Heavy wooden beams ran across the ceiling of the one-room cabin, adding to the overall rustic feel. Although the room was hot, it was still cooler than I would've expected with no air conditioning and all the windows closed.

Colter used the pump that was next to the faucet and worked it until water burst out of the pipe. I was relieved that we wouldn't have to haul a bucket from the well. He came back with a bowl of water and a rag, then took his seat on the edge of the bed. He dabbed the rag into the water, then started washing my forehead. "Hasn't anyone ever told you to push the limbs out of the way? Even your face got messed up."

I darted my gaze away. Messed up. That was a good description of me even before I'd shown up at Fang's. But did it still describe me? Didn't I feel stronger? The Darkness had gotten its clutches on me, but I'd resisted it and I'd won.

His touch was gentle, yet when he took my chin, it was firm. "Look at me."

I did. As before, all he had to do was tell me what to do and I'd do it.

"Why'd you act like that when I said your face was messed up?"

"I don't know."

"Bullshit." His blue eyes had taken on more silver. "You don't think much of yourself, do you?"

"I'm okay."

"Don't you own a mirror? Have you ever taken a good look at yourself?"

The question threw me. "Sure." But I only used it to get ready in the morning. Or to stare critically at myself. So, yeah, I'd taken long hard looks at my face. "Just because I don't gaze at myself and think I'm beautiful doesn't mean I don't think I'm okay."

"You're more than okay, but you don't get that, do you?"

More than okay. The man could've sung me a love song and it wouldn't have sounded as sweet. It was too much for me. I had to change the subject.

"Would you get me some water, please? I'm dry as a bone."

"Yeah. Although I'm not supposed to help you with food or water."

I shot him a look. "Really? Don't you think we're past worrying about breaking the rules?"

"You're right." His face transformed, brightening with his chuckle. "Yeah. Way past."

He rose and made it to the kitchen in two long strides. After rummaging through the cabinets, he found a chipped mug, then went back to the pump. "It'll taste different than city water. Better."

"Thanks." I took the mug and sipped a little. Then a lot. He was right. It did taste better. Somehow more refreshing than either tap water or bottled water. "More, please."

He refilled the mug and handed it back to me. "Okay, but take it easy. You might get sick if you drink it too fast."

"I will." But I still downed the big mug of water. "I don't suppose you've got some food? You know. Like a bag of chips or canned food? Heck, I'd even chow down on pork rinds."

"Sorry. Nope."

"Damn."

He shrugged, then took his place beside me again.

"Tell me about you, Colter Quaid. What's it like to be one of the Kings of Beasts?" Again, I meant it in a half-joking way, but he heard the serious side of my question and ran with it.

"I've never been anything else or lived anywhere else."

"So both your parents were part of the gang? Or pack? Or family? Or whatever Burke called it?" I had to admit I was a little envious. My family had consisted of myself, two parents who didn't like each other much, and—

And. It was one hell of a big word.

I didn't like to think about Alicia. It was my fault that she no longer existed.

"We're really more of a pride."

"You mean like lions in Africa? That kind of pride?"

"It's just another word meaning the same thing as a pack. Or group or gang. But we're more than that. We're closer to each other than most people ever get. We live in and around Cripple Creek, the small town near Fang's, and we stick together no matter what. I was raised with the other kids, forming an extended family. We'd do anything for each other."

He blinked, as though he'd just realized how much he'd said. I had to admit I was surprised at his sudden chattiness, too. But I liked that he'd opened up and I wanted to hear more.

"Do your parents still live here? I mean, your father?" I shouldn't have mentioned his mother. "Is this his cabin?"

"This is my family's cabin. But it's ours for the next two

nights."

Two nights with Colter. I couldn't think of anything I'd like better. Except maybe two hundred and fifty thousand dollars. Or maybe not. If only I could have both.

"Do you have any brothers or sisters?" I was being nosy, but I couldn't help it. I wanted to know everything about him.

"I have two brothers, Connor and Morgan. No sisters." He patted another scratch on my cheek. He had a soft touch when he wanted, which added to the mystery of him. I'd seen his fierce side and his sexy side. Now I'd find out about his caring side. Every side of his personality was as good as the last.

"Are your brothers part of the pride?" Pride sounded more majestic than pack did, like a pack of wild dogs. He and the others stood tall and proud, regal in the way they carried themselves.

"Like I said. We stick together."

He started cleaning my arms. I loved the way he caressed me, both healing and comforting me.

"Why'd you sniff me?"

"Because you smell good." He shot me a playful look. "*Smelled* good."

I cringed. He was right, but it didn't make me feel any better. Besides, he didn't smell so great, either.

"And I'm supposed to be your mate?" To ask had taken more strength than I knew I had. Or more curiosity. Or perhaps just more hope. "Don't you think it's taking it a little too far to call me your mate? I mean, what's wrong with girlfriend?" I was growing bolder the longer he touched me. Otherwise, I wouldn't have dared to say the *G* word.

"That's just our way. Mate. Girlfriend." His gaze grabbed onto mine. "Woman. Wife. It's all the same to us. Once the decision's made, we stick to it."

Okay, I had to admit it was a little unnerving when he talked about his pride, mates, and the whole challenge thing where I was supposed to prove I was strong enough to become one of them. Was it a mountain man thing? Or just his group taking things too far? And more to the point, had he made his decision? Or was he just playing along with the whole games thing? Did he really want me for more than just two nights?

If I would've had to make a choice at that moment, I would've chosen him.

Don't go letting your feelings get in the way. You need the money worse than you need a man. Even a man like him.

"What about you? Where's your family?"

I hated talking about my parents. They'd split up two years earlier and I was still trying to decide if it was a blessing in disguise or the end of my family. I closed my eyes, forced back the desire to let my mind welcome The Darkness, then opened them to see his expectant face.

I can handle this. I can and I will.

"My parents split up. We don't talk much." I shrugged as though it was no big deal, but it was. "I don't have any other living family and my parents couldn't care less if I got hit by a truck tomorrow." I smiled, trying to take the sharp edges off my words. "Or if I got eaten by a very large cat. I still can't believe you stood up to that animal."

"I bet you've got it wrong. About your folks, I mean."

"No. I don't." My tone came out harsher than I'd wanted.

He averted his gaze, standing to take the used water and dump it into the sink. He refilled the bowl and returned with a clean cloth. "As for the cat, most animals are more afraid of you than you are of them. I didn't do anything."

"The hell you didn't. And trust me, she was anything but afraid. She was out to taste my blood."

"Well, she didn't and that's all that counts."

Funny how it felt like he was dodging the subject. I was a pro at dodging sensitive subjects.

"Was growing up as members of the pack, er, pride like everyone else's childhood? Was it the kind of childhood you'd want for your own children?" I was pushing too far, too fast, but I ignored the warning signals and pressed on. "Is that the kind of life you want?"

His eyes clouded over, dulling the blue. "Living our way is hard, which is why we have the games. If a girl—" He scanned my body. "If a woman can't handle the games, then she can't handle the life we lead."

"That hard, huh?"

"Yeah. Real hard."

It wasn't what I'd wanted to hear. "What's hard about it?"

"It's not easy to explain. After the challenge, you'll get a better idea. But I can tell you that it has a lot to do with living on the outside, of not being like most people. Like I said, I'll explain more later."

He was dodging again, but I didn't want to push so I accepted his answer. For now. "At least tell me this. Is it worth it?"

He brightened a little. "Yeah. It is."

"Good to know."

Clearing his throat, he added, "What do you want?" His stare was intense. As though he was testing me.

"I don't know." I couldn't meet his gaze. I was afraid of seeing disappointment there. I'd had enough of disappointing others in my life. "I think as long as I'm sharing my life with the right person, then the rest of it is just white noise."

When I looked at him again, I couldn't help but think I'd answered correctly. I'd told the truth. But was he the right person?

He continued taking care of my scratches. When he reached for my ankles, I grabbed his arm and pulled his attention back to my face. Some secrets were too hard to talk about.

At least, as far as my own were concerned.

"Why'd you do it anyway? Run the cat off?"

"I told you. It wasn't a big deal."

"No, I mean all of it. The cat, the ditch, then…the other. And it was a big deal. You broke the rules for me. What I can't figure out is why."

"Because you're a big deal." He put the bowl and cloth on the floor, then brushed the hair away from my cheek. "I couldn't risk losing you."

He could've said a lot of things, but nothing would've sounded better. It was as close to a declaration of love as I'd ever had. Mike had said sweet words and talked about a future life together, but even when I thought I believed him, I never really had. Not down deep where it counted. I think I always knew we'd never last. And I'd been right. Looking at the raw yearning in Colter's face, I wanted to think he was different. And yet…

"Lose me? I'm going to leave in a couple of days. I told you, didn't I? I have to choose the money." The more I said it, the worse it felt.

"Shit. It's only money. But if you really need the money that much, then I want to make sure you know what you're giving up."

He stood, tall and strong, like a machine built for lovemaking. I couldn't help but lie there, unable to speak, unable to move. All I could do was watch and wait for whatever came next.

He toed off his boots, then reached to his shoulders and pulled his shirt over his head. I'd seen my fair share of male stripper revues, men who had practiced how to disrobe in front of women, but his simple way was a whole lot more erotic than their choreographed moves. The shirt fell to the floor and my attention followed, then flicked back to take in his muscled chest. I drifted my attention from between his pecs downward, over his tight stomach, until the sag of the front of his jeans stopped my progress.

His stomach was a hard rock with horizontal channels running along his abdomen. He tugged on the button of his jeans before thrusting the flaps open and shoving them down his iron-like thighs.

Damn, but his cock was incredible, long, thick and curved at the end. The word *cock* alone didn't say enough. His was an instrument, a tool, a weapon he could whip out whenever he wanted and bring me to my knees. Or put me on my back. Good thing I was already there.

I lifted up, ready to take off my clothes. He crawled on top of the full-size bed and stopped me. In one smooth motion, he pulled the shirt over my head, then snapped my bra free. Shyness hit me and I crossed my arms.

"No, don't. You're perfect."

No one had ever used that word to describe me. Yet, because he'd said so, I was willing to believe. At least for the night.

He laid me down and brushed my lips with his. The touch was light, but it had the effect of a fiery torch, searing over my mouth and into the rest of me. My body trembled as though I was cold, but I was hotter than ever.

I swear it was the first time I'd ever seen stars. His kiss took everything. Even the air I needed to stay alive. But I would've gladly died rather than break us apart. The other kisses before had been amazing, but this one was more intense, needier, demanding I answer him back with equal fervor.

His tongue plunged inside my mouth and I had no choice but to let it in. Our tongues met, twisting, tangling in a wild ride of need. His hands cupped my breasts, kneading them, thumbing, then pinching my nipples. I pushed my tits against him, wanting him to hold them forever.

His moan met mine as he pulled back. For a moment, our gazes locked. Silver stars sparkled in a sky of blue. If we stopped at just that much, I'd be devastated and yet, strangely, satisfied. He straddled me, then skimmed his fingers down to the top of my jeans.

He had them pulled to the widest part of my hips when realization of what we were doing made me freeze. I couldn't let him see. Not yet. If I did, it would be over before it began.

"No." I grabbed hold of my jeans. He hadn't noticed my ankles before and I didn't want to press my luck.

He didn't understand. I could see it in his eyes and in his expression. There was no way he could.

"Please. Make it darker."

"But I want to see you. All of you."

"I'm not ready."

His brow furrowed deeper, but, after a brief hesitation, he snuffed out the candles with his bare fingers. The rest of the cabin was still dimly lit, but it was darker around the bed.

"Thanks." Hiding secrets while getting naked was a hard thing to do.

His eyes glowed, his facial features shadowed. "Sure. This time. But I want to see you soon. Out in the open and in the sunlight."

I kept my real answer to myself and told him what he needed to hear. "Okay." I kicked off my shoes, making sure he wouldn't reach down and do it for me.

He pulled on my jeans and I hurried to get them and my panties off without any more of his help. Bending low, he placed kisses between my breasts. I gripped the bedspread and held on as a fresh tingle flowed over my skin in the wake of each kiss. I sucked in my gut as he made his way lower, his hands cupping the sides of my breasts while his thumbs kept my nipples growing harder.

The lower he went, the tenser I became. But in a good way, with anticipation of what was yet to come. Memories of the first time he'd gone down on me came flooding back and I was ready, aching for him to lick me.

He teased me, taking the indirect route. Kissing and nibbling, he rode over my non-existent hip bones, back to the rise of my belly, then over to the other side. What he did to me was torture and bliss all at the same time.

Yeah, he knew what he was doing.

Then it came, the moment when he settled between my legs and lowered his face to my pussy. I jerked as though it was all a surprise, but he kept me centered, holding me by the top of my legs.

"I'm going to taste you again."

I liked how he talked. Sometimes he sounded older than he could possibly be. Instead of saying "I'm going to eat you out" like most guys his age would, he made it sound nicer, even romantic.

I sucked in a breath, then let it out in a moan as he pressed not just his mouth, but his face to my heat. He hadn't touched me with his tongue, hadn't moved my folds apart with his fingers yet. Instead, I heard his slow intake of breath.

Worry hit me. After the day I'd gone through, how could I smell good? I had to stink. He'd already said as much.

"Damn, but you smell great. Just like I remembered."

Apparently, I can. Or his nose is off. Or he's just being nice.

"But…"

He lifted his head and looked at me. "No. I was kidding before. You smell amazing, no matter what. It's still all you."

Those were my last coherent thoughts. As he buried his face even closer against me, everything switched over to feelings, sensations, and emotions. Ideas and specific thoughts were no longer necessary. If anything, they got in the way.

He pushed my folds apart and dove in. He came at me hard, his tongue whipping over my clit, then sliding down to plunge into my pussy. I cried out and clutched my breasts, wishing he had more than two hands to use. Or multiple tongues.

He wasn't one of those guys who had no clue what to do with a clit. Or any other part of a girl. As I'd often thought before, he was a man and not a college boy, and he was proving me right.

His cock grew harder against my leg, telling me how large he'd be once he was inside me. I shoved my pelvis against him, earning a guttural, animal-like groan that made me feel like a woman. Like his woman.

Lifting my legs, he rested them on his shoulders, then feasted on me harder than ever. I reached for him, but couldn't get any more than the soft brush of my fingertips against his hair.

The sounds of him lapping up my juices was enough to send my body into overdrive. I couldn't stop squirming even though moving away was the last thing I wanted to do. He dragged his tongue over and around my clit, then down to spear my pussy. He sucked, nibbled, then moaned his pleasure.

"Please, Colter." I begged him, but I wasn't sure what for. Did I want him to stop eating me? No. Did I want him to fuck me? Hell, yeah. Although it made no sense, I wanted him to do both at the same time.

My body was no longer mine. He'd taken it and made it his.

When he stopped and lifted up, I groaned out a complaint, then silenced it as he yanked me toward him. His cock pressed against my entrance, once again teasing me.

I gritted my teeth and growled. "Colter, please."

He ran his palm along my leg, then before I realized what he was about to do, he'd slapped my ass.

"Oh." I wasn't sure how to react. Maddy had talked about experimenting with a few tie-me-down-and-fuck-me sessions. They'd sounded a little scary. But now? The sizzle, the pain his spank had given me had awakened a series of wonderful eruptions that ran along my leg and into my pussy. Unlike the pain that gave me release from my torment, the stings he gave me tantalized me, giving me pleasure.

He growled, sounding all masculine and beastlike. His jaw worked, jumping the muscle there as he lifted me higher, then plunged his cock inside me.

I reacted, heart, stomach, and mind in turmoil as he filled me. Wrapping my legs around him, I held on. It was a sweet ride, a tumultuous ride that took me into the highest highs I could ever have imagined. He pulled me up, bringing my breasts against his chest as he plunged again and again.

My secret, my worries were gone. I lived in the moment, uncaring what the past had done to me, unconcerned with what the future held. His nibbles at my flesh, his grip on my butt cheeks melded me to him.

He was an iron rod ramming harder and harder into me. When he slid out, I gasped in a breath only to have it thrust out of me. He stretched me, creating friction that would burn until the rush of our juices put it out. All I could do was to dig my fingernails into his skin and hold on.

The sex we shared was more than simply physical. It was a link to each other, a way of bonding us together that was both familiar, yet new. Frightening, yet exciting. I held on to him like the lifeline he'd suddenly become.

Together we moved as one, our bodies connecting to form a wave of continuous ripples and flows. It was as if we'd known each other all our lives, then had become separated and had finally found each other again. He buried his face against my shoulder and I laid my head back, eyes closed, absorbing every sensation.

Sex had never felt like this. But then, it had never been with Colter.

Together. Forever? I couldn't think that far ahead.

Had I ever had a climax before? I wasn't sure any longer. At least I'd never had one like this one, revving up inside me, ready to whirl me into the eye of the tornado.

My body prepared itself, stiffening as the lust rolled through me. I was on fire, a fluid, scorching element with no end. And yet the end was coming closer, barreling toward me at incredible speed and force.

Colter rammed into me again, then dug his fingers into my ass and stilled. His eruption signaled mine. I cried out, in joy and in protest, as my orgasm ripped outward.

Hanging on to each other, we let our bodies have their way.

Chapter Eleven

Colter

Erin lay next to me, snuggled against my side as the candles around the cabin slowly burned down. Their feeble flickering gave the room an extra coziness.

Coziness. When the hell had I ever used that word?

I caressed her hair, stroking my hand over it, then twisting a strand of it around my finger. She'd gathered the bedspread to pull over her legs. How she could be cool I didn't know. Perspiration still dotted her forehead and dampened the hair at the nape of her neck.

I was content. Ready to spend the next two nights with her before it was time to return to Fang's. She said she wasn't going to choose me, but I knew it was only her fear talking. It wasn't uncommon for the girls to cling to wanting the money, saying they'd take it instead of the man. She was skittish, like a newborn filly. But she'd change her mind. I'd make her change her mind. Then she'd choose me over the money and I'd claim her.

Burke had warned the girls that they couldn't choose the money, then have the man later. If Erin thought we could give it a try anyway, it would eat at me. I wouldn't go against the pride's law about that. To let Erin choose the money with the intention of me joining her later would put both our lives in danger.

Money didn't mean a damn thing to my people. No one individual had their own money. From investments, land acquisitions and more, we'd accumulated a vast amount of wealth that was to be used to keep the pride intact. We could literally burn money and still have more than we could ever spend. We preferred to live simply, using the land and everything it gave us to keep us alive and happy.

If a woman chose the cash over the man, then the pride would pay her—with the provision that she never disclose how she'd gotten the money. If she chose the man, then he'd claim her and she'd become one of us and never want for anything.

Nothing ever surprised me when it came to the pride. The elders wielded power and influence that extended well beyond our mountains.

Burke hadn't told the women about our wealth and influence and he wouldn't. Not until they became one of us.

I couldn't wait to see her reaction when, after she'd chosen me, I told her she'd have more than two hundred and fifty thousand. She'd be able to pay for all the education she wanted. If she wanted to leave the mountain to continue college, then I'd go with her. Later, however, we'd return home. But I doubted it would get that far. Once she was one of us, she'd want to stay on our mountain and make it her home.

How would she react once she knew what I was? I'd prepare her, easing into the revelation to keep from frightening her too much. Others had learned the hard way to talk first, convincing their mates that shifters existed. Once the girls were willing to accept the existence of shifters, then, and only then, did the men transform and reveal the lions hidden inside. Until Erin made her decision, I had to keep my secret. If—no, *when*—she chose me, I'd tell her, then shift and show her my lion. By that time, we would've grown together, our physical attraction morphing into love that would last a lifetime.

I gazed at her. Her eyes were closed and her eyelashes feathered over her cheeks. She didn't think she was good-looking. I could tell by the way she'd acted during sex. Didn't she think I'd notice when she sucked in her rounded belly, hoping to make herself appear skinnier? Why did women torment themselves about their bodies anyway? I studied her face, lingering over her lips. Maybe society wouldn't say she was beautiful, but I liked the small bump in her nose and the fact that her ears were a little bigger than they should've been. Perfection was boring. The rise and fall of her steady breaths made me happy, lifting her breasts toward me only to fall, tempting me to suck on her nipples and wake her up.

Did I have it bad or what? I figured it was both a good thing and a bad thing to be in love. It sucked because I hadn't expected to fall for anyone. Hadn't thought I'd ever risk my heart. I'd wanted to live a life free to do whatever I wanted, unburdened with a mate.

Until Erin.

I couldn't resist any longer. Bringing my mouth to her breast, I took her nipple between my teeth and sucked. She stirred and reached out to take me by the neck.

I was ready to go again, but I needed something else first. "Baby?" She hadn't said if she liked me calling her that, yet the small smile she gave me was enough of an answer.

"Yeah?"

How was I going to put this without sounding stupid? Or making her feel stupid?

"Look, I know you said you were in this for the money, but

that's all changed, right?" I sounded like a damn girl clinging to her first boyfriend. But I couldn't help it. In the space of a day, she'd taken hold of me, capturing me with one sniff.

Her smile died. Not a good sign. Then when she didn't meet my eyes any longer, I knew I'd fucked up. Yet I couldn't stop. I had to know and I had to tell her.

"Colter, I can't choose both. That's one rule we can't break. Right?" She lifted her eyebrows in a hopeful question.

My chest tightened like I was having a heart attack. "So you're still going to pick the money over me?" Even with her telling me straight out, I couldn't believe she would. Not after everything I'd done, everything we'd shared.

She pulled away, bringing the bedspread up to cover her body. "You have to understand. I need the money. I already owe a ton and I haven't even graduated yet, much less gone to law school."

"Don't most students have loans to pay off?"

She looked me straight in the eye. "This was just sex, Colter. Don't make it a big deal."

Don't make it a big deal? Fuck that. It was a big deal. I had to make her understand that we weren't just a fun thing to be forgotten once she was gone. We meant something. She was the only one I'd ever love. And if she left, it would destroy me.

But there was no way I was telling her. I still had my dignity even if it was hanging in tatters.

She had to be lying. It was the only explanation. That and needing the money.

I wanted to tell her about our money. Yet if I did, I'd break yet another rule. I was already pushing it. And if I told her, I'd never know which she wanted more. The fucking money or me.

"I know that's not how you really feel." I climbed out of

bed, going over the top of her. Snatching up my clothes, I jerked them on, then glared at her, daring her to keep lying to me.

"Colter, please. Don't do this. Can't we just have fun until I have to go back down the hill?"

Like it was nothing but a quick fuck at some fraternity house. My instinct told me she wasn't that kind of girl, but it had also told me she was the one for me. Maybe my instincts were just plain wrong.

Whatever the reason, I was done trying to convince her. A pride male never begs. Not to a woman or anyone else. I pulled myself together, crushing the urge to shake her into admitting she'd fallen for me just like I'd fallen for her.

"Look, Colter, I came to do this challenge because of the money."

"That's not the whole reason and you know it."

"You're right. I wanted to prove I could do it. I wanted to find out if I had enough strength to handle it."

I bit back my anger. She never would've made it without my help and we both knew it. If I hadn't stepped in, she'd be dead right now, ripped to shreds by Shayna. When she reached out to take my arm, I backed up. It would hurt too much for her to touch me.

"Hey, I get it. It's just fucking, right? Nothing more." If I stood there a second longer I was afraid I might change my mind and beg her to pick me. To do so would've torn my soul apart almost as much as her choosing the money would. I tugged on my boots, ready to get out of there.

"Please don't be mad."

Mad didn't cover it. Not by a long shot. "'Course not. Why should I be? It's just sex, right?" I stalked to the door, my anger giving me the shakes.

"Colter, no. Don't leave."

She stumbled out of the bed, wrapped the bedspread around her, and hurried toward me. I wanted to shove aside my anger and go to her, to feel her warmth wrapped around me again. Instead, I grabbed hold of the door.

"Be careful, Erin." Would she notice that I hadn't called her *baby*? "I won't be around to help you."

"No, please. Don't—"

I didn't hear the rest of what she said as I slammed the door behind me. I made it into the woods just as I started taking off my clothes.

Run.

Change.

Run harder. Faster.

I snarled as I hit the ground on all fours.

Erin

I dashed to the window, but didn't see Colter anywhere. My chest hurt and I couldn't force the panic down. What would happen if I didn't see him again? Could I make it on my own?

I'm not sure how long I stood at the window hoping I'd see him walk out of the forest. Long enough that my feet started hurting from standing in one place too long. The sun had set a while ago and now it was so dark I could barely see anything at all. Who knew what could be hiding behind a tree?

I'm just psyching myself out. I'll be fine. He'll come back.

Only a few of the candles still burned. The lanterns looked like they'd last a long time, but I wasn't sure. But a lack of light wasn't my biggest concern. After washing down my body as much as I could with a rag and a bowl of water, then getting dressed, I couldn't hold back the urge any longer. Spooky or not, I had to go.

I took one of the lanterns off the hook, then opened the door. The outhouse hadn't seemed so far away earlier. I shifted from one foot to the other, trying not to think about what might be lurking in the forest, and instead, concentrated on relieving my immediate need. Was there toilet paper? And what about spiders and snakes and who knew what else might be inside the small wooden structure?

Still, when a girl has to go, a girl has to go.

I pulled my courage together and stepped out onto the porch. Should I close the door? What if it got stuck? The key was still in the lock, so I pulled it out and shoved it into my pocket.

I pulled the door as far as I could without actually closing it. It wouldn't get stuck shut, but it wouldn't look like it was open if anything or anyone thought about getting inside. The idea of returning to the cabin and finding another person or an animal waiting for me made me even jumpier. And I sure as hell didn't want to fool with the difficult lock again. I hurried to the outhouse, scanning the shadows.

Once I got to the door with the crescent moon carved into it, I wasn't sure I wanted to go inside. Not only was the smell wafting outward bad enough to make me glad I didn't have anything in my stomach, but the warped, gray wood that had looked horrible in the daylight was spooky as hell at night. Did I dare risk it? Or did I do the camping method of squatting in the woods? One glance at the ominous trees made the decision easier.

The door creaked open, jangling my nerves even more. I stuck out my arm and held the lantern as far inside as I could.

Oh, shit.

It looked like the really bad version of a porta potty at an outside concert. And no toilet paper. I bit my lower lip. If my bladder hadn't been about to burst, I might've gone back inside the cabin.

Taking a steadying breath, I moved the lantern around to get a better view and saw the hook on the left wall. Obviously, whoever had built the outhouse had thought about night trips to the john. I hung the lantern there, then eased the door closed.

I pulled down my jeans and did my business as quickly as I could. My bladder thanked me. Suspending my butt over the seat—really just a hole in the boards surrounded by a ring of Styrofoam—I wiggled my ass and let myself drip dry.

The things I'll do for money.

But that was a lie. I'd known it when I'd told Colter and I knew it now. I'd come for the money, yes, and to prove myself, but I'd found him, too. Yet I wasn't ready to trust my heart again. I'd given it to Mike and, after surviving his rejection, I'd placed it behind a wall, keeping my heart safe. It was locked away from anyone who might want to capture it, then tear it apart as Mike had done.

Loneliness was a small price to pay to keep my heart in one piece.

A low growl had me freezing in place, my throat tightening as though my heart really had jumped upward. Trying to stay as quiet as I could, I pulled up my jeans, then peeked through the slats.

Oh, hell, no.

A large cat stalked across the front yard, heading straight for the cabin. Was it the same one I'd seen earlier? I couldn't be sure, but how many could there be?

I stayed as motionless and as quiet as I could. If I was lucky the stench of the outhouse would cover my aroma.

The cat took her time padding across the grass. She paused at the steps, then jumped onto the porch in one silky flow of graceful movement. She crouched, going down low as she moved closer to the door.

If I ran, she'd catch me before I made it to the trees. And if she came toward the outhouse, she could knock down the building with one shove. I could think of only one way to defend myself. If she got close enough, if she tore the outhouse down around me, then I'd try tossing the lantern at her and hope it would scare her away.

She had her nose to the door. I couldn't see well enough to know if she was sniffing to pick up my scent or if she was pushing it to go inside. If she went inside, would it be safe to run into the woods? Or should I stay where I was? I squinted, trying to see better.

A roar blasted the air, sounding as though it was nearby, less than a few feet away. The mighty noise startled me and I let out a small yelp, then slapped my hand over my mouth.

Nothing I knew could make a sound like that. Nothing I knew was so ferocious, so powerful, so commanding. The roar sounded godly, majestic, and without equal.

The cat lifted her head, then was gone in a flash, disappearing around the corner of the cabin.

I had to take my chance. If not, I'd be left standing in the outhouse all night. Easing the door open, I grabbed the lantern and ran like my life depended on it. As far I knew, it did.

Damn, how I wanted Colter. He'd keep me safe from the cat and whatever had roared. I ran as fast as I could, the rhythm of my heart doubling to pound in my ear. I burst into the cabin, then slammed the door closed behind me. Fumbling for the metal bar, I yanked it down to rest on the hook on the left side of the door and secured it before rushing to the nearest window.

What the hell had roared? I could still hear echoes of the sound in my mind and I trembled.

Colter, where are you? Please come back.

Erin

After the scare I'd gotten while stuck in the outhouse, I'd stayed up most of the night huddled on the bed with the bedspread over me and one candle sitting on a table next to me. Every bump and skittering sound had me hugging the bedspread to my chin and wishing I'd never agreed to do the games.

The money, the challenge, and then Colter. There was no denying it. Greed and lust had fucked me up good.

I must've finally fallen asleep, but I awakened with a start. Not sure if I'd actually heard something or had only dreamed it, I stayed where I was, watching the growing light outside the windows. I couldn't remember the last time I'd gotten up at sunrise. But I was glad I had. Once I felt safe enough, I shuffled over to the window and took in the view.

Who knew a sunrise could be so beautiful? I watched it, admiring the way the light shifted from a hazy glow to a full golden light the farther it climbed above the level of the trees. The world was peaceful, new and fresh.

Soon enough, however, I had to move. Leaning toward the

window, I scanned the surrounding trees for any signs of the cat or other dangers, but saw nothing except a lone rabbit out for a morning hop. My stomach rumbled, protesting the lack of food, but there was nothing I could do about it. However, the need to go again was a different matter.

My trip to the outhouse this time was uneventful. I made a mental note to check the cabin for toilet paper. Or, if I got lucky, I could ask Colter. If he came back.

My stomach growled again. But a quick search around the cabin came up empty. Aside from a can of beans and no can opener, I was shit out of luck as far as food went. Why would he have brought me to a place with no food? Was starving part of the challenge? I vaguely remembered Burke saying something about food. Exactly what, I couldn't remember.

Irritation hit me, both at Colter and at myself. I should've asked about food last night instead of winding up in bed with him. Or at least, I should've asked afterward, before he'd stormed off and left me alone. I could handle the no toilet paper problem, but no food? That was messed up.

Still, at least I had water. And if my memory was any good, I recalled seeing a bush full of berries near the path.

I made a second pass through the cabin and found an old canteen I could fill with water and take along with me on the trip back down the hill. The thing didn't smell very good, but it was better than nothing. A few cups, bowls and utensils rounded out the items in the cabinets.

Outside, I paused and gave my surroundings another quick check. If the cat came after me again, I was as good as dead. Having Colter rescue me once from her was lucky. Having him do it again would be a miracle. And I didn't believe in miracles.

Where was Colter anyway? Was he staying away to punish

me like Mike had often done? If so, then he'd learn soon enough that I was through letting guys treat me that way.

I couldn't help but believe Maddy would be proud of how I was thinking. Was I getting back to the girl I'd been before Mike? And yet, I knew that was impossible. Too much had happened. Besides, the girl I'd been before Mike hadn't been the confident woman I wanted to be. And definitely not strong. Not after what had happened to Alicia.

Alicia, I miss you like crazy. If I could change one thing, I'd take your place.

My stomach rumbled again and I tried to fill the void with water. It didn't help much. I was tired, lonely, and starving. My mood quickly took a nose dive.

Alicia, please forgive me.

The therapist my parents had sent me to, more for their benefit than mine, was certain my suicide attempt was my way of trying to make amends. She'd stressed all too often how illogical it was to think my death would bring my sister back. That it would, in fact, only hurt my parents more. She'd been right, of course, but the way I figured it, at least then my parents wouldn't have me around to remind them of their loss. And how I'd fucked up.

The pain seeped into me as I'd known it would. Thinking about Alicia always brought it back. At first, when the guilt had swamped me, I hadn't had enough strength to get out of bed. Now when I thought of her, I could still move, still react to people, still pretend I was alive.

It wasn't a good idea to think about her. If I did, I was welcoming trouble.

But there was no stopping The Darkness now that I'd let the first memory come slithering in.

I hadn't done what I was supposed to do. For one of the few times during my high school years, I'd rebelled against my parents. I hadn't wanted to babysit Alicia and I'd ignored her, taking my anger at them out on her. In the end, we'd all paid a huge price.

My lawyer had argued that I was just a kid, too. That my parents shouldn't have left me, sixteen at the time, alone with my three-year-old adopted sister. That, although other sixteen-year-old girls babysat children, taking care of my sister was too much for any teen. My parents never would've adopted her if they'd known she was mentally "deficient." Their words, not mine. And they should've known leaving her in my care would be too much for me to handle. But they'd needed "a break." Besides it was just one night. One night they could spend at a hotel, away from their problems. Their problems named Alicia and Erin.

I searched for the berry bush. The misery hit me so hard I thought I'd double over. I put my hands on my knees and took deep breaths as the therapist had taught me to do.

Let it go. It wasn't my fault.

Yet as many times as I repeated those words, I never believed them. It was totally my fault. I was the one who'd acted like a brat and ignored her, pushing her away and telling her to go play by herself. I was the one who hadn't noticed her opening the back door and toddling out to the swimming pool.

When I'd found her, floating face down, my world had gone from just plain awful to totally fucked up.

"You're to blame. You're the one who should hurt. You're the one who should be dead." The Darkness knew how to taunt me.

I swallowed back the need to cut, the urge to find some way, any way to get rid of my guilt and pain. Stopping, I closed my eyes and concentrated on dragging in big breaths.

"Just do it."

The Darkness oozed its way inside me, tugging at my mind and my heart, trying to force them to give in. I clenched my fists and squeezed my eyes shut.

Think of something else. Anything else. Don't let it win.

Colter's face burst into my mind first. Then came Maddy's and Nina's.

And then at last, Alicia's smiling one.

Incapable of speech, she could have never told me, but I had to believe she wouldn't want me to keep suffering, to keep blaming myself.

I won't give in. Not this time.

Opening my eyes, I was thrown for a moment, as though I'd expected to see my parents' living room instead of the trees. But the trees were a welcome sight. Once again, I'd come out unscathed.

I trudged into the forest, taking care to keep the branches and bushes from scratching me. It was strange to keep the slashes away. I'd been punishing myself in a similar way for years following my suicide attempt.

Keep on going. Stay safe.

Maddy? Nina? Where are you? Are you safe?

I drew in a ragged breath and wiped away the sweat dotting my brow. It was already hot and the sun hadn't risen to its peak yet.

Where was Colter anyway? Had he planned to take off last night? Or had I forced him away?

Was he with someone else? I didn't want to think so, but it wasn't like we'd made any commitments. Unless being called his mate was a commitment. But how would I know? I still wasn't sure what being his mate meant.

"Damn it, Colter. Why'd you leave me alone?"

I'd already gone far enough into the woods, but I still hadn't found the damn bush. If I went any farther, I might end up getting lost again. I turned back.

When I broke through the foliage of the trees, I didn't think. Just the sight of him sitting on the steps of the cabin put me into a run. I was against him, my arms wrapped around him before I'd realized what I'd done.

"You came back."

"Yeah. And I always will." He pulled me away from him. "You all right?"

"Yes. Although the cat, the one that started to attack me, came to the cabin last night. I got stuck in the outhouse."

"That must've been fun."

I liked his grin, even if he was teasing me. He needed to grin more often. "Yeah, not so much. Where'd you go?"

"Oh, around."

"But where?"

"I bet you're hungry."

Did he just change the subject? Still, with my stomach growling, I didn't mind. "Well, duh. I haven't had anything to eat since yesterday morning." But he wasn't holding anything. "Please tell me I don't have to hunt for my food."

He tilted his head to the side. "We can if you want to, but I brought some food and fresher water. It's inside."

I broke away from him and burst into the cabin. Sitting on the small kitchen table was a duffle bag. Next to it were several bottles of water. I pounced on the stuff, twisting off the cap and quenching my thirst.

"Take it easy. Remember? You don't want to chug it and

make yourself sick."

I nodded and took another long swig anyway. "Aren't you breaking the rules again?"

He shrugged. "Yeah. No big deal."

I grinned, beyond happy to see him. "So what's in the bag?" Unzipping it, I dug into the stash of goodies.

Potato chips, beef jerky, a loaf of bread, and a jar of peanut butter were the highlights. Then came a few apples, pears, and bananas as well as clean, untarnished knives, spoons and forks. I peeled a banana, then held it in my mouth as I continued to plunder the bag. Lifting one of the many packages, I took the banana out of my mouth and gave him a pointed look. "Ramen? Seriously?"

"I thought that's what all college students eat."

The twinkle in his eye said he was kidding. "It is. But that's the point. I have to eat this crap all the time. Why didn't you bring some hamburger? Or better yet, a steak?"

"If you haven't noticed, the place doesn't have a refrigerator. Besides, raw meat attracts predators."

"Good point." The cat had gotten too close for comfort twice and I didn't want to take any chance of bringing more large animals near me. "Peanut butter sandwiches and ramen it is."

"Check the side pocket."

I did. He'd wrapped a towel around a bottle of wine. "Oh."

"What's the matter? Do you like white wine better? Or beer?"

"No. It's fine." He was all the intoxication I needed.

"No problem. I just brought it in case you…" He shrugged again. "I'm not much of a drinker, either."

I had one peanut butter sandwich made and was already

working on the second. "Um, do you want one of these?"

He was next to me, taking away my hunger and replacing it with a hunger of a different kind. I closed my eyes for a moment to savor the way he smelled. His wasn't a bottled kind of scent. His came from being in the woods, from testosterone and everything else that made him an amazing man. When he moved to sit down, I took the other chair, scooted it close to his, then started working on the first sandwich.

"You never said. What do you want?" The blue of his eyes darkened. "I'm not talking about the games or getting the money. You've got bills, school loans to pay off, and then law school. I get that. But is that it? Don't you want anything else?"

I took another swallow of water, both because of the peanut butter clogging the top of my mouth and the need to stall. Talking about my future had never been my favorite subject. Except when Mike and I had talked about it. Looking back on it, I realized I'd done most of the talking.

"I don't know. The usual stuff, I guess."

"A husband, kids, and a home in the suburbs?"

"Maybe." I'd thought I'd wanted the typical American dream when I was with Mike, but now the idea didn't appeal to me. Life in the suburbs wasn't always easy like on television sitcoms. Just because people lived in nice houses didn't mean bad things couldn't happen.

"So do you think you'll like being a lawyer?"

"Not really." It was the first time I'd ever admitted it out loud. My being an attorney was my parents' goal for me, not mine.

"Then there's something else you'd rather do?"

"I'd rather be an artist."

"An artist. That's cool. What kind of art?"

"I love painting. I just never have the time to do it or the money to buy art supplies. Working at an art supply store is the closest I can come to it."

"Then that's what you should do. Paint, I mean."

I laughed, covering my mouth since I had food in it. "Sure. Tell that to my parents."

"Why do you care what they think?" He was intense, staring at me like he could draw the answers out of me.

Funny how he made everything seem so simple. "I don't." But I owed them. I'd taken Alicia away from them. And I'd embarrassed them. First with my sister's death, then with my attempted suicide, and after that, with the cutting.

"Tell me you'll think about doing your art."

I met his gaze and told him the truth. "Okay. I will. But no promises."

He leaned closer, making me nervous. Nervous in a good way. Now that I wasn't starving any longer, my body started revving up, heat ebbing through me, the memory of us together in bed beginning a new need. I glanced at the bed, then jerked my gaze away.

Sex was good. But sex with someone I could fall for was dangerous. Falling for someone I'd have to say good-bye to and take the money instead was just plain stupid. Fucked-up stupid. Did I dare risk getting even closer to him?

"Is that what you want, Colter? The American dream? Family and kids?" I'd learned early on how to redirect a conversation.

"In a way. But not in the city. My home is here, in the mountains."

Since Alicia's death, I hadn't felt as though I had a real home. My apartment at college was a temporary shelter, nothing more. I wondered what it'd be like to have a place I could really call home. A place where I was safe and secure. A place where I felt loved.

"But do you want a family?" Suddenly, I needed to know.

Did I want kids? Would I be a good mother? After what had happened to my sister, could I trust myself to take care of them? The answer came to me, surprising me. I wanted them. And I wanted them with Colter. I was standing on shaky ground, but all of a sudden, I was willing to risk it.

"Yeah. I'd like some kids. Four or five would be good."

"Four or five? Why not just one or two?" And yet, his wanting so many kids gave me a warm glow. Any man who wanted that many kids would probably make a good father.

"Okay. How about three or four?" His smile was there for my enjoyment.

"Uh-uh. How about two or three?"

He grinned, distracting me from what we'd been saying. "Three it is."

"Hey, wait a sec. Did you just get me to agree to have three kids?" I took a bite out of the second sandwich although I was nowhere near as hungry as before. Three children. But we were just talking. It wasn't reality.

"And no dog."

He'd tricked me into the conversation, and I was enjoying it. "Why not a dog? Don't you like dogs?"

"Nope."

"Seriously? Then we have a problem. I love dogs."

"Do you own one?"

"No. I'm too busy and my landlord won't allow pets. Not even cats."

"No cats? Why not? Cats are great."

I choked a bit just as I took a sip, then turned away as it came out through my nose. "So says one of the Kings of Beasts, right? Is that why you guys have a lion on your jackets? You really, really like pussy cats?"

"We like pussy and we like cats." His expression was dead-pan, but it was obvious he was joking. "But we don't like pussy cats."

I let loose with a very unladylike snort. "Just big cats?"

"Yeah. The king of the cats." He shrugged. "No pets. Huh. I guess you won't miss what you never had."

"I never had a lot of money, either, but I'll miss it if I don't win it." If I could've kicked myself in the ass, I would have. Colter's grin was gone.

"I told you before and I'll tell you again. You're my mate. Call yourself my girlfriend, my woman, my wife-to-be. It doesn't matter."

There was the mate thing again. "I don't understand. You're not some caveman and I'm not a cavewoman you can drag around by the hair. You can't just tell someone you barely know that they're your mate or wife."

"Sure you can. I just did."

He'd been joking before, but now he was stone-cold serious. There was not one bit of humor in his expression.

"Just because you say it, doesn't make it true. Colter, we don't even know each other. We can't. Not in a day. Hell, Mike and I dated for a long time before I realized I really didn't know him."

"Mike Rollingwood, right?"

That threw me. "How'd you know? I haven't told you about him." Or had I? I couldn't remember.

"Did you think we just picked your name out of thin air?

Or liked you on Facebook? We did our research before we sent out those invitations."

I backed up. "Damn. Stalkerish much? Nina said she'd entered our names in the challenge, but we meant to ask once we got here. Then when everyone was at Fang's, things got a little tense and I forgot. So how much research did you do?"

He didn't answer right away, giving me time to think. "Wait a second. How'd you know about Mike but not about all the rest of it? You asked me all these questions like you didn't know anything about me. Have you been playing me this whole time?" I didn't want to believe he'd do that.

"Roberta did the research, and she mentioned him, but not the other stuff. Still, I knew enough to know you needed money. That's the main reason most of you came. To get the money, right?"

"So you tricked us? Is there really any money to win?"

He strode to the window. "Erin, I didn't play you. And the money's no trick, either. If you choose the money, you get the money." He faced me. "If you choose me instead, then you get me, but not the money. It's that simple."

I shouldn't go there, but I did, anyway. "I told you I have to choose the money. But what if I take the money, then—"

"What if you take the money, then we get together afterward?" He shook his head. "I've broken the rules for you, but I won't do that to my people."

To my people. What a weird way to say it.

"So let me get this straight. You and your buddies took the information Nina gave you to send us invitations knowing we needed the money. Now that we're here and doing the challenge, you expect us to choose you over the cash, to become your mate"—he frowned as I used air quotes—"but you're not willing to meet up later? So it's an either or kind of thing? No compromise? If you really"—I stopped, almost blurting out the *L* word—"cared, then you'd want me to have both."

"I won't betray my pride." He came to me, taking me by the arms. "Once this is all over—" He grinned with a sparkle in his eyes. "Once you choose me, you'll understand why I can't do that. Why I'd never do that."

"You need to stop saying I'm your mate. I don't even understand what the word means."

"I told you. It's like a wife, but more."

"That's not telling me anything. What do you mean by more? More as in what?"

"You'll be my woman. You'll care for me and you'll have my children. You'll fuck me when I want you and you'll keep me happy."

"So being your mate will be like I'm your slave? If so, then yeah, give me the money."

"No. I'm not getting this out right. You'll be my partner, just like in a marriage. But my people never get divorced. We stay together no matter what."

No matter what? That sounded impossible. No one had ever stayed with me no matter what. Not after they found out about my secrets. Except for Maddy and Nina, of course, but they were different. "I don't believe that."

"It's the truth. We'll be bound as mates. And together, we'll make decisions and live our lives free."

"But only here in the mountains? I have a life back in Chambers and a degree to finish."

"You can do that, if you still want to. But once you have, we'll move back here. I told you. The mountains are my home and they'll be yours."

None of what he'd said made much sense, even if it did sound appealing. A man who'd stay with me forever. A family that stuck together. Children. A real home. It sounded too good to be true. Which meant, of course, that it probably was.

"Why don't you guys just meet girls the normal way and date? Fall in love then get mated. Married. Whatever."

He smiled just enough to tug at my heart. "Then I'd never have met you."

Could he have said anything sweeter? But I had to stay strong.

"I've already told you. I'm choosing the money."

"No, you won't."

He kissed me then, hard, wiping away my growing anger. His hands left my arms and came to my face, keeping my mouth on his. My head spun as the rush of my yearning swept over me. My thoughts blurred into a wild mix. I hooked my thumbs into the loops on his jeans and tugged him against me. His erect cock pushed against my stomach, urging me to lead him to the bed.

But he broke the kiss, leaving me gasping for air. "You're my mate. Just accept it. If we aren't together, we'll both be miserable."

I tried to form the right words, telling him I wanted what he did, but I couldn't. Instead, I battled the idea. I'd come there to win the money and that's what I'd do. After all, I hadn't believed the romantic bullshit about finding an extraordinary man.

Or had I?

"Colter, I'm sorry, but I'm still choosing the money."

Anger flared, ridding the blue from his eyes and changing them to metallic silver. "I could take you right now. I could claim you and make you my mate. Then you'd have no choice but to accept me."

I didn't know whether to be turned on or pissed off. I decided to be pissed off.

"Like hell. You can't make me do a damn thing." It was a dare. One I hoped he'd take.

"Don't, baby. Don't turn this into a challenge."

I glided my tongue over my lips and watched him follow the motion. "I already have." After all, he'd been the one to challenge me first.

"Fine. Challenge accepted."

Oh, shit.

He picked me up and threw me over his shoulder. A few steps later and I was again on my back on top of the bed. I struggled, determined not to let him have his way, but I was like a fly trying to beat up a dog.

Thrusting my arms over my head, he held my wrists with one hand, then reached under the small table that served as a nightstand. His body hovered over mine, close enough I could've licked the side of his face.

He held up a strip of soft leather and grinned. "Baby, this is your first lesson in being my mate. Don't ever challenge me. I always win."

"We'll see about that." It was a useless threat and we both knew it.

"Yeah. We will." Like a cowboy tying a calf, he had my wrists tied and the leather strip wrapped around one of the slats of the headboard before I knew what had happened.

I kicked and squirmed, but with him sitting on top of me, I wasn't going anywhere. The whole thing was frustrating and as exciting as hell.

Laughing, he scooted to one side, then took my legs and rid me of my shoes. My jeans and panties followed, flying to the floor. I let out a groan and kicked again, then bucked and tried to keep my legs away from him.

"Colter, look at me."

He did, taking his focus away from my legs even as he grabbed another two leather strips and started to tie my legs to the end of the bed.

Please, don't let him see my scars.

I had to keep his attention on my face. Every time he glanced back to wrap the strips around the bed slats, I bucked, then told him to look at me. I prayed I'd distract him enough that he wouldn't have time to notice my ankles.

"This isn't fair." I put on a scowl.

He tilted his head in that way I found lovable. "Fair? No one said we had to fight fair."

"What are you planning on doing?"

"This." In one smooth move, he was between my legs and using the fact that they were already spread wide to his advantage.

I sucked in air as his tongue and teeth worked to send my excitement into overdrive. I yanked on my restraints, but couldn't get free. Not that I really wanted to. His sexual expertise had me writhing under his careful command.

The heat in the cabin grew more intense, enveloping its warmth around us. I no longer cared about any challenge, his or mine. All I wanted was to have his—

Yes!

His fingers slid into my sheath and finger-fucked me, exploring my warmth. He knew exactly what he was doing, just as he had all the times before.

I lifted my head, needing to see those strange eyes, and met his gaze. What I saw there, the unbridled love, catapulted me into an orgasm. I cried out, the cries turning into whimpers as my body shuddered my climax outward.

My breathing was as rapid as my heartbeat. Every inch of me was alive, aching for him to touch me everywhere at once. Even if I didn't admit it, he'd already claimed me using only his two fingers and his mouth.

I moaned and yanked against my restraints. "Colter, damn it."

He sat up, wiped his mouth, then slid upward, trailing his fingers along my skin. His touch was electrifying, scintillating, enough to drive a girl out of her mind. If it were humanly possible, I'd live for his touch alone.

"Colter, turn me loose."

He shoved my shirt up to my neck, then sent my bra in the same direction. "Are you ready to admit that you're my mate? To say you'll choose me over the money?"

Aw, hell. Why'd he have to go there?

"You know what I said." Damn, how I wanted to choose him, but if nothing else came from the games, I'd get the money I needed. Would it be worth the price? Once it was over, once I'd used the money to pay my bills and loans, would I regret it?

The answer was as clear as glass. Love was much more important in the long run, but did his wanting me as his mate mean he loved me? He'd never said the word and, until he did, even after seeing it in his eyes, how could I believe it? I'd made that mistake once. I couldn't risk making the same mistake twice.

Still, I couldn't help but wonder. What if I did?

His tongue trailed a path around my nipple and sent the

question straight out of my head. I arched, loving the way his hand felt against my breast, his teeth nibbling at my taut bud while his oh-so-long cock pushed between my legs. If I could've lifted my pelvis and shoved his cock inside my pussy, I would have.

"You're mine." He fisted his hands in my hair. "Say it."

"No. None of it makes sense. I'm no one's mate. Not even yours."

I yelped when he brought his teeth down to bite my shoulder. It hurt, but didn't break my skin.

"I could claim you right now. Without you agreeing. You'd understand after I did it."

A flash of alarm stiffened me. He wouldn't hurt me. I knew he wouldn't. Unless I'd pushed him too far? "Turn me loose."

He lifted his head and studied me. "You're frightened."

"A little."

He stroked my temple with his thumb, keeping his gaze to mine. "I don't want you to ever be afraid of me."

The fear had come and gone. "I'm not any longer."

"Good." He pressed a light kiss to my mouth. "I'm going to fuck you."

As though he'd pressed an On button, the ache between my legs skyrocketed. "You didn't talk this much at first."

"I didn't?" He nibbled on my neck.

"No. But now you talk too much."

"Then I'll shut up. Until later."

I nodded, then gasped as he lifted up, positioned his cock, and thrust it inside me. He was huge, bigger than I remembered. Side to side, beginning to end, he filled me. The friction of his shaft worked against my inner walls.

I tugged on the restraints, but couldn't find my voice again.

Instead, I set my gaze on his as he rammed into me, his chest and arm muscles working, his clenched jaw jumping. His dark hair formed a perfect frame for his tanned face.

I could move only a little, but when I could, I matched his rhythm. My short puffs, my *uhhs* echoing around the cabin, set up an accompaniment to his soft groans. Our sweaty bodies made sucking noises. We no longer needed to speak. Instead, we communicated with our eyes and through our touches.

I was his mate. I could see that he believed it. Now if only I could believe it, too.

"You are my mate."

I fantasized that I could see those words in his strange silver gaze and I wanted to give him the answer he wanted.

Yes, I'm your mate.

And yet I stayed quiet.

When he closed his eyes, I knew he'd reached his limit. He could hold back no longer. Just seeing his body tense, his head thrown back, sent my body into another hard release. As I cried out, he shouted along with me.

Our bodies shook together as he clung to me. I wanted so much to dig my fingernails into his back, to feel his chest crushing my breasts, but the bindings wouldn't allow me to bring him closer.

As though he knew what I was thinking, he reached above me and tore the leather strip away from the bed, then did the same to free my legs. My wrists were still bound together, but at least I could clasp my hands behind his neck and pull him against me.

We melded together as his climax ended and he rolled to my side. Unable to speak, we lay together in silence, listening to our breathing and the birds outside the window. Exhausted, I snuggled against his strong body, content to stay by his side, and wished we could lie together forever.

But I knew all too well that wishes, like dreams, rarely came true.

Chapter Twelve

Colter

I hated to leave Erin so soon, but I had to. I'd stayed by her side, listening to her soft snores and caressing her hair while she slept. But the longer I stayed, the more anxious I became.

Fury had gone wild inside me when I'd seen Shayna approach the cabin, then start up the cabin steps. I'd had no doubt she'd wanted to hurt Erin. She wouldn't bother trying to scare her off. Erin's death was a permanent solution.

As much as it infuriated me as it did the other men, it wouldn't be the first time a jealous female had tried to get rid of a girl during the games. Although all of the pride, males and females alike, understood the need for the challenge, the females didn't want them to continue. Each year, more of them voiced their dissention, but the males, the rulers of the pride, always had their way. That left only one option for the female who wanted a pride male. She had to get rid of the girl before she finished the challenge and chose the man. It didn't matter if she drove her away or if she killed her, but gone for good was better.

Shayna was strong, independent, and ready to do whatever was necessary to have me. The realization of Shayna's intent chilled me.

Erin was my mate. I knew it and she knew it, too, no matter how much she wanted to deny it. But both of us knowing

THE CAPTURED HEART   217

wouldn't make it come true. If she needed the money more than she needed my love, then she'd take it. The idea made me angry, frustrated, hurt, and a bunch of other feelings I couldn't put names to. Although I'd never had to worry about money, I understood, having seen what the world was like for those who had to make it on their own. If she was that desperate, then I wouldn't stand in her way.

She was worth any kind of sacrifice. Even giving her up.

I slipped my arm out from under her, then eased out of the bed. She looked so peaceful and sexy. My cock twitched to life again, but there was no time. If everything worked out the way it should, we'd have a lifetime to spend together.

I hesitated to leave, but I doubted Shayna would return after my warning. At least not for a while. Still, I planned on being back before she could make another move. She'd run off last night after hearing my threatening roar, afraid I'd find her close to Erin. She knew I'd do whatever I had to do to keep Erin safe. If it came down to a battle between Shayna and me, I'd easily win. Fighting her was the last thing I wanted, but I wouldn't back down.

I wasn't too worried about Shayna telling the pride I'd broken the rules, either. If she'd wanted to, she could've already done so. The fact that they hadn't come for Erin told me she'd kept her mouth closed. And I doubted she'd tell them once we returned to Fang's. She wouldn't want the others to know she'd tried and failed to claim the man she wanted. She'd already suffered enough shame when she'd exposed herself to me outside of Fang's and I'd rejected her. Shayna had a lot of pride and wouldn't stand for any more humiliations.

I just prayed I was right.

The old yearning raked through me, my animal stealing into

my skin, growling and snarling its need to shift and run. Staying too long in my human body made me antsy. The beckoning call would soon overwhelm me, forcing me to shift whether I wanted to or not. It was better to heed the call and run at the first sign of my inner beast rising to the surface. It clawed at me, snarling to be set free, tearing at my will to resist. It pushed to get near the surface, to take control of my mind as well as my body. If I didn't run soon, I might shift and Erin would see the animal side of me. She wasn't ready. With everything else against us, with Shayna after Erin, I didn't need another problem.

Opening the cabin door, I took one more look at my sleeping beauty and slipped outside. I shifted enough to let my sensitive hearing pick up all the noises in the woods, then listened to see if she'd awakened. When I heard nothing, I took off running into the trees where I'd strip and leave my clothes under a bush. My animal roared, the silent sound of it rippling under my skin. I was one of the Kings of Beasts and the mountains were my kingdom.

Erin

Nothing made me feel sadder than waking up without Colter by my side. I'd fallen asleep cuddled against him and had hoped to wake up still curled under his arm. To wake up with the blanket scrunched into a pile next to me was a pitiful substitute. But I guess I should have expected it. Like I'd thought earlier, wishes and dreams rarely came true. And even when they did, they didn't last long.

I stretched, determined not to let it get me down. Maybe he

was outside. Pulling on my clothes, I hurried to the door and flung it open, only at that moment thinking that I should've checked first and made sure the big cat wasn't hanging out on the porch. Thankfully, she wasn't, but neither was Colter. A quick look around didn't help, either. I couldn't find him anywhere.

Damn.

The disappointed feeling spiraled downward into an even shittier feeling. Had I been fucked and dumped? Couldn't he have at least stayed the night? If only for dinner?

I closed the door, then turned and leaned against it. The awful thoughts came back, darkening my attitude along with my heart. The thing was, I should've known they'd come. And yet, each time they did, they caught me unaware, unprepared, and all too ready to accept them.

But not this time.

I pushed away from the door. It wouldn't matter if I never saw Colter again. All that stuff about being his mate was ridiculous. Who talked like that, anyway? Was it his version of how to get between a girl's legs?

I'd come for the money and I'd leave with the money. No man, not even Colter, could change my decision.

Even as I was trying to force that belief into my brain, I kept glancing out the windows, hoping to see him walk out of the trees. When it didn't happen, I sat down at the table, ready to dig into the duffel bag for dinner.

At least he'd left the food and water.

Damn it, Colter. Why'd you leave?

I was so fucking tired of being left alone.

My gaze slid to the wine bottle. One drink wouldn't hurt. I could drink just enough to lessen the pain starting to tighten my heart, and along with it, the urge to cut.

I jerked my gaze away from the temptation. No. I didn't need it. I wasn't sure why, but the longer I stayed on the mountain—with Colter—the stronger I felt. The next day, I'd walk back to Fang's and claim my money.

How many times had Colter said he'd claim me? And how many times had I thrilled to hear him say it?

I slid my finger along the curve of the bottle. Still, one little drink wouldn't hurt. Besides, it'd give me something to do.

My parents, Maddy, Nina, my therapist. All of them were inside my head telling me not to pop the cork and have a sip.

Alcohol was a two-edged sword. One side helped to ease the emotional whirlwind inside me, to dull the need to cut, but the sword could flip to the sharper edge if I had too much, getting me to let down my guard against The Darkness.

I took the bottle and lifted it to the light outside. It sure looked yummy. Besides, I didn't have anything else to drink except water. And red wine was supposed to be drunk at room temperature. It made sense to drink the wine.

I imagined sitting on the front porch, catching the breeze, and lounging away the rest of the day. Plus, if I saved a little for later on, it would help me get to sleep.

There were so many good reasons to drink it. But I wanted to share it with him.

If he came back.

I set the bottle back on the table, my decision made. I'd drink it later. Once I was sure Colter wasn't coming back. Or better yet, we could drink it together while sitting on the porch like a married couple enjoying the night sky.

The fingers of The Darkness tried to close in on my mind, but I fought it off. I smiled at my victory, then grabbed a water bottle and one of the muffins hidden in the corner of the bag. It would be a long, boring day, but I hoped the night would be so much better.

Still, the questions remained. Where had Colter gone? And why did I have to keep asking that same fucking question?

Erin

Hours later, I'd found my way to the porch and one of the rocking chairs. I was bored out of my mind with only the birds and a few rabbits to watch, but if a little boredom was the price I had to pay to win two hundred and fifty thousand dollars, then I figured I was getting a terrific deal.

But would I end up paying an even greater price? Once I had the money and was back home in Chambers, would I regret not choosing Colter? When the lonely nights came, as they always did, would I ache for the feel of his arms around me?

He wanted me for his mate. The word sounded old-fashioned, like something out of a history textbook. The only people I'd ever heard use the term were those on television shows or in movies. Usually when talking about supernatural beings like vampires or werewolves.

I laughed. Boredom was making me think silly things.

Colter's a werewolf.

I laughed again, setting the birds in a nearby tree into flight. The idea was fun to think about, but it was just a ridiculous notion.

What would Colter say if I told him I thought he was a werewolf? Most likely, he'd laugh his ass off, then want to see the empty wine bottle. Still, it might be fun just to see his reaction.

I swatted at a gnat and noted the position of the setting sun. It'd be dark soon. Would he leave me alone all night? Had he finally decided not to break any more rules? Would the cat come back?

I suddenly wished he'd brought a gun along with the food and water. A gun powerful enough to take down a big cat.

Leaving my empty water bottle beside my chair—I'd already gone through three of them—I headed toward the outhouse. From that point on, I'd only take sips of the next to last bottle. Maybe then I could get through the night without having to make another scary trip outside to pee.

Not for the first time, I wondered if being in the outhouse, along with its overpowering stench, had saved my life. If the cat had smelled me inside the cabin, would it have burst through a window and torn me to shreds? Or had the deafening roar frightened the beast away and saved me? Whatever could make a sound that terrifying was huge, even bigger than the large cat. The sound had reminded me of a lion's roar, but there'd been an element in its tone that had made me shiver. Strangely, I'd shivered not out of fear, but out of need. I didn't understand how an animal's roar could make me feel that way, but I couldn't deny what I'd felt, either.

I did my business, zipped my jeans, then hurried back to the cabin. My stomach rumbled again and I decided to fix myself a snack.

What if he didn't come back? What if he'd finally accepted that I had to choose the money over him? I hated to admit it, even to myself, but having him keep after me to change my mind was an ego boost.

I didn't want to lose him. If I wasn't so deep in debt, with law school looming and my parents' demanding I become an attorney, I'd pick him over the money in a heartbeat. Even now, I was finding it harder to think about leaving him behind.

He wanted to claim me and make me his mate, which sounded more like he wanted to brand me and make me his pet. It definitely wasn't my idea of a romantic declaration of love. That's what I told myself while trying to ignore the thrill it gave me.

I glanced out the window and into the coming night. What if he said he loved me? Straight out so I'd know for sure? I wanted to know I was more than a mate. I wanted to be the girl he yearned for. The woman he wanted not because she'd give him three children, but because he couldn't live without her.

I'd already given my love to one man who'd let me down. Fear and pride would keep me from doing it again.

Then there was The Darkness. How I felt about Colter was clear enough. I could love him. Hell, I wanted to love him. I perhaps already did love him. If the money wasn't an issue, I'd let my guard down and welcome him into my heart. But first, I had to know if he could handle my secrets. Would his desire to take me as his mate die once he learned about the scars on my ankles and why they were there? Would he hate me as much as my parents did when he found out I was responsible for my sister's death? Would he throw me away like Mike had done?

I had way too many questions and not enough answers.

But I knew one thing for certain. I was damaged goods. No man wanted someone like that. I'd be better off not dreaming for something I could never have. And yet, dreams were tough to kill.

The knock against the door startled me, then sent me running for it.

Colter?

I skidded to a stop a foot from the door. Colter wouldn't knock. Fear took hold, catching my breath in my throat. It hadn't actually been a knock. More like someone or something banging against the door.

Inching to the side, I crept to the edge of the nearest window and made a vow to tell Colter to put shades on them. But at least the cabin *had* windows. Glass wouldn't keep the big cat out, but it was better than nothing.

Holding my hair back, I leaned around the frame of the window and took a quick look. The moon put out enough light for me to see. I'd half expected to see the cat while hoping to see Colter. Instead, Hector stood a few steps back from the door.

I jerked away from the window. *What the hell is he doing here?*

I peeked again. He had on the same black sleeveless vest and black jeans with scuffed work boots. But all the cockiness was gone. Blood dripped from a wound in his hand.

I pulled away again, rested my back against the wall and tried to think. The door wasn't bolted. He could come inside if he wanted. Trying to make as little noise as possible, I reached up and grabbed hold of the bar. Halfway down, however, I lost my grip on the heavy wood and it dropped into place with a loud thud. I cringed, then held my breath.

"Hey, Erin? Can you open the door, please?"

Please? I wouldn't have thought he knew the word. "What do you want?"

"I need your help."

His hand didn't look bad enough for me to risk opening the door. "Sorry. You'll have to get help somewhere else." Okay, so I felt bad turning him down, but not *that* bad.

"Can you open the door so we can talk face to face?"

Every bit of me screamed to keep it closed. "Again. Sorry." If he wanted in, I doubted I could keep him out. I went back to the window and stared at him without trying to hide. He saw me and turned my way.

I hated to ask, but couldn't stop myself. "Are you all right?" His blood left red blotches on the porch.

He lifted his hand, giving me a better look at his wound. "It's not too bad." His blue-silver eyes met mine, worry glinting in them. "Colter's in a lot worse shape than me."

"What?" Colter was hurt. For a moment, I would've sworn the world stood still. "What happened? Where is he?"

He jerked his other hand toward the forest. "He's back there. He told me to come and get you." His face grew even more ominous. "It's bad, Erin. He's asking for you."

Nothing, not even The Darkness, had ever hit me so hard. It was as though his words had reached inside me and torn my heart right out of my chest. I had to go to him. "Hold on. I'm coming."

Taking hold of the bar covering the door, I shoved it high and out of the way, then flung the door open. "Where is he? Take me there."

The only thing I remembered after that was seeing his eyes change to all silver, then feeling the pain ricochet outward from my back and into my arms and legs a second after I hit the floor.

Hector had me pinned on my back. He yanked his belt out of his jeans, then undid the button. I screamed, but the sound was gone as the force of his slap slammed against my cheek, turning my face to the side.

I was disoriented, unable to focus on anything except the

two words repeating through my mind.

Oh, God, oh, God, oh, God.

This couldn't be happening. Not after everything I'd already gone through. I couldn't move. I felt his hand holding me down, much like Colter had done. But this was different. This wasn't rough sexual play. This was rape.

He shoved his hand under my shirt and bra, fondled my breasts roughly, then laughed an odd, evil laugh that had my stomach doing a sickening flip-flop. I did the best I could to kick him, but his body was too heavy on top of mine.

"Come on, bitch. You know you want it. All you college girls fuck everyone, right?"

"No! Get off me. Let me go!"

His weight lifted from me and, for a second, I stupidly believed he'd let me go. Instead, he grabbed hold of my jeans, then spun me around, putting me on my stomach. I tried to scramble away, but my efforts only made it easier for him to pull my jeans down to my ankles, then off, along with my shoes. He ripped my panties away.

"Doggy style it is, bitch."

I clawed at the rough hardwood underneath me. The harder I tried to gain any kind of a hold, the longer the scratches grew. Trying to push myself upright was useless. He grabbed my hips and yanked me backward until I was on my knees. A hand in the middle of my back forced my face to the floor.

"No. Don't. Please stop."

His evil laugh came again as he grabbed my arms and wrenched them behind my back. Keeping one hand around my wrists, he worked on his jeans, the unforgettable sound of his zipper coming down and flooding me with terror. I was stunned into silence, disbelieving what was about to happen, when I felt his bare thighs push against the back of my legs. Spreading my legs, he got between them and pressed his cock to my asshole.

I screamed, but the scream soon morphed into pitiful moans. Still, I struggled as he wrapped his arm around my legs and shoved his fingers between my folds.

"Aw, come on, bitch. Why so dry? You know you want this. Just relax and enjoy. Hell, I'll even let you suck on my cock when I'm done."

Tears of fear and of rage streamed down my face. "Stop. Colter will kill you for this."

His cruel laugh was a sound I'd remember for the rest of my life. "Don't worry about him. He won't do nothing. I have a right to claim the cunt I want. You're not as juicy as my mate was, but you'll do and I need a new mate. Lucky for you, you're it."

He wanted to claim me. My stomach threatened to bring up its contents. Instead, I squirmed, trying to throw my body one way, then the next, but he held me firm. I was weak and defenseless against his brute strength. At least my efforts made him take his hand from between my legs to hold me still.

"Knock it off." He slammed his hand down on my spine, pushing my face and shoulders harder against the floor. A growl followed, then the slide of sharp teeth along my lower back.

I fought him, trying to use every last bit of strength I had to move my body, but it was hopeless. I screamed again, putting all my frustration and pain into the sound until my throat burned. My screams turned into sobs.

"Please, no. Please."

Surprising me, he lifted away, his hold on me weakening. Had he taken my pleas to heart? I jerked, getting my hands free. Scrambling away on my hands and knees, I cried hysterically as

I got as far away from him as I could.

I took hold of the end of the table, pulled myself to my feet and turned to face him. But Hector was no longer there.

Stunned, I scanned the small cabin, half expecting him to jump out at me, to toy with me, to take me to my knees again. But he really wasn't there. I snatched up my jeans and tugged them on.

"Knock it off, man. I have every right to make her mine."

I dashed outside to find Hector holding Colter in a head lock. My first instinct was to launch my body at Hector's back, but I knew I'd do little good. Instead, I rushed back inside the cabin, grabbed the wine bottle, then raced back outside.

Jumping as high as I could, I slammed the bottle against Hector's neck. It broke, shattering wine and glass over his shoulders. His roar deafened me as I fell to the ground beside the men. I could've hit him with a feather, for all the good the wine bottle did. As far as I could tell, it hadn't done any damage. Instead of falling to the ground as I'd hoped, he turned his head and snarled at me, exposing razor-like teeth.

I stumbled backward, panic seizing me. Who had teeth like those?

Colter took his chance, using the distraction I'd caused to grab him and toss him over his shoulder. Hector landed on his back, then howled as Colter planted a kick to his side.

Colter looked at me just long enough to yell. "Get back inside!"

I didn't want to leave him, but the intensity of his look, the harsh bark of his words sent me flying to obey. Running, I dashed back inside the cabin, then slammed the door. But I didn't lock it. I couldn't lock it knowing Colter might still need me. Instead, I pressed my face against the window, ready to open the door in case he escaped to the cabin.

Colter still retained the upper hand and had Hector down on the ground. He landed another solid kick to the man's side, then added a blow to the back of his head. Hector let out a tortured howl as Colter clutched his vest and hauled him to his feet. He came up swinging, but struggled to stay upright. Colter delivered two sharp jabs to his face, making his head bob back and forth. Hector flung his arms out, flailing, but couldn't land a blow.

Colter stalked around Hector like a wolf staking out its prey, then jumped in and landed a solid uppercut to the jaw. He staggered and would've fallen if Colter hadn't hooked him under the arms and pushed him back on his feet.

"Stop, man. I've had enough." All the fight was gone from Hector. Instead, with blood streaming down his face and arms, he held up his hands in defeat and tucked his head.

"Why'd you do it? I thought we were friends." Colter kept circling him, landing one blow after another.

"It's my right, man. I saw her and I wanted her." His voice pitched higher, almost to a whine as he bent over, trying to duck each of Colter's hits. "You know how it is."

"That's the only reason I'm not breaking your neck. But I swear, man, if you ever, *ever* lay a hand on my mate again, I won't think twice about doing it."

Colter was furious and I was afraid for Hector. Not that he deserved it.

"Get going before I change my mind." Colter paced away from Hector, running his hands through his hair as though that would keep him from striking out again.

Hector took off running, weaving back and forth, falling, then getting back up. Once he'd gotten close to the trees' edge he turned around, probably to check and see if Colter was following him.

I blinked. Then squinted, determined to see better.

What the hell?

It couldn't be true. There was no way it was happening.

But it had to be real. Unless I'd hit my head harder than I'd realized when Hector had thrown me to the floor.

As I stood at the window, my focus locked on Hector, he began changing. His body blurred as he ripped his clothes away. The vest went flying into the air, followed by a toss of his boots and then his jeans. Not long after the clothes hit the ground, more changes swept over him.

His body, growing a little clearer with each minute, bent into strange angles. His tanned skin grew lighter, taking on a furry texture. Paws with long, deadly claws took the place of his hands while his torso twisted, arms and legs bending at bone-breaking angles, then reforming into shorter limbs.

I gaped, unable to believe my eyes. A snout replaced his jaws and nose while his ears shifted upward, becoming more rounded. Longer fur erupted from his hair, forming a collar around his neck. Silver eyes glowed.

In less than a minute, Hector had changed from a man into a lion.

"Colter!" He had to get away from the monster. "Run!"

Colter twisted around and met my gaze.

I clapped a hand over my mouth, terror gripping me. Shaking my head, I backed away from the window and screamed.

Chapter Thirteen

Colter

Fuck.

Hector couldn't match me in a fair fight so he'd gotten back at me the best way he could. He'd shifted with Erin looking on.

The anger I'd felt when I'd found him on top of my mate, his fangs ready to sink into her, warped into an even greater fury. Not only had he tried to take her from me, he'd exposed what we were before I'd had a chance to tell her. My beast roared inside me, ready to tear his head off. The world around me shifted into grays and blacks as the silver took over my eyes. Fangs burst from my gums and the tingle I always felt when fur covered human skin raced like wild fire over my body.

Her cry to warn me about Hector had me twisting around without thinking. My silver gaze met her stunned one.

No. Not yet.

But she'd seen me. She'd seen my fangs and the fur covering part of my face.

It was my place to tell her and I'd wanted to do it in the kindest, gentlest way possible. Hector had stolen that from me. I wanted nothing more than to tear him apart, limb by limb. But I couldn't let my animal free. Not when Erin needed me.

Forcing my lion back into submission, I dashed for the cabin. At first I didn't see her. It took a moment for my eyes to adjust from the dark outside to the flickering lights of the candles and lanterns. Once they did, however, I found her, huddled on the bed.

"Erin, baby, it's all right. He's gone."

As far as I could tell, she wasn't injured. At least not physically. The way her body shook, shudder after shudder shaking her from head to toe, confirmed what I already knew. She'd seen Hector change. She'd seen me.

"Stay away."

She couldn't have said anything worse. "Please, baby, let me explain."

She shook her head, hard and fast. "No. Get away from me. Whatever you are."

Damn Hector to hell and back. Not only had he broken the law by showing her what he was, he'd made me break it, too.

"I'm sorry you had to find out that way. But now that you have, we need to talk about it."

She pulled her legs tighter against her chest. I hurt for her more than I did for myself. "Baby, please. Let me help you understand."

"Help me understand? Understand what? That you can change into an animal? That you're not human?" She denied me again, as though shaking her head hard enough would keep me away.

"I wanted more time with you before I told you what I am."

"Oh, my God. Now it makes sense. Lions have mates, not humans."

I dared to take a step closer, but didn't take another when I saw her alarmed expression. "You're right. I'm a lion inside. People call us shifters. Except for the other girls, everyone you saw at Fang's was a shifter. They're my pride. They're my family."

"Like werewolves."

Was she starting to come around? At least she'd stopped shaking. "Yes. Like werewolves, except we change into lions."

Her eyes grew wide. "Then the big cat. She wasn't a cougar. She was a lion?"

"Right. She's a lioness. Her name's Shayna and she wants to be my mate."

It had to be my imagination, but I thought I saw a flash of anger, maybe even jealousy, come over her. But it was gone before I could be certain it was real.

"Then why don't you mate her?"

"Because you're the one I want." I came closer, making her scrunch her body even tighter. "You're the one I love."

She blinked as though I'd clapped my hands in front of her face. "Love? No. It can't be. You don't really know me. And I sure as hell don't know you like I thought I did."

"I know enough. You're smart and funny and nice. Plus, you and I have a physical thing that's beyond amazing."

Her face softened and I had the nerve to think she might be coming around. My hope ended all too soon.

"You're an animal. A wild thing stuck inside a man's body."

"Yes and no. I can change into an animal, but the man I am, the man I hope you've come to care about, is still there. Even while I'm in my lion body. Does that make sense?"

"Nothing makes sense."

I hated causing her so much turmoil, hated seeing her afraid of me. "Baby, if you believe nothing else, believe that I'd rather die than hurt you."

"You lied to me. That makes it hard to believe anything you say now. Why didn't you tell me what you were?"

Being a lion meant I had courage and my ego fought with the need to make her understand. Yet if it brought her back to me, I'd say the words few lions ever said. "Because I was afraid. I didn't know how you'd react. And because it's against pride law to tell you before you choose me." I came to her, moving slowly but firmly, hoping she'd let me hold and comfort her. "I wanted to break it to you in a better way."

She threw off the blanket, tossing it at me, then sprang off the bed. I paused, then chased after her, snagging her around the waist and lifting her off her feet.

"Let me go. I hate you. You lied to me." She struggled, kicking and flailing her arms and legs, but she couldn't hurt me. She couldn't hit me hard enough to hurt me as much as her words did.

"Calm down, baby. If you promise to stay put, I'll let you go." She stopped fighting me and I placed her on her feet. "Will you stay and let me explain?"

At her nod, I eased my hands off her. Then grabbed her again when she lunged for the door.

"No, let me go. I want out of here."

I didn't have much choice. I couldn't let her run into the woods at night. Even if Shayna or Hector weren't around, there were other inhabitants of the forest that might harm her. Running at night, she could stumble, fall, and injure herself. I had to keep her until morning and hope she calmed down enough to listen.

She let out an angry shout as I hauled her back to the bed and set her down on it. Her struggles were of no use as I took her hands and tied them together, then looped the end of the leather strip around the slat of the bed and secured her to it. She had enough slack that she could reach the knots, but I'd tied them so tightly she wouldn't be able to undo them.

"No. You can't keep me here. This is kidnapping. Untie me, damn you."

I had to move away. If I didn't, I was afraid she'd struggle hard enough to injure herself. "Once you calm down and listen to me, then I'll untie you. Besides, you have to spend the night here anyway. You wouldn't want to ruin your chance at the money, right?"

She stilled at the mention of the money. Now that she knew what I was, I was certain she wouldn't change her mind about taking the money. But it no longer mattered what she wanted. Once she'd seen Hector shift, she'd lost her right to choose. She'd have to become one of us even if she didn't want to. Yet after she changed, she wouldn't want to leave. No one ever had. Where else would they go? They'd no longer be fully human, but part lion.

Anger, fresh and terrible, gripped me. I cursed Hector. Under our rules, he had the right to sink his fangs into her, to claim her as his mate. Allowed or not, I'd never known any man who'd disrespected his pride brother enough to steal his mate. Luckily, I'd stopped him before he could bite her. I just wished I'd stopped him before he'd shifted.

If only I'd had more time with her first. More time for us to grow together. More time to prepare her to believe the unbelievable.

Her glare could've turned trees into ashes, but at least she'd settled down enough to stop fighting me. "Will you listen? And try doing it with an open mind?"

"Both of you are lions. Hector and you."

I couldn't blame her for having a tough time wrapping her mind around it. "Like I said. Everyone at Fang's, except the girls, were lions."

"But you said I was your mate."

"You are." I didn't want to get into our laws. It was better to keep the explanation uncomplicated for now. She had enough to handle. "Hector's been talking about getting another mate and I guess he decided you were the one he wanted." I'd felt sorry for him before this, but no longer.

She nodded as though everything made sense. "Lions don't live in America."

The statement wasn't unexpected. Often a girl's mind would snag on a related fact instead of trying to comprehend what they'd seen. "We're shifters, not just lions."

She inhaled, her nostrils closing in, then releasing as she let out a tortured sigh. "This isn't real."

"Baby, it is." I spoke like I'd speak to a frightened child. Most of us reverted to our childlike selves whenever fear grabbed hold of us.

"Then show me." She held her body so hard that her fingers made indents in her legs.

I'd known she'd want to see. They always did. If only we'd started this conversation with her in a calmer state. "Are you sure?"

"Yes. I have to see. I have to know I'm not going crazy."

I couldn't blame her. Humans had a difficult time accepting that they'd had sex with someone who wasn't entirely human. But she had to accept more than the sex part of it. She had to accept me as her mate.

"You're not crazy." I started to tug my shirt off, then paused, needing to make sure. "When I do this, I have to know you'll stay where you are. Don't try and get away. I won't hurt you. I promise."

She didn't respond and I took her silence to mean she'd stay put. I started disrobing, my nerves jumping. Once I was naked, I kept my gaze on hers and let my animal go free.

The change hurt at first. It always did and it always would. How could bones break and reform without pain? But I'd grown used to it a long time ago. Most lion shifters transformed before their first birthday, but I'd gone through my first shift at six months.

It swept over me as the beast inside me roared its victory. It clawed and scraped, snarling and snapping its way to the surface. The world around me blurred as it hit me, controlling my movements, trying to control my thoughts. Soon I'd think like a lion, but I'd never lose my human mind completely.

I saw Erin's eyes go wild, saw her tug at her bindings. I considered stopping the shift and reverting back, but she had to see so she'd believe. And then, she'd accept.

Claws and fangs took their place as fur spread over me. My eyes changed to all silver, ridding the world of its color and replacing it with grayscale hues. My mane burst forth and I shook my head, loving the relief it gave. Dropping to my paws, I swished my tail back and forth to shake off the lingering effects of the shift, then padded toward her.

Erin

I'd finally gone insane. That was the only thing that made sense. After killing my sister, trying to commit suicide, then cutting myself, I'd finally realized the awful truth.

I was certifiably nuts.

Either that or Colter was the one who'd dived into the deep

end of an empty swimming pool. Yet, how could I explain what I was seeing? My man, my Colter, had changed into a lion. A real live King of Beasts.

And now he'd proven it to me. What I'd seen Hector do was real, and Colter could change, too.

Shit and more shit.

I gritted my teeth, steeled my nerves, and vowed I'd make it out of the cabin alive. Maybe not with my mind intact, but at least alive.

The lion came closer. I jerked at the ties holding me, but he was right when he'd said I couldn't get free. All I could do was pray that he didn't sink his huge fangs into my flesh.

Instead, he padded over to me, then rested his huge head on the bed in front of me like a big, lovable dog. His purr was soft, compelling, and I couldn't resist it. I reached out as far as I could and brushed my fingers over his furry muzzle.

"Oh, my God."

If animals could smile, then he was smiling.

I stroked him, each pass of my hand giving me the courage to stroke him again. And again and again. Slowly, my terror receded, giving way to amazement.

This is real. Colter's a lion.

Just as I was beginning to enjoy myself, he swung his large body around, then walked back to where he'd dumped his clothes. Moments later, he was human again.

"Are you all right?"

I nodded. "I think so." Even after what I'd seen, I couldn't help but admire his body. He was all muscles and strong bones. His movements were graceful.

Like a cat's.

I'd been wrong before. Colter wasn't a werewolf. He was a

werecat.

"Good." He yanked on his shirt, then his jeans. He pulled out a kitchen chair, carried it close to the bed, spun it around to sit down, then rested his arms on the back of it.

It was crazy, but just watching him turned me on. I wanted him so bad I could taste it. But I had to know more before we could ever be together. "Okay. Talk."

He let out a breath and I could hear the anxiety in that puff of air. "I've told you some of it. I was born and raised in these mountains. The people I live with are my family, my gang, my pride. My mother and father lived here and I want to raise my children here." His strange eyes zeroed in on mine. "With my mate. With you."

The word made sense now. Or at least as much as anything did right then. "I'm your mate. A lion takes a mate."

"Right. But, Erin, please try and get this. I can change into a lion. I'm what people call a shifter, a werecat. Like the werewolves you mentioned. But I'm still a man with all the same dreams and needs of any man. I'm an animal, but I'm also human."

"You already told me all this."

"Yeah, but I want to make sure you get it straight." He gripped the back of the chair so hard his knuckles turned white. "You're my mate. I knew it the moment I got your scent at Fang's."

It had seemed odd at the time, but animals sniffed each other when they met. That, too, made sense now.

"It's what we do. When we get close to a girl we find physically attractive, one we'd consider taking as a mate, we inhale her aroma."

"So if she smells good, she's mate material?" My curiosity

helped me calm down.

"No, it takes a lot more. I've smelled other women before." He stopped and grinned. "That sounds really freaky, but I'm not sure how else to say it. Anyway, once we meet someone who has the right scent, one we can bond with, then we know she's our mate. There's more to it. Like getting to know you, but taking in her aroma is the basis for everything else."

"So you're saying it's like we were destined for each other and you knew it by my fragrance?"

"Yes and no. Like I said, I don't know how to put it just right. But once I picked up your scent, I knew you were the one for me."

"And what about me? Don't I have a say in it?"

He leaned back. "You do. You've known that from the start. You can take the money or me once you've proven yourself in the games."

Yet something about the way he averted his gaze bothered me. Was he holding something back?

The Claiming Games was more than a challenge to see if I made it back to Fang's. I had to prove I could be his mate and join the pride. No one had told us what they were, but then how could they? If they had, the girls would've run out of Fang's as fast as they could go. But I needed to hear it from him. "Proven myself?"

He darted his gaze away, then brought it back. "The challenge serves two purposes. First, you have to make it back to Fang's tomorrow. If you do, then the pride knows you're physically and mentally strong enough to become one of us. With us, just like it is with lions in the jungle, only the strongest survive. Being my mate means living as we do. It's not an easy life, but it's an amazing one."

Had I already failed? If he hadn't helped me, I wouldn't have made it to the cabin. "So that's why you weren't supposed to help me. I was supposed to get here on my own."

"Yeah, you were."

"Then why did you? Didn't you want to know if I was strong enough? Worthy of you?" He caught the sarcastic inflection I'd put on the word *worthy*.

Somehow, during the trip up the mountain and the time in the cabin, I'd realized that I was worthy of a lot things. Like being happy. Like being with Colter. Like simply being alive. But not because I made it through some challenge. I was worthy just because I was me.

"You're my mate and the one I want. Screw the games." Desire softened his face. "Besides, when Shayna started to attack you, I had to step in. I couldn't see you get hurt. And then when I saw Hector…" The muscle in his jaw twitched.

I studied him, trying to fight against my growing need to tell him it was all right. To say I didn't care what he was as long as he was by my side. I'd come to depend on him, yet at the same time, he'd made me realize I was stronger than I'd thought. Instead, I kept quiet.

"And the second purpose?"

"The second was to make sure you wanted me as much as I wanted you. If you take the money instead of me, then I'll know you weren't really the one for me. But here's the thing. I do know. You just have to want me back."

The sadness that made him bow his head bit at me. He wanted me. Really wanted me. "But I have to take the money. I told you why. I don't have a choice. If I did…" But what was the point of saying I'd choose him if I could?

"I know. Bills and loans. I got it."

"And when were you planning on telling me what you are? Before or after I made my choice?"

He didn't want to say. I could see it in his eyes. "Not until after you picked me. It's against the rules to let you know what we are until after you've made your decision. And if you chose the money, then you would've never found out."

"The why did Hector change when I was watching? He broke the rule." I had my suspicion, but I needed him to confirm it.

"He did. I'd like to believe he shifted in the heat of the moment, but I think it was to get back at me and to scare you. Maybe it was a little of both. I don't know. I wanted to tell you what I was on my own terms and he took that away from me. I never wanted to frighten you."

I nodded, having guessed right. "He did a damn good job."

"Are you saying you want me to leave? Are you still afraid of me?"

"No. I'm not. Not anymore."

Relief flowed off him like water over a dam. "Yeah?"

"Yeah. In fact, seeing you as a lion—after I got over the initial scare factor—was pretty amazing."

He grinned bigger than I'd ever seen him grin.

If only I could choose both. As unbelievable as it sounded, I wanted him. Animal side and all. "I said it already, and I'll say it again. You don't know me. How can you just by sniffing me? What if I have horrible things in my past? Secrets that would make you want to run from me? What then? If I say I want to be your mate and you find out how awful my secrets are, will you dump me?"

He narrowed his eyes. "Do you really think I'm that kind of guy? I'm sorry if other guys have messed with you, but I'm not them. There's nothing you can tell me that would make me turn away from you."

"Now you're talking bullshit. Everyone has a breaking point." I couldn't believe him. If I did, I'd open up too many wounds, making my heart vulnerable for yet another loss. And more pain. So much pain I doubted any amount of self-harm would relieve the pressure. I hated to do it, but I started crying.

He was by my side, wiping away the tears I couldn't reach. "Baby, it's okay. You can tell me. Whatever's eating at you won't scare me away." His smile was soft, comforting. "After all, I'm one of Kings of Beasts. I'm strong. Want to hear me roar?"

I laughed through the tears, but the heartache that had captured my heart so many years earlier came back too fast for me to fight it. The pain led, as it always did, to The Darkness creeping in, ready to squeeze my heart in its grip until I had no choice but to open the wounds and let it out.

"No, baby. I can see you pulling away from me. Trust me. I won't let you down. Tell me what's wrong."

I shook my head, unable to set it all free. I didn't want to lose him. I couldn't lose him. If I hadn't realized it before, I did now. I knew him and I loved him.

But if I did, if I finally gave in and told him, he might leave. Then The Darkness would take everything I was until nothing was left. I'd been too close to the edge of oblivion before. If I came close yet another time, I was afraid I'd have no resistance and would plummet to my end.

His words caressed me as he untied my hands, then drew me against him. I curled into his hold, needing him to keep me safe from myself and from his possible rejection.

"Please, tell me. I swear I'll make it right. Whatever it is, however long it takes, I'll change it. Tell me."

I had to know. If he was going to reject me, then I wanted it to happen right then.

"Look." I swallowed, hard, and pulled my jeans up to my calves. Could I trust him? Or would he leave me like Mike had done?

He took a good, long hard look at my ankles, and frowned. "I saw those scratches before. It's okay. Everyone gets cut up trying to get through the forest." The smile he gave me was one of bemusement as though I was a silly child for worrying.

"You don't understand." Why did it have to be so hard? Why didn't he know what they meant? "Look again. Harder. Look at my scars."

He searched for an explanation, then bent lower to examine my ankles. Once he had, he slid his fingertip over the scars, going from one to the next. "I don't understand. Who did that to you?"

I guess self-harm wasn't something they did in the pride. "No one. I did it to myself. I cut myself."

He leaned away from me.

Oh, no. Please, no. Not again.

He was still confused when he lifted his gaze to mine. "But why?"

The Darkness surrounded me, taunting me for being stupid enough to show him.

"Haven't you ever heard of self-harm? Of cutting? It helps to relieve the pain inside me."

"I don't understand. So you hurt yourself to make yourself feel better? That doesn't make sense."

He wouldn't understand. Not many people could.

"It's what I do." I'd had to talk about it with so many people. My parents, my therapist, Maddy and Nina. I didn't have it in me to talk about it again. Not even with Colter.

He leaned even farther away from me. But that was all right. I'd expected as much. Yet when the concern on his face slowly changed to anger, my gut twisted in agony.

I'm losing him.

"What did you expect?" whispered The Darkness.

"What else, Erin? Tell me everything. I have to know." Unlike before, he wasn't asking so he could comfort me. Now he was demanding.

What did I have to lose that I wasn't already losing?

"I was sixteen when my parents left me alone with my sister, Alicia. She was three." I closed my eyes for a moment, rocking with a fresh wave of self-loathing. I hated myself for how I'd failed not only my parents and Alicia, but now Colter. Why shouldn't he hate me, too?

"And?"

His tone was so harsh, it sliced through me as easily as a razor did.

"She was my adopted sister and she had problems. We weren't sure why, but she didn't learn like other kids. I should've watched her, but I was too busy doing my own thing. And I was angry at my parents for making me stay with her. She was a pest and I didn't want her around." Shame and guilt, so often my companions, washed over me.

"What happened?"

I couldn't look at him. Couldn't bear to see the judgment in his eyes. "She fell into the swimming pool and drowned. By the time I realized she was missing, she was already dead."

I wasn't sure if it was wishful thinking on my part, but I imagined his body relaxing. Had he leaned a little closer?

"And you blame yourself?"

I glanced at him as though he'd asked if rain was wet. "Of course I did. I was supposed to take care of her."

"You were just a kid. It's your parents who should take the blame."

I laughed even as the tears ran down my cheeks. "Tell that to them. No, wait. They wouldn't want to hear it. Not from you, or me, or anyone else."

"So that's why you did…that…to your body?"

"*That* is called cutting. You can say the word without getting hurt, you know." Pain mixed with guilt and shame to flare into anger. "It helps me release the pressure boiling up inside me. I have to let it out." I didn't add the rest. He wouldn't understand how my cutting kept me safe from doing something worse to myself.

"Okay, okay. I'm sorry." He dragged a hand through his tousled hair. "Is there more?"

"Are you sure you want to know?" I wanted to strike at him, but held back. Right then, I was angry at him for making me tell him. I zeroed my gaze in on him like the sights on a rifle.

He glared back at me. "Yeah. I need to know."

I didn't dare ask him if he still wanted me as his mate. Instead, I threw it all at him, daring him to say the words, wanting to hurt him as I hurt. "No, that's not all. Before the cutting, I tried to kill myself."

He jerked back as though I'd physically struck him. "You tried to commit suicide?"

"Yeah. I tried to off myself." My laughter had a hysterical edge to it. "Obviously, I wasn't very good at it. Yet another thing I've failed at."

He stood there, staring at me like he'd never seen me before. As if I was the one who'd changed into an animal. "How could you do that?"

"How could I do what? Cut or try to off myself?" My feelings were dead, incapable of handling the torment his words threw at me. And yet, I still hurt. Amazingly, it was possible to be dead inside and still feel pain. "I told you. To stop the pain."

"And did it?"

"For a little while. But it always comes back." I shook my head and looked down. I couldn't stand to see his haunted expression. Yet, still, I had to know. Whatever he'd felt for me was gone. I was sure of it.

"That's fucked up."

I looked up, surprised and, yet, not. "Yeah. It is. But you wanted to know."

"Maybe you aren't strong enough."

I sucked in a hard breath. He was about to say those awful words. The words that would finally break me. "Maybe I'm not."

He stalked over to the window and grasped the frame. Tucking his head down, he groaned.

His pain broke through the wall I'd built to hide from the rejection I knew was coming. Watching the way my secrets affected him tore at my core. I'd done that to him. I'd taken a strong, courageous man and twisted him up inside. My anger was gone. Only the shame and guilt remained.

"I'm sorry, Colter. I'll understand if you don't want me as your mate now."

He was across the room in a flash, bending over me and making me fall back on the bed. Fear whipped into me as his eyes changed to a glowing silver.

"I won't let you hurt yourself." His hair fell forward, his face hardening. "If you want to be my mate—"

"I do." I hadn't realized just how much until that moment.

"Then you have to finish the challenge. It doesn't matter what's happened or that they'll—" He pulled back a little, then groaned an agonized sound.

All at once, I was sure he wasn't telling me everything. I shook off the feeling. I trusted him.

"Forget everything else. I need you to finish the challenge on your own. From this point on, you have to do it without my help. No matter what goes down." He pushed away and paced to the other side of the cabin. When he turned to look at me, I saw the torment on his face and in his eyes. His jaw worked as though finding it difficult to speak.

"But why? We've already broken the rules. Why is it so important that I do the rest of it on my own?"

"Because…my mother killed herself."

Stunned, I wanted to move to him, to wrap my arms around him, but I couldn't. "I'm so sorry, Colter."

He cast his gaze down and fisted his hands. "I shouldn't have helped you. I should've found out whether or not you could make it on your own. But now? Shit."

I didn't know what to say. Instead, I remained silent, waiting for him to tell me.

"My mother went through the challenge and mated my father. But what no one knew until later was that he helped her." He struggled to speak. "Just like I helped you."

His chest heaved with the effort to breathe. And still I kept away from him. For his sake. Not mine.

"You have to change when you become my mate."

"You'll change me?" Amazement and not a little fear shook me. "I'm going to be a lion? Holy shit."

"As my mate, yes, you'll become one of us."

"Like I said. Holy shit." Would it hurt? Would I like it?

"But listen, Erin. My mother was a human just like you. When she chose my father as her mate, he claimed her and changed her. But in the end, she wasn't strong enough to handle being one of us. Being a lioness was too hard for her. When she finally couldn't take any more, she took her own life."

"And you're afraid I'm not strong enough."

"I don't know how, but we have to think of a way out of this. I love you too much to risk it."

Shock hit me, pounding into me and making me tremble. "Say it again."

He started to ask what I'd meant, then understood. "I love you."

At last, I rushed to him. But I couldn't hug him as I'd wanted. Instead, I had to make him understand. "I love you, too. And I want to be your mate."

"But—" His gaze dropped lower to my ankles, then back up.

"But you don't want to risk it. You don't think I'm strong enough. You think I'll do what your mother did."

He nodded in such a slight manner that, at first, I wasn't sure he'd actually moved. "I couldn't stand it if you did."

"Does that mean you don't want me to pick you? That you don't want me?"

He stared at me, his face filled with worry. "I'll always want you. No matter what." He let out a tortured sigh. "But there's a problem. Now that you've seen Hector and me change…"

"What? They'll keep me here forever?" I chuckled.

"Yeah. They will."

I'd only been joking.

"It's one of our laws. They can't let you leave now that you know what we are. They can't risk the outside world finding out about us. On top of that, if they find out that I helped you, they won't consider you worthy of being one of us. You'll be forced to change because you know what we are, but you'll never be fully accepted as one of us. Damn it. This is fucked up."

"Then we have to hope they never find out. That Hector won't say anything about me seeing him. I'll make it the rest of the way by myself and pick you. They'll never find out and they'll accept me. Right?"

"I just don't know."

"Do you think he'll keep quiet?"

"I think so. Like I said. What he did, changing in front of you, is against our laws. He knows he'll catch hell for it so he probably won't say anything. But Hector's unpredictable." He shook his head and groaned. "I've broken the rules. If they find out, I'll have to face the consequences."

"Like what?"

He held back, not wanting to tell me. Instead, he said, "Let's not worry about it. I'll be okay. Shayna and Hector won't say anything. They can't without it coming back to bite them."

"What about the other? Isn't forcing himself on me against the laws, too?"

"No. It's not."

"You're kidding."

"Until you choose me, you're fair game. Although I've never heard of anyone ever doing that to another pride member. It's considered uncool, but it is allowed. As long as he does it before you make your choice back at Fang's. But Hector's different. The woman he chose for his mate was injured and died during the games. I don't think he ever got over it." He studied me as though he'd never seen me before. "Now that I think about it, you look a lot like her."

"Great. Just great."

"We'll just have to hope he keeps his mouth shut. If he does, they won't force you into doing anything. But you have to make it on your own from this point on."

"I will. I'll prove to you and to them that I'm strong enough." The money no longer mattered. What I wanted, hell, needed was to prove myself to him and, most of all, to myself. But would that be enough for him? Or would he still be worried that I'd do the same as his mother? "Give me a chance, Colter."

He swallowed hard. "Do you..." He cleared his throat. "Do you still cut yourself?"

"Not for a while now." Shame filled me again, but he had to know. "After my boyfriend found out, he dumped me and I almost started again. Are you going to do the same thing? Are you going to dump me?"

He answered me. Not with words, but with a kiss. I leaned into him, gripping him as tightly as he held me. The kiss was feverish, needy, promising everything and anything.

When he tugged me away from him, he stepped back and put his hand on the door. "Prove it, Erin. I hope you can. For your sake, more than mine."

I didn't have time to argue. Besides, what could I have said? Instead, I watched him as he left, striding to the trees without once looking back.

Chapter Fourteen

Colter

Suicide.

I could've handled almost anything, but not that.

I didn't care where I went. Moving on autopilot, I let my memory take me deep into the woods. The farther I went, the faster I ran. My pulse pounded in my ears as loudly as my feet pounded against the forest floor. I didn't want to think, didn't want to hear her voice in my head. Hell, for a while, I didn't want to know Erin existed.

Even worse, I didn't want to remember. But memories, being the elusive thing they were, couldn't be stopped.

"No, Colter. Don't go in there."

I was a headstrong kid of six years and full of my lion's courage. Full of the innocence that makes all children believe they know better than their parents. I ignored my father and shoved my way through the throng of people standing outside my parents' bedroom.

My laughter rang out from the joy of living in a world that gave us our freedom to run, to play, to roughhouse, to shift into our cat forms whenever we wanted. I'd just found a four-leaf clover and couldn't wait to give it to my mother.

"Stop him."

But it was too late. By the time any of the pride could reach me,

I'd already barreled past Burke and into the room.

At first, I couldn't understand why my mother was asleep. The smell of copper stung my nostrils. She lay on top of the bed, but I'd seen her in bed before.

This time was different.

Her eyes stared at me, unblinking, without the usual warm glow of love in them.

"Mommy?"

For a young lion, my voice sounded weak, pitiful, afraid. Dark stains covered her wrists. The same darkness surrounded her hands and stained the sheet.

"Colter, come with me."

I shook off someone's hand on my shoulder and dashed to my mother. I knew the closer I got, the sooner I'd realize she was playing a joke.

That had to be it. She was playing Statue, the game where the "it" person had to stay as still as possible, unmoving until the other could make them blink or flinch.

"Mommy?" I passed my hand in front of her face. She was really good at Statue. Yet terror inched its way inside me. I shoved it away, determined to make her move.

"Tickle, tickle." I'd get her now. She'd never been able to stay still whenever I tickled her under her chin.

I wiggled my fingers, then jerked my hand away at the chill of her skin. She didn't blink or flinch.

"Son."

I didn't want to hear my father's voice. He sounded too sad. Not like his usual strong self.

I tried again, confident I could make her blink. And yet, when I touched her eyelashes, a move that had never failed to work, she remained still.

"Make her move, Daddy." My whine followed but sounded far

away.

"Come, son."

My father tried to pick me up, but I struggled against him and broke free. If I let him take me away, I'd lose at Statue.

Down deep, I realized I'd already lost so much more.

Later, once I was older, I understood. He hadn't had the strength left in him to pick me up. I wiggled out of his hold and grabbed my mother's arm. Then yanked my hand away.

Why was she so cold? My mother's skin was never cold. Not as a human or as a lioness.

"Colter."

I started crying when Burke, then a younger man, lifted me into his arms and carried me past the sorrowful people and out of the house.

I slammed to a stop, my breath burning my throat. Desperately, I searched the woods as though I could find an answer to all my problems in its green depths.

She hurts herself. She tried to kill herself.

Like my mother. The only difference was that my mother had succeeded.

The roar started somewhere far inside me. Slowly, growing stronger by the second, it inched its way upward, through my abdomen, into my chest, then up my throat until, at last, the sound exploded from my mouth.

I tore my clothes from me, seeking solace in the only place I knew it existed. I needed to run faster, harder than I ever could as a human. Naked, I transformed, then landed on all fours. Shaking my mane, I let out another gut-wrenching roar and started running.

Erin

I wasn't surprised when Colter didn't return last night. If he wanted me to prove I could make it the rest of the way through the challenge, then he couldn't help me any longer. And that was okay. I'd come to Fang's not only to win the money, but to prove how much stronger I was now. I had to prove I could, once and for all, put the past behind me, and keep myself safe.

Still, I wasn't a fool. I knew The Darkness would always be with me. My goal wasn't to rid myself of my demons, but to keep them locked away, to tame them, and put me in complete, unyielding control. When I made it to the finish and accepted Colter as my mate, I'd free my captured heart, retaking it as my own.

It didn't matter if the pride found out that I knew what they were. As soon as he'd left the cabin, I'd known. How could I leave him? He needed me as much as I needed him. If—*when*—I became Colter's mate, I'd come and live in the mountains with him. I'd pay the bills and loans back some other way, even if it took me a lifetime.

I'm going to be a shifter. A lioness. Holy shit.

As scary as the idea was, I knew it was what I wanted. Colter was what I wanted. Not in the clingy, needy way I'd wanted Mike, but as an equal, a real partner. A mate.

I sat on the porch eating a muffin, and smiled at the sunlight. Although it had taken a long time for me to fall asleep, I'd gotten enough rest. The excitement of making it back down the hill, along with the thrill of seeing Colter's face when he realized that I'd made it on my own, filled with me with enough energy to last several days.

Taking a bottle of water along with me, I made my way down the steps. Halfway to the tree line, I turned around and gave the cabin one last look. Would Colter bring me back after we mated? I hoped so.

It was funny how the word fit now. Like I'd been born to be his mate. Seeing Hector change into a lion had terrified me, but seeing Colter in all his magnificent glory had done the exact opposite. He'd been a gentle giant. A wild animal that would protect me. A man who would love me no matter what. A man who was willing to do whatever it took to keep me safe. From the moment he'd changed, I'd known he'd never hurt me.

It was strange, but going back downhill made me sad. If given the choice, I would've stayed at the cabin with Colter for as long as he wanted, even with the outhouse and without modern conveniences. I wasn't ready to return to civilization. But I had a challenge to finish and my mate to claim.

Running, then walking, I passed by the clearing where I'd seen Nina, then on to the ditch where I'd fallen, landing on the spider web. The makeshift bridge Colter had placed over the ditch was gone, but that didn't stop me. Instead, I followed alongside the edge and finally found a place where I could jump across. I laughed, happy that I was making it on my own.

I took it slower, making sure to keep the branches from tearing at my skin. I'd already suffered enough physical pain and I didn't want to take any more. I kept moving, my eagerness to see Colter spurring me on. My excitement built, knowing I was getting closer and closer to Fang's with every step I took. After what seemed a lifetime, I found the small grassy clearing where I'd seen the large cat.

No, not a cat. Shayna, the lioness.

It was easy to believe I could've withstood her. At least, I would've given it my all, going down with a fight. But I wasn't delusional enough to think I would've won. She could and would have killed me with one quick swipe of her paw.

But Colter had interfered, broken the rules, and saved me.

I took a moment to spin around and see the world in a different light.

Shifters are real. And I'm in love with one.

I'd seen two men change into lions and I knew what I'd seen was real. I thrilled at the idea of becoming one of them even if it scared me a little. Would it be painful? Could I tell Maddy and Nina? Was Nina going to complete the challenge and become a shifter, too? And what about Maddy? Would Nina and I have to keep our secret from her?

I paused at the edge of the other side of the clearing and scanned the path ahead. Gathering my determination around me like a cloak of protection, I stepped onto the path and picked up my pace.

Soon, I was surprised to find myself humming a tune. I was, for the first time in a very long time, really, honestly happy. Not just pretending to be happy for Maddy or Nina. After The Darkness had taken me the last time, I'd learned to put on a smiling face, learned to say what my friends wanted to hear. But I'd never felt truly blissful before. Even when I'd thought I'd found the love of my life in Mike, I'd never experienced this kind of joy.

Colter had given me that and now I had to give him the same thing. Only by making it through the games would I be able to give him the happiness he deserved.

Keeping my head down so I wouldn't stumble over the stones buried in the ground, I kept going, eager to see him. I wasn't aware of her presence until it was almost too late.

Her snarl brought my head up and sent my heart racing. But I stood my ground. Running wouldn't do any good anyway. She'd catch me before I could turn around.

"Shayna, leave me alone."

The glowing silver eyes blinked. Did she understand me? I couldn't remember if Colter had said anything about how their minds worked while they were in their animal bodies. She growled, her tail swishing back and forth, as she laid back her ears. She eased forward, crouched and ready to attack.

I backed up, knowing that if I didn't keep her in front of me, she'd pounce and take me down. Yet instead of following the path back the way I'd come, I eased into the bushes. I glanced around, hoping to find another fallen limb to use as a weapon.

If she attacked, I'd get in one good blow before dying.

She growled and moved at my pace. Was she toying with me? Was she delaying the attack to terrorize me first?

And yet I wasn't afraid. I'd faced more awful things than her before and I was still alive. I'd do everything I could to stay alive now.

"You have to stop. Colter doesn't want you as his mate."

She growled again, showing more fangs. Did I piss her off? I sure hoped so.

"Even if you kill me, he still won't take you as his mate. And he'll know you're the one who murdered me."

Her tail was low, her ears twitching as she crouched even lower, ready to spring. Frantically, without trying to draw attention to what I was doing, I let my fingers brush over the limbs around me. I searched the ground, hoping to find one limb big enough to do damage, but not too big that I couldn't swing it hard enough to hurt her.

I couldn't find anything I could use as a weapon, so I had to resort to bargaining with her. "If you turn around and leave, I won't tell him you tried again."

She shook her head, refusing my offer, then stopped and crouched even lower.

My head pounded, my chest tightened, and I knew in the next moment she'd launch her body at me, claws flexed and fangs ready to sink into my flesh. "Shayna, you don't want to do this."

She was already in the air before I'd finished speaking. Ramming into me, she knocked me off my feet, taking my breath. I landed in the middle of a bush, my arms thrown outward, my fingers spread, my eyes closed. Branches jabbed into my back and wrapped around me.

When I opened my eyes, she stood over me. Her silver eyes glinted with savage hatred and saliva dripped from her fangs to splatter on my face. Her low growl, soft, yet menacing, blew warm air over my skin.

I'm going to die.

Yet, unlike all the times before when I'd let The Darkness take me to the edge, the choice was no longer mine. I said a quick prayer, hoping there really was a God in Heaven, then prepared to die.

I love you, Colter.

The lioness put her face closer and snarled. I met her gaze and fisted my hands, ready to fight as best I could. When my right hand closed over the rough bark of a thick stick, I took the chance that it would be enough.

Glaring at her, I curled my lips back in a human snarl. "Go to hell, bitch." I brought my arm up as hard and as fast as I could.

Her eyes widened a moment before she let out a yowl and jumped off me. Whirling around, she fought to get my makeshift spear out of her side. Blood covered the area around the spear. Fur caught on branches as she screeched and thrashed, but she couldn't get it out.

I scrambled to my knees, searched for yet another branch and found one with a jagged end. Getting on my feet, I charged her, ready to take advantage of my chance to strike again.

She saw me coming and, with an ear-splitting roar, thrust her body out of the thick bushes and back onto the path. I rushed after her, feeling more powerful than I ever had, but by the time I'd made it to the path, she'd already disappeared into the forest.

I dropped to my knees, my second spear still in my hands, and let out a victorious cry. I'd faced her and survived. My body shook from the adrenaline coursing through me.

If only Colter could have seen me.

Scanning the woods, I hoped I'd find him watching, but I didn't see anything. I hadn't seen anything when I was going up the hill to the cabin, but he'd been there. If he wanted to stay hidden, he would.

"I did it, Colter. I fought her off."

I listened, but there was no response.

Would she come back? If she did, she'd be more determined than before. I didn't think I'd mortally wounded her. At least, I hoped not. If she attacked again, I'd defend myself, but I didn't want to believe I'd taken a life.

Struggling, I got to my feet and resumed my journey, going faster, even when the branches scratched at my skin. Scratches wouldn't hurt me. And they wouldn't be my way to release my internal pain any longer. I'd have to fight against The Darkness again, maybe for the rest of my life, but now I knew I could beat it.

I was stronger. Braver. Ready to handle anything life threw at me.

Colter

Not helping Erin was harder than anything I'd ever done. I'd followed her from the moment she'd left the cabin, determined to let her make her way on her own no matter what. If she was going to be strong enough to be my mate, she had to prove it. She had to bring out the lioness inside her.

After I'd run most of last night, I'd finally realized what I had to do. I'd thought of nothing else all night and had come to a decision. Even though I'd helped her, even if the pride never found out that she knew what we were, I still wanted her as mine.

More than for the money or for me, she'd come to fight an internal battle to conquer her demons. I couldn't rid her of her demons for her. If I did, she'd never find her own strength. Instead, she'd turn to me to fix her problems and, in the end, she'd resent me for it. Worse still, I'd resent her for not becoming the strong mate I needed.

But I'd always be there for her. Comforting her, helping her as much as she'd help me fight my own demons. We'd never be free of them, but we'd learn to tame them. We were mates. We were pride. We'd fight together and be stronger than when we were apart.

Although I wouldn't help her make it back to Fang's, I

couldn't stay away. I'd watch her just as I'd done on her ascent up the hill, but this time I wouldn't interfere.

And then I saw Shayna.

It took everything in me not to warn Erin. I wanted nothing more than to jump between the two of them and take Shayna to the ground. Shayna took her time, playing with Erin, scaring her, wanting her to beg for her life. Fighting against my natural instinct to protect my mate, I'd watched in horror as the lioness attacked, knocking Erin on her back.

I got closer, ready to break my vow. I could never let Erin die. No matter what the consequences. I crouched, ready to kill one of my own.

And then, Erin's hand closed over the pointed branch. Her arm came up, driving the spear into Shayna's side.

I'd never been prouder.

Stepping back into the cover of the forest, I watched her, smiling as she let out a victory cry as any lioness would've done. Then she got back on the path and continued her journey. All that was left was to see if she'd choose me over the money.

Erin

I still couldn't believe it, not even after stepping out of the woods and into the parking lot. After running, then walking, then running again down the hillside, I'd made it all the way back to Fang's. I hadn't had any more problems. Shayna had stayed away and I'd managed not to fall into any ditches or run into any snakes.

Had I killed her? I hoped not. But if I had, I wasn't to blame. She'd brought it on herself.

A couple of the girls I'd seen going up the hill when the games had started stood next to their men. Although they looked as though they'd gone through hell and back, with bruises and cuts, they also seemed wiser, calmer, and more confident than they had before. Did I appear the same way?

"Erin."

Nina jumped on me from behind, enclosing me in a tight bear hug. I twisted around so I could hug her back.

"You made it." She grinned from ear to ear.

She checked me over and I did the same. Her hair was matted and she was dirty, but I didn't see any major injuries. I assumed I looked as disheveled as she did, but who cared? Looks didn't matter. Only strength did.

"Right back at you." I pulled her close and got a whiff of her body odor. "Damn, do I smell as rank as you do?"

She laughed. "Worse." Glancing over my shoulder, she searched the small group of people standing outside Fang's. "So? Where is he? Where's your man?"

My man. Damn, but that had a good sound to it. I tugged at my hair, and then dropped my hand. I looked around, but I didn't see Colter. My gut twisted. Had he given up on me? If I could tell him how I'd stood up to Shayna would it bring him back? Would it make him proud to have me as his mate?

"I don't know." But I wouldn't let it get me down. "Where's yours?"

She pointed at the tall blond that had pulled her aside when we'd left Fang's two nights earlier. He gave her a wink, then answered Burke's call for the men to come inside the bar. Burke's hard gaze fell on me, yet instead of bowing my head, I thrust out my chin, daring him to speak to me. Daring him to call me a bitch. Instead, he tipped his head in greeting.

"Have you seen Mia?"

The women had been left outside. It wasn't difficult to take in the five of us that remained. Had the others already gone home? A chill slid over me. Or had they failed? Were they lost in the woods? Hadn't Mia completed the challenge?

Fear summoned up The Darkness. Yet, amazingly, I pushed it away with ease.

"Oh, no." Nina had come to the same conclusion.

I took her hand and squeezed. "No. Let's not go there. We don't know anything yet."

"You're right. Wow, listen to you. You're a regular Ms. Optimist."

"Hey, you two."

Nina and I spun around to find Maddy coming around the side of the building along with a handsome dark-haired man. Together, we pulled her into a group hug.

"Ow. You're breaking my bones."

She was dirty and banged-up just like Nina and I were, but she'd never looked more beautiful to me. "I thought you went home."

She dragged fingers through her hair, combing out a twig from the snarled mess. "I did. Then about a mile down the road, I had the cab turn around and come back. You didn't think I'd let you two go through this without me, did you?"

"But wasn't it too late?"

Her attention shifted to the man. He'd just opened the door to enter Fang's when he raised a hand to Maddy. She smiled, then returned the gesture. "Nope. He was still waiting for me. I guess he knew I'd come back."

"Then we all found a man?" Nina practically hopped up and down. "This is so exciting. We found love. All three of us."

She edged closer, dropping her voice to a whisper. "And you both know what they are, don't you?"

Maddy's expression said it all. She knew as well as I did. "That they're the Kings of Beasts MC?"

"No. I mean…" Nina grasped for words. "That they're what they *are*."

"Yes, Nina. We know they're lions. On the inside and on the outside. But keep it quiet. The others might not know yet." Again I searched for Colter, and again I came up empty.

"I still don't believe it and I've seen him change several times," added Maddy.

Nina darted her gaze to the other two women who were a few yards away. But her excitement couldn't be restrained. "But you saw him? So he broke the rule, too?" asked Nina.

"I guess we got the bad boys of the pride." I shrugged and laughed, then lowered my voice again. "I always did love a bad boy."

"Amen to that, sister." Maddy reached her hands out to us.

We stood, hands clasped, each lost in the wonder that were our men. Lost in silence, we simply stood, enjoying being back with each other.

"Erin, get in here."

I jumped at the sound of Burke calling my name. For a moment, I hesitated, unsure if I wanted to go. But I wouldn't let him scare me. Not any longer. "I'll be back."

Burke waited for me at the door, holding it wide, then motioning me inside. I strode into the dimly lit bar to find the men standing near the walls as they'd done the first time I'd entered Fang's. It was unnerving to see their attention focused on me. Hector was among them, but he didn't look at me. Colter stood next to Roberta near the bar's counter. I smiled at him, but he didn't return it.

Burke led the way over to the bar, then crossed his arms and confronted me. "We know Colter broke the rules. That he helped you, keeping you from injury, even from death." He narrowed his eyes. "Think before you answer."

I glanced at Colter, who stood, tall and proud, next to a statuesque woman who held a hand to her side as though favoring an ache. Colter slanted his head at her, telling me what I'd already guessed. It had to be Shayna. If I'd stabbed a human in the same way, they would've been dead. Or at least flat on their back in a hospital. I met her gaze with my own and told them. "It's true. He did."

Shouts and calls for exile erupted around us. Exile? So that was the consequence for helping me? I turned cold. Yet I knew Colter would understand that I couldn't lie. There was as much strength in telling the truth as there was in completing the challenge. As much as it might hurt us, I'd had to tell the truth.

Burke's face twisted into a grimace. "Fuck. Colter, you know how it goes. Do you admit it?"

Colter was calm and my pride swelled. "Yes. Shayna attacked her on the way to the cabin and I saved her." He looked past me to Hector standing behind several of the other men. "Then when Hector tried to claim her as his own, I fought him off her." His mouth curved. "Although she did her part to get rid of him."

He didn't mention Hector's change and neither did Hector. If either one of them had said anything, it would've been fine by me. I wouldn't lie about that, either.

More calls to exile Colter echoed around me. My heart broke to hear them, but there was nothing I could do except tell them the rest of it.

"Shayna attacked me again on the way back to Fang's and I fought her off. On my own. See?" I pointed at her. "She's trying to hide where I injured her, but you can tell, can't you? And Colter didn't help me then. Doesn't that count for anything?"

"Did she fight you off, Shayna? Without any help from Colter?" Roberta stalked over to stand in front of the scowling woman.

Shayna couldn't meet her eyes. "Yes. But that doesn't change anything. He still helped her."

Roberta grabbed her by the arms, forcing her to look at her. "Why would you tell us this? You're willing to have him exiled? Because he chose another? You don't know for certain that Erin will choose him over the money."

Anger and hurt burned in Shayna's eyes. "Why wouldn't she? He loves her. Anyone can see that. I won't lose him, especially not to that human cunt."

Human.

I froze, fear stiffening me. I kept silent, hoping no one else would notice what she'd called me.

The men around us had quieted down to listen. Once she'd stopped speaking, they started talking amongst themselves, but it was easy to see they hadn't liked what she'd said. Some of them spoke of Colter refusing to mate her and of her failure to get rid of me. Shame filled her face as she overheard them.

I stood tall and proud, ready to take whatever fate they decided for me. But I couldn't let them hurt Colter.

"Please, listen to me." I waited, seeing if Burke would stop me, but he remained coolly silent. "Don't punish Colter for my weakness. Let him stay. He loves the pride and the mountains. I'll leave and never come back. Without the money and—" It killed me to say the words, but I had to. "And without him."

"That's not how it works." Burke lifted his hand, stilling the others. All of a sudden, he narrowed his eyes at me. "You know what we are."

I swallowed. "Yes."

Growls and roars erupted around us. Burke's eyes flashed solid silver. His lip lifted into a snarl as he turned toward Shayna. "You attacked her in your lioness form."

It wasn't a question, but Shayna's slight nod was all the confirmation he needed.

I'd fight my own battles from now on, but I wouldn't lie and I wouldn't keep any more secrets. "There's more. I saw Hector change after Colter fought him off. But I didn't know the cat was Shayna until Colter told me. He had to. I was freaking out after seeing Hector change."

Several of the men whirled toward Hector. He hunkered down and eased farther into the shadows.

Burke raised his hand, quieting the rest of them. "We'll deal with Hector and Shayna later. As for the bitch, the law is clear. She's lost her right choose. She'll become one of us."

He paused, seeing if I'd argue. I only nodded, accepting his ruling.

"As for Colter." He turned to him. "Because of your interference in the games, you will leave here and never take a mate. You'll never see her again. If you try and get together, you'll both pay a heavy price."

It was Colter's expression that told me what Burke meant. They'd kill us. I was certain of it. Simply because we loved each other enough to be together anywhere and anyway we could, they'd do whatever it took to keep us apart.

"No." I choked, unable to say anything more. I'd found the man I loved, only to lose him.

Colter stalked toward Burke, his eyes blazing more silver than blue. "Once I'm gone, will you accept Erin as an equal? She completed the last part of the challenge and fought off Shayna's second attack on her own. And she fought bravely against Hector. She deserves to be a full pride member."

Burke was already shaking his head when Roberta spoke up. "The rest of the females and I won't treat her any differently than anyone else. And the men won't, either." Her gaze slid over the men before settling on Colter. "I promise you that."

A murmur arose from the men as Burke glared at his mate. But no one, not even Burke, went against her.

"Leave, Colter." Burked turned his back on the man I loved. I watched, horrified, as the other men and Shayna turned their backs to him. Two of the men hesitated and I wondered if they were Nina's and Maddy's mates who had broken the same rule. But I'd never tell. Roberta and those two men were the only ones who didn't turn their backs on him.

"No, please. I'll do anything you say. I'll become one of you. Please, punish me any way you want, but let Colter stay."

Growls and roars erupted around us. Burke's eyes flashed solid silver. His lip lifted into a snarl.

"Colter, wait outside," ordered Roberta.

"What the fuck for?" Burke glared at his mate. "I've already made my decision."

She waved her hand in dismissal. "You, too, Erin. Wait outside."

Hope was a cruel thing, teasing, offering a chance where none existed. I grabbed hold, determined to make that hope a reality. Following Colter, I hurried outside where the other girls still waited.

"What's going on?" Maddy glanced at Colter, who stayed at

my side.

"I'm not sure. Colter and I broke some of the rules."

Nina and Maddy exchanged a look as they realized that their men could face trouble, too.

I couldn't let go. I'd hold on to the flickering light of hope for as long as I could. "But Roberta's doing something. Maybe she's changing their minds. I don't know. Do you?" My hand slid into Colter's.

"I doubt it. The rules have never been changed." He pulled me against him. "We have to face facts. You have to stay and I have to leave. And I wouldn't count on getting the money you need." He was trying to make a joke, but it fell flat.

"Fuck the money. All I want is to stay with you. I don't care what they say. I'd rather risk my life than lose you." They'd have to kill me to keep me away from him. "Let's leave right now. Before they come out and force you to go."

"I don't want that kind of life for you. We'd be hunted and, if they found us, they wouldn't hesitate to do whatever they had to do to protect the pride. I won't risk your life."

I pulled away from him, angry that he wasn't willing to put it all on the line like I was. "Damn it. Don't you get it? I'm the one who decides what I want to do with my life. Not you and sure as hell not them."

At least I'd made him smile. "It would mean running away. As far from your family and friends as we could get. We'd have to disappear. Are you really ready to give up your life?" His smile grew. "I thought you wanted the money over me."

I shrugged, ready to play his game. "They're not going to give me the money anyway. So I might as well take what I can get."

He laughed as my confused friends looked on. "Oh, so

that's it. You're not getting the money, so you're settling for me. Gee, thanks."

I was through playing around. I uttered a growl, then clutched his hair and yanked.

"Hey."

"Listen up, Colter Quaid. I've spent too many years beating myself up about everything. I never thought I deserved anyone like you. But, damn it, after all I've been through the past few days, I now know that I do. I want you and I'm going to have you. Tell me you'll claim me no matter what they say. Claim me before one of them can."

"You're braver than I am, Erin Pierce."

I gave him a quick kiss. "I guess I am. Say it. Tell me that, no matter what, we're in this together."

Colter had just opened his mouth to respond when the call came.

"Back inside, you two." Roberta held the door open.

He took my hand firmly in his and led me toward our fate. Maddy, Nina, and the other women watched us go. As soon as we stepped inside, Roberta waved us toward the bar.

I held my head high and walked alongside my man. Whatever they said, we'd face together, whether they liked it or not.

We all looked to Burke, but it was Roberta who came to stand in front of us. "We call ourselves the Kings of Beasts. But where there are kings, there are queens and I'm the queen of this pride."

Burke was stone-faced, as were most of the men.

Roberta arched an imperious eyebrow. "We've never had any woman find out what we are before she made her decision. The rules of the games are clear and have been that way for years." She scanned the room almost as though daring anyone to contradict her. "But it's time for a change."

It was hard to breathe, hard to think. All I could do was hold onto Colter's hand even tighter.

"Others have interfered in the games just as Colter did. Some were exiled, but others weren't. Sometimes we turned a blind eye if no one spoke up about it. If Shayna hadn't said anything, we would've let it pass this time, too."

Why would they do that? If Shayna hadn't told them, would they have even known?

"From now on, no one, male or female, can interfere in the games for any reason." She tilted her head at Shayna. "But if someone does, then the male has a right to protect his future mate. It's what a man, a king, should do."

Colter cleared his throat. "Then I can stay." It wasn't a question as much as a confirmation.

"Only because we haven't punished others in the past. Exile will no longer be the punishment. Instead, your standing in the pride will be lowered." She crossed her arms, but her smile lessened the harshness of the gesture. "Do you understand?"

Colter and I nodded together.

"You'll stay with her as your mate," added Burke, who came to Roberta's side.

I almost let out a cry of joy, but managed to slap a hand over my mouth just in time.

Burke gave me one of his infamous glares. "As for Hector and Shayna, they'll lose their standing in the pride, too. Respect and position for all three of you will have to be earned back with time."

He bent his neck to one side then the other. "All this shit's giving me a fucking headache. Zack, get the rest of them inside."

We all watched as Nina and Maddy led what was left of the participants into the bar. I smiled at my friends, letting them know everything was all right.

Colter pulled me to him, then turned to face me. "I'll go first."

"Whatever. It's already been decided, but shit, go ahead. Makes no difference now." Burke hopped up on top of the counter. "Let's just get this damn thing over with. Rake, slide me a beer."

The man behind the bar poured a tall glass of beer, then handed it off to Burke. He downed it in one long drink, then wiped his mouth with the back of his hand. "Get on with it, damn it."

Colter held both my hands. "You know how I feel and what I want. Tell everyone your choice. Would you have chosen the money or me?"

I'd come to the games to win the money, but that had only been part of my reasons. Finding love had drawn me as well, but that, too, wasn't all of it. After all I'd gone through, I'd finally realized what I'd been hunting was so much more. I'd found the strength to live my life on my own terms without the fear of The Darkness overwhelming me again. Yet without Colter, what kind of life would I have?

"Screw the money. I choose you."

Cheers erupted around us again until Burke once more had to call a halt to it. He picked up another mug of beer and slammed it back. "Surprise, surprise. She chooses the man." His glittering gaze met mine and a small smile lifted the corners of his mouth. Then he frowned and turned to the others. "Who's next?"

As much as I wanted to see what Nina would do as she took her place in front of the bar, I let Colter pull me outside. Picking me up, he whirled me around, enclosing me in a tight hug. I laughed and held on until, at last, he set me down on my feet.

"Are you sure? What about all the bills and school loans?"

"I'll figure it out later."

He narrowed his blue-silver gaze at me. "Now that no one's listening, tell me the truth. Would you have chosen me over the money?"

"You, of course. I may have lost out on the money, but look what I'm gaining. A whole bunch of big kitty cats."

"Damn." He glanced back at the bar. "Don't ever say that again."

"Okay. I won't. As long as you let me pet you tonight."

"You, my mate, are fucking amazing. But I have to tell you. Don't worry about the money you owe."

"What do you mean?"

"Now that you're one of us, we'll pay everything."

"Seriously?"

"Of course. We take care of our own."

"And what about getting my degree?"

"If that's what you want, I can live in town until you finish. It'll be hard and we'll have to come to the mountains a lot to let our lions run, but we can do it. Once you graduate college, then law school, we have to come back to the mountains to stay. Agreed?"

"Okay." But I was finished living my life out of guilt. "And if I wanted to skip college and law school and paint instead?"

"Then paint." He tilted his head and gave me a searching look. "But what about your parents? What about becoming an attorney?"

"What about them? This is my life and I'm going to live it my way."

"You've come a long way since the start of the games."

"Yeah, I have. And it's only the beginning." I cupped his face and planted a kiss on his lips. My body tingled as he swept his tongue inside my mouth.

I hated like hell to ask, but I had to. "And about what I told you?" To my relief, he didn't turn me loose.

He kissed me hard and fast. "It'll be hard, but I'll do my best to understand. If you're willing to try and fight it."

"I will and I am. But don't expect miracles overnight."

"I won't." A glint of mischief was in his eye. "So what do you want to do right now?"

I gave him my sexiest look. "I want you to take me back to the cabin and make me yours."

"Are you sure? I have a place just outside Cripple Creek with electricity, running water, and an inside toilet."

"No. I want the cabin. Later you can show me your place."

"Our place. What's mine is yours from now on. But are you sure you want to go back to the cabin?"

Playfully, I slapped him on the arm. "Stop asking before I change my mind."

"Okay, okay." He swept my hair back, his expression growing serious. "Have you thought about how the change happens?"

"Actually, I have." I'd come to the conclusion that it had to be similar to how werewolves changed people. Of course what little I knew I'd gotten from the movies, so it was all just speculation on my part. "With a bite?"

"Yeah. With a bite. The bite hurts, of course. And your

body's going to go through a painful transition, but the pain only lasts a day or so. Think you can handle it?"

What else could I say? I'd go to hell and back for him. "Sure I can."

"Okay, then, let's go to the cabin."

"What about my friends? I should tell them where I'm going."

He glanced at the bar just as Maddy and a handsome dark-haired man came out, hands locked together. She was radiant, a woman in love. A woman who only had eyes for the man she adored.

"Trust me, baby. They won't even know you're gone."

Chapter Fifteen

Erin

I shook my hair, then ran my hands through it, detangling it with my fingers. I never would've dreamed I'd be taking a swim in a pond, but I'd had enough of my filthiness. The sponge bath at the cabin hadn't been enough. When Colter made love to me the next time, I wanted to smell like a woman and not like something that had crawled out of a pile of garbage. I'd be clean, refreshed, and ready to get down and dirty with him.

He waited on the shore, his gaze never leaving mine. I didn't want to say anything, but I was a little disappointed that he'd taken his swim, then gone back to the shore instead of making love in the water. My disappointment left me as I saw the size of his erect cock, ready and waiting for me. His wet hair sparkled in the sunlight and water droplets glistened on his tanned skin. Crouched down, he looked like the wild beast that he was, ready to attack his prey. I was happy to be that prey.

Acting sexy had never come easily to me, but I did my best as I pushed through the water and strode onto the ground. Water streamed down my body, my nipples hardening as the breeze lightly touched them.

"I wanted to swim with you."

He grinned, looking like a Cheshire cat, then leapt upward, his muscles springing into action. I could see the catlike movement in him.

Colter grabbed me, encircling me in his oh-so-strong arms, and crushed his mouth to mine. I closed my eyes, savoring the tanginess of his flavor and the firmness of his mouth. His nude body was hard against me, making me think that if I leaned against a mountain wall, it wouldn't have been any harder. He was beyond anything I'd ever dreamed of, all man and wild animal rolled into one.

His kiss deepened, his lips growing more intense, more demanding. I cupped the back of his neck and took his tongue inside. It circled mine, clearing my mind of everything except him. His hands found every curve and hill of my body, and for once, I wasn't worried about the added pounds I carried. He loved me for me. Like no one else ever had. And I loved him just as much.

I yearned for him, not only for his body, but for all of him, man and animal. To have him beside me for the rest of my life still seemed like a dream, but I was willing to take the risk of the dream dying. Yet with Colter, I knew the dream never would. He stirred a fire inside me that knew no limits and would never burn out. If we hadn't needed to come up for air, I think we would've stayed, our bodies pressed together, until we died.

His eyes boasted silver flecks and the desire, the unrestrained lust I saw, made my own craving claw at my stomach. Would that craving grow stronger once I was changed and became like him? I couldn't imagine how it could get any more intense, but I couldn't wait to find out.

"If I don't stop now, we won't make it to the cabin."

"What cabin?"

He touched my cheek. "Don't say that if you don't mean it."

"What cabin?" I repeated and answered his grin with one of my own.

"Mate, you're one sexy woman. But I want to make sure you know what's going to happen. We haven't talked about what it's like to be a werecat. Not just how it is to change, but the rest of it."

"Yeah, I get it. Didn't you say it's like how a werewolf changes?"

"It's the same for all shifters. Still, have you really given this enough thought? I need you to be ready."

"Colter Quaid, are you trying to get out of changing me?"

He slid his fingers into my hair and held me. "Don't make this into a joke, baby. You have to be sure."

"How can I make you understand? I am sure. I want to be like you. I want to be close to you in every way. Besides, it'll make it easier for the kids."

The silver was gaining in his blue eyes. "Yeah, I'm sure all six of them would like having their mom be a shifter, too."

"Wait. Six? I remember something about three. Or was it two?"

He nibbled on my chin, then slid his mouth over to tantalize my earlobe. "We can decide later. Right now, I need you. If I don't get to fuck you right now, I'm going to blow."

I didn't try to contain my delight. "Well, we wouldn't want you to blow. Besides, I need you just as much. Take me, big guy."

His deep breath shuddered through him. He gritted his teeth, fighting to hold back. "You drive me wild."

"Is that you or the animal inside you talking?"

"We're one and the same."

I tried to bring his mouth to mine, but he captured my

wrists. "We should talk first. There's so much you need to learn."

"I'd rather we do it first and then talk."

"You, woman, are the real animal."

"Yeah? Okay, then, fuck me and make me roar." I didn't want to wait another minute. "We have a lifetime to talk. You're my man and I'm your woman. Your mate. Everything else I need to know can wait."

"You are definitely my mate."

"Then get to it and claim me."

"Damn, but you're hot. I remember thinking how sexy you were when I saw you in Chambers."

"I remember seeing you, but I never thought once you'd remember me."

"Of course I did. You were the best-looking girl there. You were at some coffee shop along with Maddy and Nina. And some stupid college guy."

With Mike.

Funny how it no longer hurt to think of him. How could I have thought I was in love with someone like Mike when I deserved a man like Colter? My thoughts, my strength, my life had changed so much since I'd come to the mountains. And all for the better.

His gaze smoldered as he took in my breasts. "You're more beautiful than ever." Scooping me off the ground, he carried me to a grassy area that was shaded by the pines above us. I laid my head against his chest, placed my hand over his heart, then traced the lion tattoo. Was his heart beating as fast as mine? I was pleased to find that it was.

He gently lowered me to the grass and sat down beside me. The scene was so serene, so peaceful, with the quiet of the forest surrounding us and the light breeze blowing our hair. His strong face hovered above mine and I reached out and caressed his cheek. He leaned into my palm, closing his eyes, then opening them to reveal the love there.

He kissed me again, softer at first, but then heat, passionate and real, scorched my lips. I grasped at him, moaning, voicing my need to have everything he could give me. And I swore a silent promise that I'd give more than he gave me. Fire erupted between my legs, burning even hotter as the wetness grew. I slid my hands along his shoulders, over the mounds his muscles made.

Colter broke off the kiss, then touched my lips, sliding his thumb along the seam. "I have to ask you. Are you okay? Do you promise to stay with me forever? I don't know what I'd do if you ever left me."

He was asking me to be his for the rest of our lives. Still, I caught the real question in his tone.

"You don't have to worry about me. I won't leave you."

"You understand, right? We're stronger together than either one of us is apart?"

I kissed him quick, needing to reassure him once again. "You've taught me how to live and how to fight to stay alive. I can't promise I won't have rough times, but I do promise I'll do my best."

We held each other for a while, giving to the other what we'd found in ourselves. When he leaned back, his eyes sparkled with silver.

"I always meant to ask. Do your eyes always change to silver when you're turned on?"

"Yeah. That's how you'll know."

I glanced toward his crotch, then back up. "Oh, I think

there's another way." I touched the skin next to his eye. "Will my eyes turn silver after you change me?"

"Yes. You'll have blue-silver eyes from then on."

"Cool." Maybe he was right. Maybe we needed to talk more first. If I could wait that long. "What's it like when you're in your lion form? You still know me, don't you?"

"Like I said, the animal and the man are the same. You can't have one without the other." He flicked his tongue down the side of my neck, tickling me, and turning me on all at the same time. "You don't have to worry. I'll still know who you are."

He lifted me without any warning, placing me on top of him. His cock pushed into position, easing against my folds. I flattened my hands against his chest, letting my hair play over my shoulders.

Colter sucked on one nipple, flaring lightning quick bursts of lust into me. He gripped my ass, then tugged me closer. Although I wanted him so much it hurt, I couldn't resist the urge to tease him, thrusting forward both to rub my breasts over his face and to keep him from entering me. The sunlight played over his face whenever the shadow of my body didn't take it away. The warmth of the day washed over us, but it was nothing compared to the heat we made between us.

"I need you so much."

He gripped my ass with both hands, forcing me to stop moving. He could kill me if he wanted, breaking my neck as if it were a twig, but if there was one thing I was certain of, I was safe in his hands. "Tell me what you want, Colter."

"I want to eat you up." His growl rumbled under my hands.

I sizzled, the swirl of desire spinning outward until it took my mind as well as my body for a ride. "How? With your cock or your mouth?"

"I'll get around to both sooner or later."

Another growl, deep and masculine, thrilled me. "Fuck. Now." Looking into my eyes, he brought me down, piercing my pussy with his cock.

All at once, breathing became more difficult, thinking impossible as he commanded my body, making it respond to his every touch. I could do nothing more than to ride him and hold on with everything I had.

"Colter. You're going to make me—Oh, shit, please, please."

"Please what, baby?"

"Fuck me. Harder."

My body trembled, sensations racing to fill every inch of me. I arched, offering him my breasts and he accepted, drawing a nipple into his mouth. I shoved against him, urging him to plunge harder, faster. His grunts came with each thrust as he answered my call.

Colter shoved into me again and again. I screamed in joy, in need, in ecstasy, uncaring if everyone in the world heard me. We moved as one, each reveling in the pleasure we gave each other. Our bodies slid together, rocking as the rider and the ridden. His mouth found my tits again as his fingers explored my butt, then slid over the rise and into the crevice.

I'd thought myself stronger, but I wasn't sure I could hold on much longer. He was doing most of the work and yet the energy surging through me would soon hit the wall and break apart. I clung to him, keeping the delicious agony going, my body moving on its own. Wonderful, time-bending sensations washed over me and all I could do was to savor them.

"I don't know how much longer…"

"Baby, I have to…"

I stared at him, unable to think, but I knew what he meant. "Do it, Colter. Claim me."

"Are you sure? We can wait a few days. If I go much farther, I won't be able to stop." He opened his mouth. Fangs flashed in the bright sunlight.

"Do it. Claim me. Make me like you."

A groan rolled out of him as he plunged into me. I felt him drive deep and far, skimming over the tender spot inside and shoving me over the edge as he shot his hot cum into my sheath. I fell apart then, my body caving in to his demands as my climax went wild, tearing through me.

When he opened his mouth again, I laid my head to the side, welcoming what would come. He sank his teeth into my flesh and, at first, panic seized me. The Darkness rolled in, ready to reclaim me, telling me not to trust him. I dug my fingernails into his back and held on, pushing the awful blackness away as I gave myself to my mate. My skin burned like a branding iron had been set against my neck. The burn continued, rushing into me, sliding down my shoulder and into the rest of my body. I screamed, but it wasn't long before my screams soon turned to whimpers.

Colter

I cradled her against me, covering her with our clothes. She was beautiful, her dark lashes layered over her blush-filled cheeks. Her hair spread over my arms as she curled toward me. She'd wake up soon and I'd convince her to forget about the cabin for now and go to my home on the outskirts of Cripple Creek.

I caressed the wound in her neck. While she was asleep, I'd

added my own healing kisses to it. My bite would change her within the next two days. It would be painful, but I'd be there, making sure she had everything she needed. The others would stay away, respecting the time and the energy it took for my bite's saliva to enter her system and transform her into my mate. Her friends were probably going through the same thing. She'd sleep off and on during that time, sometimes crying at the anguish tormenting her body, and at other times feeling strong and ready to run. I couldn't wait to run with her, her long strides matching mine as I showed her my mountain home. She'd share in the freedom I loved and it made me laugh. I hadn't realized it before. Had, in fact, thought myself already free. But until she'd captured my heart, I hadn't known what real freedom was like.

She moaned in her sleep and I held her tighter, my gaze falling to the slashes on her ankles. The fresh ones came from the branches, short cuts that had no rhyme or reason. The others ran in parallel lines of faded scars.

It bothered me that she'd gone through what she had, but I had to believe I could help her put it in the past. Together, with the animals inside us to give us power, we'd fight against the darkness that threatened her. Even if we only won some of the battles and not the war, I'd stay and fight along with her. Already, I could feel my own darkness, the awful memory of my mother's death, easing. I'd found my mate and, because of her, I was stronger, too. I could think of my mother without it tearing me to shreds inside.

"Hey."

I smiled down at her. "Hey yourself. How are you doing?"

She stretched, lengthening her body, then coming to a sitting position. "Good." She paused, searching. "Really good, in fact. Is that normal?"

"Yeah." The sunlight was starting to fade. "We'd better get going to my home. Not the cabin, but my real home."

"But—"

"No buts. I don't know about you, but I want a toilet I don't have to share with spiders." I swept her hair over her shoulder. "Besides, the next couple of days are going to be rough. I want you to be comfortable."

"That bad, huh?"

I was pleased when I didn't see fear in her eyes. "Yeah, it is. But you'll get through it."

"Can we come back to the cabin later?"

"Sure." I stood, taking her along with me and handing her clothes to her. I took my time getting dressed, stopping often to admire her body.

Once she was ready, she gazed around her. "You know what? I was never big on nature, but I'm really starting to get into it."

"You'd better. We're going to spend a lot of time in the woods." I slid my arm around her. "Come on. Let's go home."

Erin

Transformation was like giving birth. At least, that's what it seemed like to me. Everyone talked about how wonderful it was, but very few told you that it hurt like hell. I found out the hard way.

After two days of alternating between excruciating pain and elated happiness, I made it through to the third day. I didn't remember much except for Colter being there whenever I cried out. He was there in the middle of night, holding my sweaty body and applying cool cloths to my forehead. He was there in the morning when I emptied my belly of the food he'd just given me. I remembered his voice and his touch. And I remembered feeling loved, completely and absolutely.

When I woke up on the third day, he was still there, sitting in the chair next to my bed.

"Colter?"

His eyes opened at once. Was his quick reaction part of being a lion? Always ready to leap into action? I'd soon learn the answer for myself.

"Hey, mate."

The sound of that one word warmed me.

"So this is your home?"

"No. This is our home."

I studied the small room with simple wooden furniture. It wasn't much, yet at the same time, it was perfect. "Think you can give me a tour?"

"Sure."

He moved to sit beside me, cupping my hand between his two, giving me comfort even when I didn't need it. I tried to sit up and a wave of nausea hit me. "On second thought, I think I'd better stick close to the bathroom." Memories of stumbling toward the bathroom door came rushing back.

He frowned at me, studying me hard. "Do you still feel like upchucking?"

"Upchucking, hurling, kissing the porcelain throne, vomiting, and everything else you can call it. Yeah. Is that normal, too?"

His frown deepened. "No. It's not. By the third day the transformation is complete. You should be feeling great."

"Wow. Do you mean I can change into a lion now?"

"Give it a try in a few days. You don't want to push yourself too fast. We have all the time in the world. And the word is lioness. Some of the men get their fur up if you call yourself a lion. It's a male thing."

"Oh, then, I'll definitely have to call myself a lion in front of Burke. You know. Just to piss him off."

"Shit. That figures."

I leaned against the headboard, but didn't pull my hand from his. "Have you heard from Maddy and Nina? They probably think I dumped them for a man." We'd promised we never would, and yet I'd done it.

"They're fine. We'll check on them tomorrow, okay?"

"Okay." I yawned, a sudden tiredness wiping my energy away. "Maybe I need to sleep a little more."

He gave me the same concerned look.

"Don't tell me that's not normal, either."

"No, it's not."

I wasn't worried until he widened his eyes. "What is it? Tell me."

"You're tired and you're still sick to your stomach." He leaned closer to me, put his nose to my neck, then drew in a long, slow breath.

"Okay, now you're scaring me. Why'd you sniff me?"

"I'm not sure, but…" He shook his head, his smile making me feel a little less nervous until he sniffed me again. "No. I take it back. I've never smelled that scent before, but it's just like I've always heard it would be. Sweet, sugary. You but with something extra."

"What?" I pulled out my hand and slapped his arm. "Damn it, Colter. Will you just tell me?"

"Baby, I think you're pregnant."

Pregnant. I couldn't speak, couldn't think past the word echoing over and over in my mind. "But how? I mean, we've only been together a few days."

He squeezed my hand. "I know it's fast and all, but with us, it happens fast. And it's a good thing, right?"

Was it? I had to force my gaze away from his to be able to think. Yet the answer, just as it had been when I'd first met him, was clear enough. I was a strong woman, a powerful mate, but I couldn't keep the emotions from overwhelming me.

I looked into the blue-silver eyes of the man I loved and started crying. "Yeah. It's a very good thing."

About the Author

Bestselling author Beverly Rae lives in Georgia along with her husband and her "fur" babies. She began writing early, first with poems, then with song lyrics. Later, after she'd found her own real romance hero, she penned her first book and hasn't stopped writing.

Beverly's books range from the contemporary to the paranormal. Some are hotter than others. Some are darker than others. Some of them have a touch of humor. But they're all written from her heart, with a belief in a happy ending.

To learn more about Beverly Rae and her books, please visit www.beverlyrae.com.

Send an email to Beverly at info@beverlyrae.com or follow her on...

Facebook at:
https://www.facebook.com/beverly.rae

Twitter at:
www.twitter.com/Beverly_Rae.